CRUSHING ON YOU

Other Books by Sara Breaker

Young Adult Sweet Romance
Just an Alternate
Change of Mind
That's So Sweet: Campus Players

New Adult Sweet Romance
Insert Happy Ending
Holiday Blues

Hale Valley Sweet Romance series
Switch on Christmas (a prequel novella)

CRUSHING ON YOU

SARA BREAKER

Zeta Indie Publishing

Contents

1 Chapter One - Transient   3

2 Chapter Two - In Theory   12

3 Chapter Three - Impact   24

4 Chapter Four - Pointless Endeavor   34

5 Chapter Five - Blast from the Past   41

6 Chapter Six - Distractions   50

7 Chapter Seven - Grown up   56

8 Chapter Eight - What Works   64

9 Chapter Nine - Stereotypes   78

10 Chapter Ten - Winter Fair   92

11 Chapter Eleven - To Friends   107

12 Chapter Twelve - Helping Hands   119

13 Chapter Thirteen - Reveal   131

14 Chapter Fourteen - Relapse   144

15 Chapter Fifteen - Not a Date   159

16 Chapter Sixteen - State of Bliss   177

17 Chapter Seventeen - Roaring Party   192

18 Chapter Eighteen - Follow-up   210

19 Chapter Nineteen - Empty   224

20 Chapter Twenty - A New Year   236

21 Chapter Twenty-One - Sparking Joy   247

22 Epilogue   258

About The Author   264
Sneak Peek: Holiday Blues   267
Sneak Peek: When They Do   271

crush /krʌʃ/

verb: to pulverize

I

Chapter One - Transient

"Jeez, how many years do you have to write this stupid paper of yours?"

Ingrid Harmon gave her younger sister a pointed look. "It's only for a month, Sam." She hauled a small suitcase up onto a chair before unsealing it with a loud zip.

Sam raised her eyebrows as she surveyed the sunny room. Another large half-unpacked suitcase sat on the double bed and three humungous heavy-duty boxes claimed most of the fake hardwood floor's surface.

"Then why does it look like you're coming home to stay?" Sam mused aloud, tiptoeing to carefully pick her way across the mess. "I don't know if you got the memo or not, but since you moved away for college seven years ago, this became officially—and *solely*—my room."

"I just wanted to make sure I had all the resources I needed to finish." Ingrid moved over to pull out several volumes of thick reference books from one of the boxes.

"I still don't understand why you had to come all the way back home for this," Sam said. "Weren't there enough sociological subjects over there at your illustrious Ivy League university?"

Ingrid was fully open to attributing her sister's ignorance to the fact that Sam was only in her final year of high school. "Sam, if I thought for a second you would understand, I would explain it to you." She turned to pin her favorite print 'We see what we want to see' onto the corkboard wall.

"Hey! Don't cover my Shawn Mendes poster!" Sam hurried to move Ingrid's poster off to the far corner.

"Whatever happened to 'sharing is caring'?"

Sam stuck her tongue out in insolence.

"Look," Ingrid began. "Mom was going to nag me to come home for Christmas anyway. I'm just a little bit early."

"And staying longer." Sam was still making a face before she waved her hand. "Whatever. Better not mess with my stuff. I like everything how it is."

"But this room is already a mess!" Ingrid pointed out. "It used to be neat as a pin when it was *my* room."

Sam huffed. "I have my own organization system that only I understand."

Ingrid scoffed in incredulity but her sister merely whirled to exit the room. As she did, Sam nearly ran into the petite brunette who had come straight up the stairs, all the way from the neighbor's house, likely without even knocking at the front door first.

"There she is."

Ingrid's lit up as she met her best friend's gaze. "Felicia."

Arms crossed over her chest, Felicia had a smirk on her face. "I thought I could hear the refreshing sibling rivalry from next door. I can't believe you're back in Hale Valley!"

"Why is everyone talking like I've been gone for years?" Ingrid asked as she returned her poster to its original position on the corkboard wall. "I'm here like every other major holiday."

Walking into the room, Felicia shook her head. "Not really. I'm pretty sure you missed Kate's awesome promotion party, and Nadia's baby shower, or that time when Mrs. Klein was spreading that rumor about the town orthodontist having an affair with his dental hygienist."

"Those are not major holidays," Ingrid argued. "Also, you know how busy I've been." She put her hands up in resignation. "Then again I knew when I'd decided to go to grad school that my social life was basically over. We're lucky to have time to eat between research and writing rambling papers."

"Sure. That makes total sense. Just abandon your family and friends." Felicia nudged a box on the floor with her toe.

Ingrid gave her a shrug. "I am here right now, aren't I?"

"Ingrid!" A voice floated up the stairs. "Are you here right now?"

Ingrid turned to yell back. "Coming, Mom!"

She blew out a breath to assess the mess she'd made. Funnily enough, Sam's original clutter still dominated the room. She picked up her old netbook laptop off the desk before mumbling, "Note to self. Finish unpacking later."

Ingrid led the way back downstairs with a warning to Felicia as she followed suit. "Watch out for the decorations."

Felicia jerked her hand back before she ruined the festive red and green boughs twisted all around the staircase railing. "I see your mom is going traditional this year. Was last year's theme teddy bears?"

"No, that was two years ago. Last year was 'Frozen'." Ingrid wiggled her eyebrows.

Felicia laughed. "Oh, that's right. Your dad was so allergic to that fake snow foam."

Ingrid grinned. "Yup. My dad's still off on his soon-to-be-annual fishing trip with his buddies and won't be back until the end of the week. He surely doesn't want to be around all this crazy preparation beforehand."

"Your dad is a very wise man," Felicia quipped and they both laughed.

Mom was at the dinner table, surrounded by golden party favor bags she was stuffing with noisemakers and little trinkets. "Sam, could you turn the TV down, please?" she called out to her daughter, slumped onto the plush living room couch across the way.

Sam's response came in a displeased grunt, some crunching of potato chips, followed by the remote control beeps as the volume reduced.

"Hey, Mrs. H." Felicia popped over to hug her.

"Oh, hi, Felicia, dear. Nice to see you."

Ingrid went to hug her mother next. "Mom, she's always here. She's here more often than me."

"I am the surrogate daughter," Felicia claimed with a haughty grin.

Mom turned in her chair, golden bows still in hand. "Ingrid, honey, don't forget you're supposed to set up the video calling for those who can't make it to our party this weekend." She gave Felicia a big smile. "We even have cousins and aunts flying in from Australia and Germany this year."

"Can't wait," Felicia cheered.

"You're sure you're not working that night, right, Ingrid? You changed your plans so suddenly." Mom's tone tinged on authoritative. She spoke louder so that Sam could hear. "This is our big family reunion, girls. Your attendance is not optional."

Ingrid chuckled. "Mom, you know I wouldn't miss it. Someone has to help you make sure things run smoothly, police the cousins, make sure Grandma Ellen stays away from the karaoke machine." She gave Felicia a knowing look. "Make sure to bring up common controversial topics for the Aunts to fight over instead of among themselves."

Mom laughed.

"I keep forgetting how overtly critical all your extended family can be," Felicia smirked. "Why do you all bother having these big family reunions at Christmas again?"

Ingrid and her mom exchanged knowing looks before responding in unison, "Presents!" before both laughing.

"It's once a year," Ingrid went on. "They can pretend to make nice for one night. They can start squabbling again in the New Year."

Felicia noted the little laptop Ingrid slid into the bag she'd plonked on the table. "Maybe someone will finally gift you a new laptop, you cheapskate," she chided.

"Hey, this netbook has seen me through some hard times," Ingrid pointed out. "And it's so handy, I can bring it anywhere. They don't even make them this small anymore. Everyone's obsessed with tablets now or whatever. Besides, you know I make peanuts at my job."

"More peanuts than *my* job at the mall, as you well know, as it used to be your job too," Felicia piped up and they both laughed.

Ingrid noticed Sam, splayed out on the couch, her eyes focused somewhat dully on what she was watching. "And what's wrong with Little Miss Cranky Pants?"

"Sam has a crush on some football jock in school," Felicia volunteered.

Sam jumped in her seat to whirl around in complaint. "Felicia! I told you not to tell Ingrid. She's just going to ruin it."

Ingrid's eyes widened in excitement. "Sam! Why didn't you tell me earlier? This was exactly what my elective paper was all about! Juvenile infatuation and gender relations in subcultures of contemporary society. I can totally help you get a new perspective!"

"Ruining it," Sam piped up before slumping down on the couch again.

Ingrid insisted, "I'm not trying to ruin it. I just want you to see the truth. I promise it will make you feel better in the long run." She walked up to the back of the couch and looked up at the TV screen. "It's just like this show, see?"

Sam threw a pillow at her without looking. "You do *not* speak ill of the new MacGyver!"

But Ingrid caught the pillow and just laughed. "You realize he's not really that guy," she pointed out. "Hot guys like that are very rarely scientific geniuses *and* action heroes." She bent her head down to block Sam's view. "The producers are appealing to your hormones. I bet you that actor is not even smart. Just because he knows how to pronounce all those complicated words." She straightened up again to throw up her hands. "It's a script!"

Ingrid began to pace behind the couch. "It's not real! Same thing goes with all the heroes in those romance books you read. They are *not real*. If you don't realize that, you might end up spending every waking moment virtually in love with them, or researching absolutely everything about them, as though you had a snowball's chance in hell."

"Well, clearly, I don't have to worry about that because I'm not as crazy obsessive as you are," Sam shot back.

"The hair does a lot. I promise you," Ingrid went on without hesitation. "I'll teach you a trick right now. It's like ninety-eight percent effective." She pulled out her phone, searched for a photo, and then covered the top. "Here. This is how that guy would look bald. Do you still think he looks cute?"

Felicia craned her neck to look and burst out laughing.

"See?" Ingrid turned to show her mom the picture.

Mom made a face. "I'm afraid I have to agree with your sister."

"See? I knew Mom would agree with me." Ingrid grinned.

"Mom doesn't always agree with you. She didn't agree about getting our ears pierced," Sam supplied. "And that time when you insisted that we not buy an air fryer because it's just a trend and you think ovens work better."

"Ovens do work better!"

Mom hissed at Sam. "Don't start with her. You know how competitive your sister can get." She began grouping some party bags on the table as she asked her question. "What's your dissertation about again, dear?"

"Felicia, if you please?" Ingrid prompted.

Felicia cleared her throat ceremoniously. "Everyday life social structures."

"It's analyzing how people are perceived based on their social networks. For instance, stereotypes and social response," Ingrid explained.

Sam faked a loud snore on the couch.

Ingrid ignored her. "Take Einstein, for example. He's super brilliant, so of course, people also assume he's kind and generous and whatever. But the truth is he was a bit of a jerk! He didn't care for people's opinions, even ones that were right, as long as they were contrary to his."

"Or you're just bent on seeing the worst in people," Sam sneered.

"All I'm saying is: never meet your heroes," Ingrid proposed. "I'm not saying everyone is terrible. I'm just saying there's a reason stereotypes exist."

Sam huffed as she slumped deep into the couch once more. "Whatever. Finish your paper and go back to school. I want my room back solo."

Mom's eyebrows rose. "I thought you were getting a job closer to home?" she asked. "Ingrid, I don't want to have to worry about you every day with that long drive across two states. I heard from Mrs. Jenkins at the community center about this new job opening—"

Ingrid's eyes popped wide in wariness. It was rare in a week when her mother didn't try to persuade her to take some job in town, suitable or not. "Aaand that's our cue!" She jumped to leave. "Felicia?"

Felicia gave Mom a wry grin, already stepping back and motioning to the door. "Uh, see you later, Mrs. H." She let Ingrid tug her away. "Ingrid and I are going to go check out the decorations in the town square."

"Either way, Sam." Ingrid grabbed her shoulder bag with her other hand on their way out. "Feel free to read my paper if you want to get over your little school crush," she offered. "And definitely keep it in mind before you go falling in 'love'—" She gestured quotation marks with her fingers, "with this fictional, made-up guy."

"Boo! I swear to god, Ingrid, if you ruin another show for me," Sam whined. "Why can't you just let the dumb people enjoy their entertainment?"

"I'm just saying it's basic human—"

"Go away, Ingrid!"

2

Chapter Two - In Theory

"Where the heck is all the snow anyway?" Felicia was looking around in distaste.

Ingrid's hands were stuffed in her pockets. She gestured with the bottom half of her puffy jacket. "What do you mean? There's snow right there."

"There's slush right there," Felicia corrected as they walked along the street. "Hale Valley is supposed to be a perfect winter wonderland. But this is some kind of late winter we're having right now. Everything looks so...dreary and...not white."

Their beautiful small town of Hale Valley was usually 'holiday card' picture-perfect and at its best at Christmastime.

Usually.

This year, even the classic gazebo in the park, despite the plethora of fairy lights strung all across its roof, seemed lackluster without its icy frosty topping. Deciduous trees stood

12

awkwardly, bare and brown, in the square right by the Christmas tree farm lot that was only half-full while people milled around in arguably fewer layers of clothing than they ought to have been wearing for the season.

A few townsfolk were at the Soundshell garden surrounded by step ladders, boxes of colorful ribbons, and giant fake gift-wrapped boxes.

"Oh look, they're setting up the Christmas Wishing Tree." Ingrid pointed across the block to the plain green giant fir that within the next few days was surely going to be filled with sparkly handwritten note paper. "It's going to be so beautiful."

"You missed last year's tradition," Felicia reminded her as they stopped for a moment to watch the tree harness and support get fastened down. "Like the point of it being a tradition is that you must always do it."

"Sorry." Ingrid made a face.

"Then again so many things are changing around here. Dean said I was being too overly dramatic about certain policy upgrades at the mall the other day and I wasn't even. He thinks every time I tell him about my day, I'm asking him to fix something." She gave Ingrid a pointed look. "He actually said to me 'calm down'."

Ingrid laughed.

"You do *not* tell someone who you think is upset to 'calm down'," Felicia pointed out. "And since I wasn't even upset at the time, him trying to tell me to calm down just riled me up even more." She threw up her hands in frustration. "What do you think I should do with that?"

"Seriously, Fi. You don't want me to intervene again. But

you have to look at it from his point of view. Male brains just aren't wired to work a certain way. If they even sense a hint of a problem, their instinct is to just fix it. There's probably an entire gender studies course about that."

Felicia pursed her lips, displeased but resigned. "You're so good at this. If it wasn't for your constant couple's counseling, I bet Dean and I would have broken up after that first month."

"And now it's been almost a year. Congratulations."

Felicia colored slightly. "Dean makes me crazy sometimes but I do love him."

Ingrid thumped on her back. "Just focus on that. It'll all be alright."

She grinned again before she wrinkled her nose in sympathy. "Can I say it's just ironic that you are so good at giving relationship advice when...?"

Ingrid's chest tightened at Felicia's prompt and she gave her a sober look.

Because Felicia knew the real reason Ingrid had to move back home to work on her dissertation.

Ignoring her question, Ingrid started walking again. "Let's check out the new library conservatory."

Likely aware Ingrid needed to talk about this, Felicia didn't let it go. "Was Stewart happy about you coming back here? I thought he loved all that micro-managing and hands-on nit-picking of stuff?" she drawled with a derisive chuckle.

Her ire instantly building, Ingrid stopped walking again and she couldn't help her voice pitching up a few notches. "He basically kicked me off our project! What was I supposed to do? I couldn't just stay there. And besides, it's more than that. He never listens to my ideas."

Felicia gave her a knowing look. "Ingrid, wake up and smell that pretentious cold brew he keeps bragging about drinking exclusively. I told you Mr. Perfect is not all that he seemed. You should have broken up with him months ago."

Ingrid cringed almost involuntarily. "I did! I mean, sort of. Stewart and I are...taking a break. Like we're not dating anyone else but we're just getting some space and stuff."

Felicia's eyebrows rose in glee. "Really? Thank god! Have your senses finally caught up with you? Seriously, Ing! You study people for a living. I really don't know what you of all people see in that jerk."

"He's brilliant!" Ingrid argued. "He's very motivated. I know you never liked him but he challenges me. He pushes me harder to achieve more."

"Sounds like he's pushing you off a cliff," Felicia huffed.

"I'm serious. If it wasn't for him, I probably wouldn't even be thinking about competing for one of the TA slots in Professor Braun's top sociology team next year and they're only taking two."

"Isn't that halfway across the country? I'm sure your fancy degree can you get another job that won't need you putting up with Stewart's pretensions," Felicia rationalized.

"Look, you just don't understand. This is the most prestigious team in our field. Why would I want to go anywhere else?"

"You are so weird. You're the only person I know who wants to do research for a living."

"People fascinate me." Ingrid sidestepped a puddle. "You

get to analyze social interactions as a whole and tinker with the basic building blocks of communities. You get to solve the mysteries of why society does things!"

"Blah blah blah." Felicia waved drearily. "So what is it? Stewart hates the new stuff you added?"

"He thinks I'm wasting my time and that the new angle is stupid," Ingrid relayed, her tone dull. "Of course, he wants to stick to his original idea, which is so very not original by the way. It's so boring and derivative. Every other grad has already covered it. The only problem is he and I had proposed jointly to our adviser so we'd need to be in agreement."

"No offense, Ingrid. Stereotypes as a topic does sound a bit non-intellectual."

"Because you're just thinking about the lowest-hanging fruit again," Ingrid explained. "This study is about social structures at the micro level in the form of norms and customs. If we could assess how some of these methodological ideas are relevant for present-day cultural developments, I mean, the possibilities..." she trailed off in wonder.

Felicia blinked at her. "You—just said a whole bunch of gibberish." She waved her hand. "Which is why I choose to focus on the low-hanging fruit. And because the stereotypes part *is* the most interesting part in it."

"See?" Ingrid grinned in satisfaction. "Stewart just wants to tackle the same old boring high-brow academic relics. I want to explore something accessible. Something that gets real people interested. Something people will actually understand."

Felicia shrugged. "Your juvenile infatuation paper was surprisingly readable."

"*Thank* you!" Ingrid threw up her hands. "Didn't I tell you childhood crushes are nonsense?"

"Oh boy, here we go." Felicia rolled her eyes.

"It's just like I was telling Sam. She probably barely knows this boy. All she has is his appearance, a few bits of gossip regarding what he's like, and she's gone and imagined a whole other guy with all kinds of crushable qualities." They passed by the jogging group from the Senior Recreation Center and Ingrid lowered her voice. "Qualities that most guys don't even possess. And honestly, I bet she wouldn't even have noticed him at all if he wasn't a popular jock."

"You mean like your first ever biggest high school crush, Connell Matthews?" Felicia prompted with a knowing grin. "Look, I understand. This topic hits you at a very personal level."

"Exactly!" Ingrid declared confidently. "I know I use this example all the time but it is a *perfect* example. I idealized the crap out of that guy! And I knew next to nothing about him. Nothing real anyway. I spent years fawning over this image of him I had in my head—a completely different non-existent, *imaginary* guy." Stopping to let the fake Santa's sleigh cross the grassy path, Ingrid shook her head in derision and self-mocking. "So much wasted time and energy."

Ingrid didn't even want to stop to remember all the dumb shenanigans she had gotten up to in order to get Connell's attention in high school. In her mind, there was just a never-ending string of absolutely mortifying and embarrassing incidents that she would rather not remember.

"Like why did I even like him for so long?" She couldn't help but go on. "It was a total mystery. I knew absolutely nothing about him. It was just a façade I was seeing. That's why I was so dedicated to analyzing that topic to death until I'd learned to get over that guy. Problem solved."

Felicia patted her back in consolation. "Yes, yes, I remember. Your lifelong goal and big success. You achieved closure by changing your mindset. Congratulations."

Ingrid grabbed Felicia's arm. "Oh god, remember that one time I'd heard basketball practice finished late, and I waited two whole hours at the bus stop? And you remember what kind of freaks hung out at the bus stop. I basically risked my life just for one stupid glimpse of him. I didn't even know what I was expecting!"

Ingrid certainly hadn't expected anything at all from him. She was vividly aware he had been way out of her league. The only saving grace was that each time, she had managed to stay completely under his radar.

Ingrid was sure she had been discreet. She'd never openly 'stalked' him. The only people who knew about her so-called obsession were close friends, and possibly family, as she had no doubt brought home a sneaky photo of him once or twice in the past, newspaper clippings of sports events, and class pictures.

Felicia laughed at the memories. "I know, right? And given all the schemes we cooked up, I'm still amazed that Connell Matthews never caught on that there was anything more to it, or suspected anything, or ever asked why."

Honestly, there were times when Ingrid did wonder if Connell Matthews was at all aware or had caught on that she was one of his most avid fans. Some days she had even wondered if maybe he'd humored her more than most or at least appreciated her subtlety. That maybe he'd meant to linger around her a bit longer than the others for whatever reason.

Ingrid smacked her forehead with her palm. This was exactly the dumb thinking she'd had to keep in check. Thoughts that had no logical basis whatsoever. She had been delusional to imagine that she had been special to him in some way.

"Like he could pick us out of the crowd of hundreds of his admirers. Like that DJ in that rom-com movie. That would never happen in real life. Or more to the point," Ingrid added. "He was probably so used to the random fangirling attention that he never once gave any of it any second thought."

"Although, we all certainly inflated his already healthy ego. Who wouldn't want to be around more of that, right?" Felicia was already preoccupied with her phone. It wasn't the first time she had heard Ingrid's litany about this and knew it likely wouldn't be the last.

Ingrid took a deep breath. "I'm sure if Sam lets me help her, she could totally get over this little crush of hers right away. It's another big fat stereotype. All these shiny jock types are the same."

"Oh and look, your other college hottie crush is on the news again." Felicia held up her phone showing an internet sports magazine article headline with the name 'Joshua Knowles' in big block letters next to a tall, handsome, built, blond young man posing in full football gear. "Gotta say, Ing, as far as stereotypes go, you certainly do have a 'type'."

Ingrid laughed. "What do you want from me? I was a very dumb kid."

"But even I heard about the number Joshua Knowles did

on your college roommate Laura." Felicia shook her head. "'Douchebag' doesn't even come closer to a term to call him."

"Exactly! But does anyone think badly of the great Joshua Knowles?" Ingrid prompted. "'Youngest Ever Quarterback to Make Pro'? Of course not. And he doesn't even deny it himself. He's entirely happy to parade around as he is. He's even trending right now. This could be huge for my dissertation. I'm just waiting for Joshua's agent to call me to set up an interview time. He's the perfect case study for my paper. The only problem is he's super hard to get access to."

"Are you still waiting on that? You're going to run out of time. Why don't you find someone more accessible? Someone closer to home." She pursed her lips. "Maybe someone like...Connell Matthews 'the man' himself?"

Ingrid paused to consider it. "Our advisor did say that the most authentic results would be personal but..." As much as she wanted her results to be authentic, she was also trying to avoid making them *too* personal.

Felicia went on. "Come on. Confronting your oldest, biggest crush ever, breaking down how you got over him? That sounds like it would be a big draw. And people do love a good train wreck."

"That would be what Stewart would call 'psychology fluff.' And also why exactly would it be a train wreck?" Ingrid put her hands on her hips.

Felicia merely gave her a meaningful look.

"Come on, Fi. That was so many years ago. Did you *not* understand my elective paper?"

"Um, I'm going to say no," she admitted before waving it away. "Whatever. It's just I was there, Ingrid. You were literally obsessed with this guy. You spent most of your formative years fawning over Connell Matthews. I guess I'm just wondering if you're avoiding the issue because there's a chance you might still be hung up on him."

"I'm not *not* using Connell Matthews for my study because I'm still hung up on him, Fi. It's because Joshua Knowles is a much bigger fish—better fish."

"So prove it."

"Prove what?"

"You're doing representative sampling for your dissertation too, right?" Felicia asked. "Give Connell one of those surveys. He certainly fits the profile. It's just a little questionnaire, isn't it? No big deal. Unless...you're not as over him as you say you are," Felicia added coyly.

Ingrid groaned. "Connell Matthews is not going to answer my stupid survey. I'm sure he's got better things to do."

"It's not about the survey," Felicia stated. "I just want to see if you can do it. Have you really gotten closure? Like, do you even remember the crippling anxiety you used to have from the mere sight of him?"

"We are not sixteen anymore, Fi."

Felicia put her hands up. "All you need to do is make contact. Email him the survey for all I care. Personally, I would love to read about what he's up to nowadays."

Ingrid narrowed her eyes.

Felicia could be quite devious and manipulative. Ingrid had a sneaky suspicion that there was more to it than Felicia was letting on. But at this point, Felicia had already sparked Ingrid's curiosity about the matter, not to mention her competitive streak, and Ingrid rarely backed down from a challenge.

Ingrid let out a haggard sigh of resignation. "Fine. How do you propose we go about tracking Connell Matthews down? He could be out of the state or even out of the country right now. These are legitimate academic papers, Fi. They have a direct impact on my dissertation, ergo my life? I'm a busy person and I'm not going to wait around for you to lo-jack him to satisfy your curiosity, wasting even more time with—"

Head ducked down, Felicia was already tapping on her mobile phone. "Oh look, he's right in town, playing basketball near Holly Grove this afternoon." She whacked Ingrid's arm with the back of her hand. "We could just casually walk past and you could get all your answers."

"What?" Shocked, Ingrid craned her neck toward Felicia's phone. "How the heck do you have his location right now already?"

"Duh. He does regular check-ins on Facebook. Did you forget those many, many afternoons of our youth we spent tracking his every move?"

Ingrid rolled her eyes. "No, I didn't forget those absolutely embarrassing childish stunts that were such a complete waste of time. I swear I lost so many years of my life on it. I'm just surprised he's still doing that. He really is still every bit of a self-absorbed narcissist, isn't he?"

Felicia nodded. "I couldn't even believe he's in town either. I thought he was planning to stay at Oxbridge, playing basketball for the minors by now or something, but I think something happened to his scholarship."

Ingrid gave her an incredulous look.

"What? I know you've stopped researching him for your own personal reasons but it doesn't mean I have to. I'm curious about people too."

"Mm-hm." Ingrid pursed her lips. "What's Dean going to think about you stalking some other hot guy all over the internet, huh?"

"Please. Dean knows he's the only one I've been stalking since we were kids."

The phone in Felicia's hand dinged and she glanced down to check her notifications. "Uh-oh, speak of the devil. Dean's looking for me. I better go to Grandpa K's." She pocketed her phone and gave Ingrid a mock salute.

"Sure. I'll catch up with you guys there later." Ingrid nudged Felicia's shoulder.

"Are you sure you'll be fine to go talk to Connell Matthews by yourself?" Felicia's forehead was creased.

"Fi, I'm a grown-up. I can take care of myself. Besides, Dean needs you. Go." Ingrid waved her away. "Tell him he still owes me for that thing from last Thanksgiving."

3

Chapter Three - Impact

Ingrid passed by quite a few people walking in the cheery town square, taking advantage of the gentle chilly breeze on the rare sunny winter day. One of the great advantages she'd always loved about Hale Valley, being such a small town, was that everything was almost always only one convenient short walk away.

As she crossed Holly Grove, the repeated pounding of a rubber ball echoing against the court floor and the energetic squeaking of shoes indicated that she was headed to the right place.

Looking up, her quick scan of the ten or so bodies playing basketball found 'the man' himself—tall, blond Connell Matthews, just as he intercepted the ball for a rebound.

He took a step back into a lay out to launch the ball into a perfect arc straight swish into the basket.

Like it was choreographed.

Like it was some kind of scene from a movie and he was the star.

Except interestingly, after years of conscious training, Ingrid's stomach no longer burst with butterflies at the mere sight of him, and for a real moment, she was relieved.

The way Felicia had been building it up had frayed Ingrid's nerves, making her doubt she would even be able to do this, making her doubt her conviction.

But Ingrid had been right. It had been so long ago. She was no longer the mousy nerd in high school that fluttered every time he smiled, and craned her neck whenever he walked past. College had pulled (more like forced) her out of her shell, and her acceptance into one of the top grad schools in the country had given her enough confidence that she wasn't just some dumb nobody.

She could totally do this.

It was just work.

With that assurance and a nod to herself, Ingrid set up her laptop on one of the stone benches at the picnic area lining the basketball court. She figured she would just wait for a water break, approach the man-of-the-hour, give him the calling card with the QR code so he could respond to her survey over the internet, and she'd be back home before dinner.

Easy peasy.

A few other sweaty guys were hanging around the benches across the basketball court, gulping down bottles of water, roughhousing among themselves as they waited for their next turn to play. A couple of groups of younger girls were also watching the game themselves and it didn't take a Ph.D. to figure out why.

Sure, one or two more hot guys were playing ball right then too but it was no doubt mainly Connell Matthews who was drawing in the crowd.

Ingrid had seen him play basketball so often in the past, she knew exactly what she would see if she looked up to watch. He would dominate the court like he owned it. He was very determined, very creative, always graceful, and always mesmerizing.

Irrelevant things she already knew, so she simply focused on her work.

She bent her head to re-read a few responses she had already recorded while the game continued, and after a few minutes, she'd drowned out the whoops and yelling coming from the game as she took down a few preparatory notes.

That was if Connell Matthews might be part of the study now, she had to adjust a few assumptions and parameters so that—

"WATCH OUT!"

By the time Ingrid looked up, it was too late.

The spinning orange ball came hurtling at her face.

"Aahh—!" Ingrid toppled back off the bench, her laptop clattering to the concrete floor. Her vision blurred and the world spun a little bit as she landed on her back with a thump.

There were some shouts, some hasty steps thudding on the pavement.

Before she knew it, strong arms were braced around her back to prop her upright.

"Oh, shoot—I'm so sorry. Are you okay?"

Ingrid barely registered the deep, rich voice that was

tinged with genuine concern. She blinked hard, trying to get her ears to stop ringing. The sore spot on her forehead where the ball hit her was most likely red, except since she was also flushed from embarrassment, people probably couldn't tell.

Was she okay? Seriously?

Mortification flushed right through her. So did a rush of about a dozen flashbacks of utterly embarrassing past incidents involving Connell Matthews. Why did she always have to be embarrassed around him?

This was one of the reasons she had been adamant to get over her senseless crush—to avoid getting into any more of these situations, and for a moment, she was incensed. This was all Felicia's fault!

Ingrid should have known better than to listen to Felicia and let herself get manipulated in the first place. And now look what's happened!

Ingrid squeezed her eyes shut to get her bearings back as she stifled a groan in ridicule. "Is that a rhetorical question or a shocking indictment of whatever educational institution you're a product of?"

At her dry retort, a slightly bemused chuckle seemed to catch in his throat. "What?"

When Ingrid opened her eyes to meet his gaze, his forehead was wrinkled with worry, eyebrows furrowed as he looked her over.

It was curious. Naturally, she had seen so many pictures of Connell Matthews in the past but seeing those eyes, in person, mere inches away, Ingrid still froze at the gorgeous blue of their color, causing a flustered stir in her stomach.

Connell's hair was matted to his forehead and his neck

from sweat but Ingrid had most definitely never been quite this close to him to appreciate the chiseled cut of his jaw and those high cheekbones.

His muscle-T basketball hoodie hid nothing of his broad shoulders, that strong chest, and those toned arms. As an athlete, he had always been fit but in the last seven years, hot-as-hell high school jock Connell Matthews had certainly grown up.

His arm was still around her back to help her sit up and somehow, a faint scent of his cologne had survived the basketball game. At his proximity, sixteen-year-old Ingrid's heart skipped a beat.

Oh, crap.

Jumping to straighten up in her seat and sliding away from him, Ingrid shook her head to snap out of it.

Honestly, Ingrid, she scolded herself. She was a twenty-four-year-old Ph.D. candidate who had written a paper on none other than demystifying juvenile crushes. She absolutely should know better. She put a hand up, still blinking hard. "I'm fine. I'm good."

Connell watched her warily for a moment as if to make sure she really was fine and good before tilting his head to one side. "It's Ingrid, isn't it?"

She blinked again. "What? Uh, yes. Hi." Then she paused. "You know my name." It was more a statement than a question—definitely a surprised statement.

Connell broke an easy grin. "You...got awards a lot. In high school."

Ingrid's words still failed her and she could only give him a skeptical look in return.

His expression shifted to unease. "We uh went to high school together? I'm Connell—"

"Yes, I know who you are," she cut in before she could stop herself from sounding too eager. "You were the most popular guy at Lincoln High. We've crossed paths once or twice. I once had to join your class for a museum field trip because I got confused with the buses?" It was more like she had pretended to make the mistake of joining another class's trip just because it was his class—but that was beside the point.

"Oh. Really?" It was his turn to look surprised.

Ingrid barely managed to tamp down an eye roll.

But of course.

And despite her vindication, her heart went thud in her stomach. One of her theories was finally confirmed.

As she had fully expected, except for her vaguely familiar name, he didn't know her at all.

When it seemed he'd lingered around her in the past or showed her favor, it had all been a big fat coincidence—which was exactly the point! All those years of wondering if he'd noticed her or if he'd accidentally on purpose done something to get her attention? The truth was that he hadn't.

Connell Matthews had lived his entire life without any impact or influence whatsoever from her.

"Yeah." She smirked a little. "Don't worry about it. I wouldn't have expected someone like you to remember."

More shoes squeaked from the court.

"Matthews! Are you playing ball or what?"

Connell bent over to pick up the ball and tossed it back to the other guy who was wearing both a #23 basketball jersey and a prompting look on his face. Connell gave him a curt nod. "Gimme a sec."

Ingrid moved to retrieve her laptop but Connell jumped to get it first.

He made a face when the gadget rattled in his hands. "Oh, that doesn't sound good. Were you working on something important? I'm happy to pay for the damages. Um, do you—need help to recover your work? I hope you didn't lose too much."

Restoring her laptop, Ingrid frowned as she tapped on a few keys to try to wake up the machine—to no avail. Her ancient netbook had finally given up. She let out a haggard sigh. "Oh boy, there's no hope for you, my friend." She flicked the laptop screen down to close it.

He grimaced again. "Um, let me know what I can do to help."

She waved it away. "Nah, this was an old laptop. Besides, all my work is saved in the cloud so I didn't lose anything."

Connell looked confused for a moment but then he nodded his head. "Oh, right, sure. The cloud. That's good."

Ingrid pursed her lips. He had no idea what the hell she was talking about. But it only further supported her theory. Connell Matthews didn't have two sticks in his brain to rub together to make a small fire.

"You have to let me pay you back for the laptop. I insist." He spotted her cellphone still safely on the table, picked it up, and handed it to her so she could unlock it. "You should have my number."

"Connell," his friend hollered again. "Come on!"

Having swiped her phone unlocked, Ingrid's gaze flicked

up to the group of guys waiting before she glanced over at Connell with a puzzled look. His forehead creased in deep concentration as he entered his number into her phone and dialed.

From somewhere across the court, a cellphone ring echoed, playing something like a *Skrillex* song for two seconds before cutting off. "There." He tapped a few more buttons to save his name, looking satisfied, before handing her back the phone. "Now we have each other's number."

"Great."

Connell was still talking. "You don't live here anymore, do you?"

"Oh. No." She stood up.

"Are you just home for the holidays?"

"Something like that." Ingrid started to gather her stuff. Her fight-or-flight response was insisting that she run away and hide immediately.

"Me too," Connell piped up. "I mean, I lived in Philly up until recently," he amended. "But right now, I'm just staying at my Mom's until I can sort my stuff out."

"Oh. Really." Ingrid nodded noncommittally.

He shrugged. "It's perfect anyway. I can't exactly afford to pay rent for a while and my mom is always happy to do my laundry."

She almost couldn't bite back her smirk.

Slacker. Typical.

Leeching off his parents.

Check. Check.

Her dissertation was going to kick so much—

"Oh!" Ingrid alerted, only then remembering the one

reason she was even here in the first place. "Actually, I'm working on my Ph.D. dissertation in sociology and I could use your input on my paper."

The surprise in Connell's blue eyes was tinged with pleasure. "Really? Me?"

She laughed at the obvious shock on his face. "I just need to get you to answer this...survey." She fished out the business card from her pocket with the QR code. "Don't worry. It's nothing difficult. It's not like a math test or anything."

He checked the card in his hand. "Sweet. What's it about?"

She paused for a second. Somehow she had a feeling the layman's interpretation would not land well: how she had identified him to be part of a representative sample of dumb jock stereotypes and she wanted to analyze how this characteristic impacted his life and the people around him.

Careful, Ingrid.

"I'm um—gathering information about people's uh...high school experiences and what it's been like since," she fibbed since that was mostly right.

"Wow." He whistled, studying the card again. "'Ph.D.'...that sounds a little intimidating."

At his impressed expression, Ingrid felt compelled to elaborate. "Oh, I don't have it yet but that's what I'm studying for. And it's not as glamorous as it sounds. I can barely afford to pay rent too on what *I* make, but just..." She grinned before her gaze wandered off. "The study of people fascinates me. Everyone is just so weird—it's wonderful."

Connell looked amused. "I like that."

His gaze on her was making her jittery all over again.

Ingrid glanced away, clearing her throat. She pointed to

the card to shift his attention. "So the guide was on my lap-top in case you needed help with any questions but..." She tapped her chin. "I suppose I can just leave you a copy of the explainer and you can feel free to do it whenever. There's an address where you can mail it in and—"

"An explainer?" His forehead was creased again.

"Oh, that's a sheet that has more detail about each question in the survey. It also has the definition of terms, methodology...stuff like that."

Connell was chewing on the inside of his cheek, his eyes glued to the QR code card once more.

Ingrid furrowed her eyebrows, regarding his confused expression. "Would it maybe be easier if I talked you through the survey?"

Looking a bit sheepish, he met her gaze with a nod. "Well, just so I know I'm doing it right? I'm pretty sure this is like the *only* time I would ever be asked to help on a Ph.D. thing and I wouldn't want to mess it up."

"Oh." She glanced to one side to try to recall her schedule. "Um, yeah, okay, sure. How about...we meet up tomorrow? I'll go sort out a laptop that isn't broken and we can go through the questions together. I can call you later to set up a time."

A dazzling smile formed on his face. "Sounds great! Thank you."

"Uh, th-thank *you*," Ingrid chimed in with a shrug.

She rubbed the still sore spot on her forehead as she walked away. She almost couldn't believe what had just happened.

What did she just get herself into?

Or more accurately, what did a specific someone just get her into?

4

※

Chapter Four - Pointless Endeavor

"Felicia Mae Sanders!" Ingrid's yell out was punctuated by the jangling bells above the door of the quaint little brick building as she stepped inside.

Festive fairy lights and tinsel lined the big arched windows. Boughs of holly crept up the building's original support beams. The cast iron pot belly fireplace in the center of the room had been left to die out, barely crackling any more.

Owned by Dean's grandfather, 'Grandpa K's' was the first classic, small-town diner and bakery in town. The best one in Hale Valley. Though in recent years, a few additions had been put in to modernize the place, like the fenced-in children's play area that was big with the local moms in the mornings, and the gaming nook in the back decked out with a couple of consoles and a modest-sized TV screen.

Though the gaming area was more like Dean's idea for a way to pass the time whenever the diner hit the lull late in the day, such as this afternoon when one last table was still occupied and only one other customer was at the till ordering half-off end-of-the-day pastries to take home.

But not even the permanent aroma of decadent baking and freshly brewed coffee for the late shift could quell Ingrid's confrontational energy.

Ingrid marched right to the back where a bunch of bean bags was strewn on the floor. Felicia and her boyfriend Dean were lounging—one bean bag and game controller each. A plate of yesterday's gingerbread cookies was sitting on its own bean bag.

"Hey, Ingrid! Good to see you back in Hale Valley," Dean called out, even as his attention never veered away from the game screen.

Ingrid ignored him and went to stand right in front of Felicia, hands on hips, blocking the TV. "You knew Connell Matthews was in town, didn't you?" she demanded with a hoarse hiss, her eyes darting up furtively to make sure nobody else in the diner could hear.

"I heard something about it." Felicia's grin was akin to the Cheshire cat's.

"You totally orchestrated that!" she accused before something dawned on her. "And you," she prompted Dean. "Did you even need her for anything earlier?"

Dean's grin was just as mischievous. "I wanted to be around my girlfriend. Is that so bad?"

"Aww, you're so sweet." Felicia leaned over to give him a peck on the cheek.

Watching them, Ingrid feigned an annoyed retch in her mouth. "You guys are terrible."

Felicia was still grinning, her attention returning to Mario Kart. "So, how was the blast from the past?"

Ingrid plopped down onto a fourth bean bag with a sigh. "Well, I'll tell you." She reached over to grab a gingerbread cookie from the plate. "He's that exact same immature jock guy from high school."

"How is he?" Felicia asked. "I heard he transferred colleges or something. He spent a few years in Philly and now for some reason, he's back in town too. Didn't he say why?"

Ingrid munched through words. "I didn't ask."

"You didn't ask him anything?"

"No. Why?"

"You weren't curious?"

Ingrid tilted her head. "I'm not trying to research his life, Fi. It's been literally years since I stopped stalking his information. And there's no reason for me to want to find out more about him other than what I need for the paper."

Felicia's eyes twinkled. "Did you tell him you're currently single?"

"Ingrid's single now?" Dean piped up, incredulous.

"Shockingly, it didn't come up in our two-minute conversation. Besides, I'm not single *per se*," she corrected.

Felicia shrugged. "Well, you've been on a break like you said and everyone knows what that means."

"Does it mean I can make fun of Stewart's preppy ascot now?" Dean prompted. "Seriously, what is this, the seventeenth century?"

Ingrid let out a haggard groan. "Oh yeah, sure, now that

I'm single, let me just go hit up Connell Matthews for a date, shall I? Sure. That's going to happen. Talk about a pointless endeavor."

"Why must it be pointless?" Felicia asked.

Dean leaned back in his bean bag to interject. "Hey, I don't know this guy but I thought you said he was, and I quote: 'permanently attached to the hip' to some Serena Walker, Miss Head Cheerleader." He made a face. "Miss Prom Queen. Miss 'I Peaked in High School.'"

"Exactly." Ingrid gestured to Dean, nodding with emphatic agreement. "And if you had gone to school with us instead of your fancy private school, you would have thought the same thing." She met Felicia's gaze again. "I would have imagined the two of them should be married by now."

Felicia's jaw dropped and she finally put down her controller to whirl around and give Ingrid a pointed look. "Didn't you hear? You even predicted this yourself," she relayed. "Connell Matthews broke up with Serena. And she's gone off and gotten engaged to a doctor of all people—probably plastics. That must sting Mr. High School Basketball guy."

Ingrid waved her away. "That's unverified gossip—which either way has got nothing to do with us."

"Hey babe, did you stop playing?" Dean shook his sandy blond hair out of his eyes, still focused on the screen.

An elderly, silver-haired man wearing a ruffled red 'Kiss the Cook' apron shuffled out from the kitchen door carrying empty bread crates, and Ingrid's eyes lit up.

"Grandpa K!" She jumped from the bean bag to hug him.

Grandpa K was a fixture on Hale Valley's Main Street. Everyone knew him and he knew everyone. It helped that he was a natural people person and was still very quick-witted after all these years.

"Is that Ingrid?" Grandpa K's smile wrinkled the corners of his eyes. "I told you kids she'd come back to Hale Valley. They all do."

"She's just home for vacation, Gramps," Dean explained as he stood and took the crates out of Grandpa K's arms.

"Oh, I see. Better than nothing, I guess." Grandpa K patted her shoulder before training his eagle eyes on the plate of cookies on the bean bag. "Dean, those look like a fresh batch of cookies, not the ones from yesterday."

Dean shot the girls a telling guilty look before slinging his free arm around Grandpa K's shoulders. "Ah! Gramps, you should take it easy in your old age. You're seeing things. Why don't we sit you down in your comfortable chair and—"

Grandpa K gave Dean a suspicious look. "Old age, eh? I'm as sharp as I was when I was your age and this whole neighborhood was four houses and a town hall." He glanced over his shoulder at Felicia and Ingrid. "Tell you what, girls. I'll send Dean back with a batch of that new cinnamon pretzels recipe I'm trying out, especially for the holidays." He shot his grandson a pointed look. "Let's see if Dean doesn't eat them all first."

Dean merely flashed a sheepish smile.

"This rascal…" Grandpa K went on. "You remind me of myself during the war. Most days, you couldn't get me to share my rations even if you were saving my life."

Felicia and Ingrid laughed as Dean escorted his grandfather back through the kitchen, their conversation trailing off.

"He's such a sweetie." Ingrid gave Felicia a grin as she sank back down into the beanbag.

Felicia slumped in the same bean bag Ingrid was on, nudging her to make space. "Hey, so what else happened, you know, with Connell Matthews?"

Ingrid rolled her eyes, her mood instantly tensing. "Well." She took a deep breath. "Long story short: he hit me in the face with the basketball then gave me his number to offer to replace my broken laptop."

Felicia burst out laughing. "What? Sounds special."

Ingrid frowned again as she felt inside her pocket for her phone. "That reminds me. I need to set up an appointment for tomorrow so I can take him through the survey."

Felicia's eyes lit up. "Well, then it's a good thing he gave you his number. Also, I *cannot believe* you have Connell Matthews's number." She wiggled her eyebrows in mischief.

Ingrid groaned. "Oh, Fi. Why do you keep making it like this is more than what it is? It's just work."

"It's just you've been mooning over this guy for nearly a decade."

"I think the word you're looking for is 'mooned'—past tense," she pointed out before pausing with a grimace. "Wait, that sounds wrong."

Felicia laughed.

"In any case!" Ingrid threw up her hands. "He was just an infantile crush—again, a meaningless thing. This was exactly the topic of my other paper, remember?"

"Whatever, Ing. If you want I'll totally shut up about this but only if you tell me your heart was beating normally when you saw him at the game today." Her brown eyes were challenging.

Ingrid gave her an unamused glare. "He hit me in the face with a ball! My pulse was racing due to my anxiety levels being so way up!"

Felicia laughed again.

Ingrid swiped her phone unlocked and stopped short. "This just all feels eerily familiar." She gave Felicia another look, recalling the one time two years after high school graduation when she had cold-called him just to ask what his basketball jersey number was because she had simply forgotten. "I don't want this to be another crazy stunt involving Connell Matthews. I have had enough of those to last me a lifetime."

"You said so yourself. It's just work." Felicia's expression had that sly, mischievous tinge again.

"Exactly." Ingrid nodded and scrolled through her contacts list to find where Connell had saved his number. But despite herself, the moment she tapped on the green call button beside Connell's name with the smiley emoji, her pulse did race.

5

Chapter Five - Blast from the Past

Ingrid had been so used to the view of the back of his head, having watched him from afar for years in school that it was easy for her to pick him out from a crowd.

She had arrived with ten minutes to spare but Connell was already in front of the building where they had agreed to meet up. His arms were folded across his chest in a way that was straining the fabric of his crisp, pale blue, long-sleeved shirt.

Like, he seriously should have gotten it one size bigger.

Naturally, he was amidst a group of giggling girls. An easy smile on his face as the girls stared up at him and hung on to his every word.

He certainly seemed to be enjoying it.

Then again, he was no doubt used to it by now.

Adjusting her hold on her binder, Ingrid walked over. It was very disconcerting, since in every other instance in the past, she would have had no problem walking toward him given that she would have usually been merely trying to walk *past* him on the sly.

God, maybe she *was* a stalker.

But now knowing that she was walking up *to* him while he was waiting *for* her finally triggered the butterflies in her stomach that she had managed to tamp down for the last seven years.

Tsk, Ingrid. So much for that.

She hadn't seen Connell since high school and just this week, she had now seen him twice.

And even if there was no denying she *may* still be sort of attracted to him, she reckoned it was completely normal.

The guy basically oozed charm and sex appeal. It wasn't even his fault. He probably couldn't help it.

Really, it was up to Ingrid to get her head back on straight and see the forest for the trees.

Connell's eyes lit up upon spotting Ingrid and he broke away from the crowd. "Hey." He gave her a cool nod.

Shaking her head briskly to clear it, Ingrid recalled the comprehensive analysis points she had outlined in her last paper, reminding herself exactly why she was no longer into him. "Hey," she smiled tentatively. "Thanks for doing this. I know people can be busy during the holidays."

"It's no problem."

"Um, okay, so, shall we sit down somewhere so I can ask you some questions?" she suggested.

"Sure." He motioned her through the sliding glass doors.

Ingrid should have recognized the address when he'd given it to her as their meeting place. She stopped in her tracks as soon as the distinct whiff of air conditioning and old carpet wafted over her. "Um, this is a bowling alley."

"No, this is *the* bowling alley. Don't you remember this place?"

Her walking slowed. "Yeah, my friends and I used to come here too—in high school."

Connell's grin was wide. "And it's barely changed since." He led the way through the corridor and Ingrid couldn't help her jaw dropping as she followed suit.

He wasn't kidding about the place having barely changed since high school.

Loud crashing of pins and muted yells came from the left where there was a set of bowling lanes right by a staircase that Ingrid knew led upstairs where the pool tables and gaming casinos were. Pop music blaring through the speakers from the music videos displayed on several large TV screens mounted along the walls mingled with the clacking of billiard balls and general merriment from the sparse weekday crowd.

"What are we doing here?" Ingrid had to ask.

"I'm meeting some friends later so I thought I'd save the trip and meet you here too."

"Oh." She nodded in understanding. "Okay, sure, that makes sense." She did a double take when they passed a festive billboard advertising 'Hale Valley's Best Hot Cocoa Contest.' "Oh wow, they still do that?"

"Of course. You like hot chocolate?" Connell asked.

"Who doesn't? My friend Felicia and I used to hit every

shop at the annual Winter Fair to try out each one and then make our own little tally."

"You're going to be around for the Winter Fair?"

Ingrid nodded again, eagerly this time. "Yeah, I saw the decorations in the square. Every year that decorating committee just outdoes itself, doesn't it? I mean I've been to many places but I think Hale Valley is still the most picturesque town during winter. Even Stewart said once that Hale Valley was like a winter wonderland and *he* can be really picky." She couldn't help a roll of her eyes. "It's just a shame there's not much snow yet."

"Stewart?"

Ingrid blinked, caught off-guard. "Oh, um... my...boyfriend."

"Ah. The lucky guy."

Ingrid stopped short but she figured her correction of 'up until recently' was neither relevant nor expedient so she just replied, "Um...yeah. So, hey, listen—"

"Oh, look!" Connell pointed across the way. "They've installed a new basketball game." He strode toward the game, waving her over. "Come on, I challenge you to some hoops."

Ingrid frowned even as she followed behind him.

While she was grateful Connell could squeeze her into his no doubt busy social schedule, she should have known he would find the first opportunity to slack off. This was going to take a bit more doing than she'd thought. "Um, wait, I do need to ask you some questions."

"That's fine. Just put it down over there for a sec and shoot some hoops with me. Best out of ten."

Ingrid couldn't help her mouth dropping open a little. "That's hardly fair. You played on the varsity team."

He smirked. "Afraid of a little contest, are we?"

That triggered Ingrid. Did he think she was simply going to fangirl over him while he shot some hoops? He probably thought she felt lucky enough to be in his mere presence. Did he think she was some spineless pushover nerd that wouldn't stand up for herself?

High school Ingrid might have flustered a lot and been meek and insecure.

High school Ingrid was not here.

She tilted her head to regard him with a cautionary look. "Oh, you really don't want me to turn it on."

Connell broke a grin. "Oh, yes, I do."

"You want me to be competitive?" She put her hands up in warning. "I'll tell you right now, I have a very obsessive personality. I can be a very sore loser and a very sore winner. It's not healthy at all. Once I'm into something, there's no digging me out."

He laughed, challenge in his eyes. "Really?" He didn't seem in any way threatened.

Undaunted, Ingrid shot him a narrow-eyed look. "How about we play a real game?"

"What did you have in mind?"

The Daytona drag racing video game was very definitely over fifteen years old. Ingrid was almost surprised that it was still in the venue and fully functional, but about six tokens later, she was 2-0 up on Connell Matthews.

Ingrid smashed her foot down on the pedal when the green traffic light lit up the screen signaling 'GO' on their third race. Her heart was pounding in her ears combined with the loud zooming and screeching of the tires as her car wound the speedway circuit. She pulled on the clutch and spun the wheel, frowning in caution as a car came weaving across the road to slam against the side of hers.

"Stop bumping me!"

Connell laughed. "What? You're the one bumping me!"

"Learn to drive—"

"Hey, no fair!" His car squealed and tumbled sideways, crashing into the fake digital crowd. "Oh—I just crashed." His chuckle was half-groan as his screen flashed 'GAME OVER' in big red letters.

Connell sat back in his seat but then he let out another chuckle when he glanced over at her.

Still wholly focused on the videogame with her eyebrows furrowed, Ingrid was concentrating on not sliding her car against the raceway, easing the wheel a little bit left and right to adjust for her increasing speed.

"Hey, look, I think you're about to set a new speed record." His voice near her ear all of a sudden made her jump, almost causing her racing car to crash as well. She hadn't even noticed that he'd gotten up to stand beside her seat.

"Hey, watch it!" Connell grabbed the wheel over her shoulders to help steer.

"What are you doing?"

"I'm trying to help," he claimed.

Connell's immediate proximity was blitzing her brain. He smelled so good. The scent of his cologne—the same intoxicating one from high school, by the way—was conjuring up all sorts of flashbacks in her mind, like the several times she'd sneakily stood next in line to him at the cafeteria.

Except Ingrid's competitive streak was on overdrive. She hadn't played this game in years but she absolutely could not lose today. She knew the next and last turn was the trickiest part. She gritted her teeth in annoyance instead.

The jerk was going to mess up her game!

"Stop it, you're making it worse!"

"No, I'm not."

"Yes, you are!"

Letting go, Connell started to laugh. "I am so not!"

At the playfulness and hint of guilt in his tone, Ingrid couldn't help a laugh herself. "You totally are!" She spun the wheel and slammed on the pedals until her car finally coasted across the finish line banner and fireworks erupted on the screen.

HIGH SCORE.

She blew out a breath, dropping her hands, before turning in her seat to give him a haughty look. "I believe I just beat you, Mr. Matthews."

Connell merely shook his head in mirth. "You never told me you drag-raced outside of your grad school studies."

"Please." Ingrid pushed up off the seat. "I've spent many a high school afternoon wiping the floor with some of these noobs."

"Impressive." He gave her a nod. "How come I never saw you around here back in high school? You must have played here so often to be this good."

After a beat, Ingrid shrugged. "I don't know," she said— even though she knew exactly why.

Connell would have been with his friends at the time. He would have been with Serena. All the time. Hence: fully occupied. She doubted he would have necessarily paid anyone outside their group any attention.

"I suppose that must have been my fault. I hardly ever socialized outside my small group of friends back then." Connell had a strangely rueful look on his face.

Ingrid blinked. "Uh...you're probably right." There was a surprising level of self-awareness in his statement that she found herself staring up at him in marveling for a second longer than she should have, and when he glanced over, she startled and looked away.

A corner of his mouth turned up. "Come on. Help my poor bruised ego. Shoot some hoops."

Pursing her lips, Ingrid checked her watch. "Um." She supposed one more game couldn't hurt.

Although once they got there, Ingrid didn't even have a chance.

Mr. Basketball was eager to shine.

Connell didn't even bother looking as he began sinking baskets cleanly one after the other, his grin already wide. "See? Do you see what I'm doing? He shoots, he scores!"

Ingrid rolled her eyes. "You're such a show-off." She couldn't help shaking her head in mirth once again.

Ingrid's phone rang and she jumped to check.

Joshua Knowles.

Upon reading the caller Id, Ingrid sat up straighter in her seat. "Oh, shoot."

"Shoot?" Connell asked.

"No, no." Ingrid shook her head, gesturing to her phone.

Finally! The pièce de résistance of her dissertation had finally made contact.

She swiped to answer the call right away. "Hello, this is Ingrid Harmon speaking."

"*Please hold for Mr. Barrett's office.*"

"Yes, of course!"

For some strange reason, she was somewhat relieved.

Challenge or not, Ingrid didn't have to get Connell's input on anything. Joshua was the big fish.

With the phone in the crook of her shoulder, she gave Connell a wan smile. "Oh, hey, I have to take this call. I should probably go first."

"But I was winning!" Connell protested with a lopsided grin.

"I really am so sorry. Would you mind if we rain check?"

Breathless, Connell straightened up and ran his hands through his hair. "Okay, sure. Call me whenever."

"And next time, I think we should start with the questions," Ingrid proposed directly, her exasperation almost leaking into her tone. "Just to make sure it gets done."

"Whatever you say, Professor."

6

Chapter Six - Distractions

"I'm back!" Ingrid called out, shrugging off her jacket as she stepped through the front door.

"Ingrid!" her mom yelled out. "We're all in the dining room."

Ingrid was expecting her family to be sitting down for a meal, but she stopped in her tracks when her eyes fell on her mom, Sam, and even Felicia at the dining table, with piles of those golden party favor bags and the clutter of dozens of little trinkets yet again.

"What's—going on?" Ingrid approached the group, trying to make sense of the mess. She met Felicia's gaze and quipped with a grin. "And don't you ever go home, Fi?"

"Sam and I were watching more MacGyver, what?"

"Aren't you my best friend? Not hers?"

"I'm everyone's friend," Felicia replied haughtily. "That's just who I am. You don't have to be jealous. There's plenty of me to go around."

Ingrid shook her head in mirth.

"Either way, we needed all the help we can get. It's DEF-CON One." Mom shoved about a dozen bags her way.

Ingrid slid her prompting gaze over to Sam. "Because why?"

Sam replied by tossing another half a dozen bags in her direction. "Apparently, Uncle Gene and Aunt Sheila aren't going to make it to the party this weekend. So remember those keychain party favors, the ones with the leaf waving that looks like—"

"The ones that say 'High, everybody'...?" Felicia bit her lip.

"Look, I thought they were maple leaves, okay?" Mom announced defensively.

Felicia held one of the distinctive leaf-shaped trinkets up so Ingrid could see and she stifled back her chuckle.

"Oh!" Ingrid's eyes widened. "Yeah. I can see how someone could make that mistake."

"They might be considered 'offensive'," Felicia mocked with her fingers as quotation marks and a sly grin.

Her mom nodded. "And they're going back in. If your stuck-up snob Aunt Sheila is still jet-setting around, maybe everyone else will just think it's funny." Mom pushed her chair back to get up. "I need to find some more of this gold ribbon. Sam, come upstairs and help me look. Ingrid, you help Felicia with this."

Ingrid could only shake her head in incredulity as her mom and sister headed upstairs. She blew out a breath, slumping into a chair as she set a couple of bags closer to her side. "Sure. I guess I should at least get something productive done today."

The exasperation from the day's events must have stayed on Ingrid's face that Felicia's eyebrows shot up. "How did the survey with Connell Matthews go?"

"Didn't."

Felicia gawked. "You didn't finish?" She abandoned her party favor bag and turned to face Ingrid with a curious prompt. "What were you actually doing?"

Ingrid huffed in frustration. "He's just really...immature. Such a slacker. He doesn't take anything seriously. This is turning into a bit of a mission. He was too distracted today."

"He was too distracted or too distracting?" Felicia smirked knowingly. "Didn't you just come from the bowling alley?"

She waved her hand to dismiss it. "Yeah, he was meeting some friends there and then challenged me to shoot hoops."

"That's hardly fair. He played on the team."

Ingrid threw up her hands. "I know! That's why I kicked his ass on the racing game instead."

Felicia must have noted the hint of a sparkle in Ingrid's eyes that Felicia's jaw dropped in amusement. "You had fun! You had fun with immature jerk Connell Matthews."

"Oh wow, here she goes again. Making a big deal out of nothing." Ingrid stood to get something to drink from the kitchen.

"Nothing? You call that nothing?" Felicia chased her down. "Your scale is so skewed, my friend. I mean, if this had happened to one of the 'groupies' back in high school—remember them?"

Ingrid's eyes widened in recollection. "Oh my goodness, yeah, the 'groupies.'"

Felicia leaned back against the kitchen counter beside her as Ingrid poured some juice. "That gaggle of Connell Matthews fans who made absolutely no effort to hide the fact that they loved him so much, doing his homework for him and fainting every time he smiled or something. And they didn't care about Connell and his jock friends harassing the freshmen, through all the loogies and wedgies, cheating on tests, cheating on their girlfriends."

"No kidding. It's such herd mentality, and the opinions of the popular girls just became consensus, boosting Connell's reputation even more," Ingrid rationalized, making a face at a now-empty carton of juice in her hand and putting it away. "Ironically, it's not much different now. You know this is exactly how trends are born." She shook her head as she mulled the fact over in relief. "Well, at least we know I wasn't the most embarrassing of the lot."

Felicia was biting back her chuckle. "Even after that time that you nearly fell on your face trying to show off in P.E. class just because Connell was in the gym too. Or that time you tried to slip a note in his locker and almost got caught by security picking the lock."

Ingrid buried her face in her hands. "I swear to god, Felicia. I am never letting you dare me to do anything ever again in my entire life. You do realize a lot of this could also be seen as having been *your* fault?"

"Hey, if I'm guilty of anything, it's only to being the most supportive best friend a girl could ever have." Felicia put her hands up innocently. "So you told him you broke up with Stewart, right?"

Ingrid made a face. "What does that have to do with anything?"

"Just in case, you know." She shrugged. "Maybe after all this time, Connell's tastes have refined from shallow cheerleaders and snobby socialites."

Ingrid laughed at the ridiculous notion. "Look, regardless. Maybe today with Connell was...fun," she conceded. "But fun doesn't help me finish my paper." She dismissed it with a wave. "Meanwhile, back in the real world, I finally got a call back from Joshua Knowles' agent's PA."

"And?"

"They say he would be interested in participating but they wanted me to propose some dates. His PA thinks he won't be available until summer which would be too late for me. She said she'd call me back though."

"Bummer."

Ingrid sighed again. "Oh well, I sort of knew it was a long shot." She pursed her lips in deep thought. "You know, I was already thinking if Joshua Knowles said no, I could have gotten Connell Matthews to participate—as a backup case study as you suggested. He was never an option because I never thought I'd get this opportunity to pin him down. But if today is any indication, it's looking like it's all moot anyway," she concluded as she headed back out to the dining area.

Felicia snatched a cookie from the cooling tray by the oven before following suit.

"Felicia, those are for the bake sale fundraiser," Mom called out. She and Sam had already returned to the table with several spools of gold ribbons.

"Oh. Oops." Felicia gave her a sheepish grin.

Fortunately, Mom was already preoccupied with the party bags to grill her any further.

Felicia sat next to Ingrid and elbowed her. "Hey, when are you going to see Connell Matthews again?"

Frowning, Ingrid inspected the party favor bags closest to her. She was perfectly happy to bookend her 'blast from the past' with that awkward exchange at the bowling alley. "I don't know," she replied distractedly. "Maybe it'll be better to find another case study altogether. I mean, if Joshua Knowles is a no-go and Connell is just too hard basket, I have to check my candidate list again."

Mouth full of cookie, Felicia merely nodded. "Mm-mm. Well, whoever it is, let's just hope they don't ask too many questions about how they were selected. It's not exactly flattering to be a representative of this particular stereotype."

Ingrid cast a sideways glance at the scattered notes and haphazardly stacked books she'd left lying open on the coffee table in the living room. "In any case, I can't afford to be distracted anymore. Stewart's paper is probably complete." Her resolve mixed with a bit of worry at her assumption. "I don't mind losing to Mr. Basketball in shooting hoops but I will definitely mind losing to Stewart. I need to get my act together."

"After the party," Mom interjected loudly.

Ingrid grinned in concession. "After the party. Yes, Mom."

7

∽∾

Chapter Seven - Grown up

Despite the rest of the town library still under construction, the new conservatory was a classy, well-lit, open space surrounded by a curated collection of plants and flowers. It was perfect for intimate parties and events with the skylight providing light and warmth during the day and a spectacular view of the night skies in the evenings.

It was as good as their cozy little town could do.

And it certainly suited Ingrid's family reunion's some fifty-strong guests.

Ingrid thought her mom had outdone herself for this year's affair. It was a crisp and clear evening. Mom had gotten her interior decorator sister Aunt Angie to spruce up the place with holiday cheer.

They couldn't quite get a Christmas tree into the space but

every other corner of the conservatory was dressed in gold and silver ribbons on evergreen boughs. The casual reading area had been pushed aside to make way for catering tables adorned with tea lights in little golden bowls. Dad had spent all morning blowing up gold and silver balloons for the 'grand' balloon archway at the entrance beside a table heaped with glittering gaily-wrapped presents. Everything sparkled from the glow of the simple modern chandeliers hanging above, the ambiance enhanced by the elegant Christmas piano music playing from the built-in speakers.

Since the 'honor' to host the Christmas event for their family changed every year, Ingrid thought it was safe to say, her mom was definitely winning.

She would have been sharing in the glow-basking of the evening's triumph, except Ingrid was preoccupied with other things.

Sam hissed at her by the potted plants. "What are you still doing here?" she asked as she rushed off toward the table of gifts. "You're supposed to be setting up the slideshow."

Head bent, Ingrid was checking her phone messages.

It had been a few days since she'd sent a handful of follow-up requests for participation to her backup case study candidates, but so far, everyone was too busy or not interested.

She chewed on her bottom lip, swiping into Joshua Knowles' PA's message thread to make sure she hadn't missed any.

No such luck.

She groaned and slipped her phone back into her chain-mail shoulder bag.

While dinner was being served, Ingrid was supposed to

put on the set of video greetings on the projector from their family members who couldn't attend tonight's festivities.

On her way to the table with the laptop set up, Mom met her by the sidelines. Being hostess of the evening, her mom's face was creased with agency and worry—warranted or not.

"Ingrid." Her mom sounded like DEFCON One again. "Cousin Monica just told me that she thinks the vegetarian truffle macaroni and cheese might have meat in it. Do you think the caterers mixed up some of the food trays? Or maybe they've mislabelled something? Or maybe they've forgotten altogether that there should be vegetarian platters?"

Her mom seemed to be on the precipice of hysteria already, panic painted on her face about the impending disaster.

Ingrid pursed her lips. She didn't attempt to soothe her mom as she knew it would be virtually impossible. Instead, she gave her a reassuring nod. "Don't worry, Mom. I'll go fix it." She rushed off, catching Felicia's glance from across the room, and Ingrid just made a big show of shrugging.

With a knowing smirk, Felicia simply mirrored her shrug and then went on to help some people to the buffet tables.

This hadn't been the first "emergency" of the night and if her mom's history was anything to go by, it wouldn't be the last either.

Ingrid wove her way around some mingling guests toward the kitchen near the annex connecting the conservatory to the main library.

It could have been the shift to the sudden dim light from the bright light in the conservatory, or it could have been the fact that she wasn't looking where she was going, that Ingrid nearly ran straight right into somebody coming out of the hall leading to the restrooms.

Ingrid's eyes popped wide as she recognized him. "Connell!"

Connell had been preoccupied with his suit jacket and was just as surprised when he looked up to see her. "Ingrid?"

She couldn't help giving him a top-to-toe once-over.

Connell Matthews was *so* wearing that suit. The charcoal black tailored jacket and matching black tie emphasized everything heart-stopping about him—his broad shoulders, his toned chest, that stupid cleft on his chin. He even looked a bit taller. And whatever product he had put in his hair made him look like freaking James Bond.

Self-conscious, Ingrid snapped her open mouth shut and she had to shake her head to clear it. "W-What are you doing here?"

"Oh, I'm...working."

Her eyes lit up in relief. "Oh, thank goodness! Are you a waiter at this event? I seriously need to sort out an impending vegetarian platter issue to make sure my mother's head doesn't spontaneously explode." She tugged on his sleeve, explaining the situation as they made their way to the kitchen.

"Of course." Connell raised his hand to call the nearest server by the window. "Hey Trudy, can someone please double-check that the vegetarian appetizers have gone out?"

A uniformed server came up to the two of them. "Excuse me, Mr. Matthews."

Ingrid froze.

Mr. Matthews?

"Harry said they had to move some of the tables to make

space for the dessert bar but now some of them are too far from any power outlets."

After a moment's thought, Connell replied, "There's a set of cold appetizers about to come out that you can swap those trays with. They don't need the heating element to be on," his tone confident and authoritative.

Ingrid's jaw dropped again and her face flamed.

Oh crap.

"And make sure all those power cables are out of people's way."

"Sure thing, boss. I'll get right on it."

"Thanks, Stan."

Once the server had rushed off, Connell met Ingrid's wide-eyed gaze again, but there was also uncertainty on his face. "Uh, sorry about that."

Ingrid covered her face with her hands. "Oh my god, you run this place." She gave him an imploring look. "I am so sorry I assumed—ohmygod—" She cringed again, looking away. "Why doesn't the ground ever swallow you up when you need it to?"

Connell chuckled. "Hey, don't worry about it. Besides, I don't actually run the place. I'm only catering this event." He gestured around them. "The restaurant, it's...sort of my business."

What? Ingrid had to stop her jaw from dropping once again. "Great! I mean, wow! I mean congratulations. I mean— oh dear god, why aren't I being swallowed by the ground yet?" She dropped her gaze in horrific mortification.

He was still laughing when his gaze distracted across the room. "Oh, someone needs me." He moved to leave but first turned back to ask, "Hey, is this your family's party? The booking is under a different last name—Taylor or something."

"Oh, that's my mother's maiden name."

His eyes lit up. "Ah, that's why I didn't recognize it." He glanced across the room again, frowning in seeming displeasure, but gave her an apologetic look. "Listen, I have to take care of something but I'll come find you later, okay?"

Ingrid's eyebrows furrowed. Why? She wanted to ask but he had already left. And she couldn't help herself from watching him walk away.

She should have noticed that the cut of his suit was significantly different from the uniforms that the servers walking around were wearing.

Significantly.

Connell looked like he'd walked right off a magazine photoshoot for GQ or Armani—the front cover of the magazine photoshoot.

Ingrid tugged on the neckline of her minimal cocktail dress.

Did it suddenly get hot in this room? Maybe she needed to get someone to turn on the air conditioning.

Ingrid blew out a breath to clear her head before heading back toward the laptop to get the slideshow ready.

Except even from way across the room, Ingrid couldn't help her stray glances toward Connell who was busy discussing what appeared to be important details with several people. His forehead was creased in concentration as he gave out instructions.

He wasn't on a basketball court, but he still looked fully in charge, as though he knew exactly what he was doing. It was very disconcerting to adjust to the thinking that Connell Matthews could possibly talk authoritatively about something other than basketball. That perhaps Connell Matthews had actually seriously grown up.

At that moment, Connell glanced over and met her gaze. It was as if he knew she'd been staring at him.

Oh crap. Ingrid flinched and looked away.

It was difficult enough to focus on the trivialities of the party. She couldn't quite wrap her mind around the fact that Connell Matthews was within the same four conservatory glass walls as she was. She was suddenly acutely aware of everything surrounding her, every flutter of any hanging decoration, every breeze stirring the curtains, every clink of every glass or utensil.

Fortunately, Felicia came over right then, snapping Ingrid out of her downward spiral with a start.

"Hey." Felicia popped a piece of cake in her mouth and spoke through her mouthful. "Apparently, your little cousin Victoria has been rooting around the table of presents and sneaking peeks inside packages. Sam said she's already torn through a couple..." she trailed off, assessing the look on Ingrid's face. "What's up with you?"

"Mm? Nothing." Ingrid dropped her gaze to the laptop, tapping a few keys, and after a few moments, the video feed flickered onto the projector screen. "Sam's supposed to be the one keeping an eye on the gifts. I did tell her to bring tape and extra wrapping paper."

Felicia grabbed her arm. "Oh my goodness."

"Now what?" Ingrid nearly froze at the alarm in Felicia's voice.

But Felicia seemed to be tongue-tied.

Ingrid gave her a weird look before she glanced over her shoulder in time to see Connell Matthews striding toward them and her mouth turned dry too.

One hand in his pocket, Connell was walking toward them with his usual confident gait. Never mind that he was drawing several other guests' attention simply by walking across the room. It was as if the entire venue had to shift to accommodate his commanding presence.

Felicia swore under her breath.

Yes, Felicia. So much yes.

8

Chapter Eight - What Works

"Hi again." Connell arrived with a smile so dazzling, Ingrid could barely look right at it.

"Hey..."

"I had some free time so..."

Ingrid couldn't help another puzzled look.

"I thought I'd come over so you could give me one of those super confused looks," he finished, teasing. "Why do you keep looking at me like that?"

Ingrid dropped her gaze at once. "Oh uhhh... I get really dry eyes. Sometimes it's hard to focus," she totally lied.

Felicia's eyes were still wide. "Hi. Connell. Matthews."

He shifted his gaze toward her and narrowed his gaze. "We went to high school together too, right?"

Felicia's head bobbed in agreement. "Yes, hi, I'm Felicia."

Connell responded with a nod. "Felicia, nice to meet you. You must be...Ingrid's best friend?"

More head bobbing.

"Why are you here?" Felicia was in awe.

"My restaurant's catering this event." He gestured toward the food tables.

Felicia turned to Ingrid with a highly meaningful look. "Oh, would you look at that? Isn't that great?" She met Connell's gaze with a big smile. "The food is so good. I love those little cheesecake things."

"Thanks, Felicia." His smile seemed genuine.

Felicia glanced from Ingrid to Connell and back again. "Well, I think I'll—oh look, I think I'm needed over there. Gotta go. It was great to see you. Connell Matthews." She gave him a mock salute, turning to leave but not before grabbing Ingrid's arm to whisper hoarsely, "Ask him out!"

Ingrid made a face. What on earth even was she talking about? She shrugged Felicia's hand off her arm and Felicia slinked away with a self-satisfied wave.

Ingrid could only shake her head in disbelief before turning back to him. "Sorry. That was Felicia."

Connell's gaze was focused somewhere over her shoulder.

Her eyebrows furrowed as she turned to one side. "What is it?"

His gaze slid back to meet hers. "Oh. Nothing. I hadn't seen your hair like that before."

"Oh." Self-consciously, Ingrid reached up to check on her hair. At the salon earlier, her sister had insisted that they both go with the fancy updo hair. Even though Ingrid had noted that it was unnecessarily high-maintenance. Although, no doubt, with her rushing around all night, her hair probably looked nothing like the elegant coiffure it was supposed to be.

Connell gestured to the table with the video presentation. "Did you get a new laptop?"

"Oh." Blinking again, Ingrid explained almost automatically. "No, that belongs to the library. Sometimes they show documentaries and slideshow presentations on the projector for school projects."

"Oh, so you didn't bring a laptop today? Shocking."

She caught the mischievous glint in his eyes and her jaw dropped in disbelief. Connell Matthews was making a joke at her expense. "Are-are you making fun of me?"

He bit his lip, his shoulders shaking in mirth.

"Let's not forget whose fault it is that I don't have a laptop anymore," she posed pointedly.

He had to stifle his chuckle. "Touché."

She waved her hand. "I know you think I'm just a total nerd who got all those awards in high school, right?"

He wrinkled his nose. "Ah, I'm sorry about that. I didn't really know you all that well back then." An almost diffident smile turned up the corners of his mouth. "But it's...nice to finally be meeting you."

The uncertainty in his tone took Ingrid aback but before she could wonder what he meant, there was a tap on her shoulder.

"Ingrid, there you are."

Jumping at the startle, Ingrid whirled around. "Mom!"

Mom grabbed her arm, her voice was hoarse. "Gene and Sheila just arrived."

Ingrid's eyes widened. "I thought they weren't coming."

"Well, they're here. I've sent your dad to stall them. We have to fix all the party favor bags to remove the you-know-what's again."

"Oh, you've got to be kidding me," she groaned in exasperation. "Can't we just fix the two bags they're going to get—" Ingrid stopped short already understanding her mother's continuous pointed nodding. "Right, of course...they're going to compare the bags and speculate about why the others have something else."

Mom clicked her tongue in knowing derision. "Sam's going around trying to catch the bags that have already gone out. Could you take care of the rest of the ones still on the table? Discreetly? Right now?"

Connell cleared his throat. "Is there something I can help with, Mrs. Harmon?"

Mom peered at Connell as though he was a lab specimen. "Is this cousin Marco?"

"Oh! No, Mom." Ingrid shook her head. "His restaurant's the one catering our event."

Mom beamed in delight. "Oh, how wonderful! Your services come very highly recommended at the country club. They say you're the best up-and-coming caterer in town. Are you the owner of *Bourbon Streets*, young man?"

His delight at the compliment was evident in his smile. "Yes, Ma'am. Connell Matthews." He held out his hand to shake hers. "Pleasure."

Mom shook his hand but her head quirked in puzzlement, looking to Ingrid. "Ahh...why does his name sound familiar? Do I know him? I thought it sounds familiar..."

Alarmed, Ingrid snapped to attention.

If her mom hadn't overheard her and Felicia talking about him the other day at the house, there was no doubt that Ingrid would have mentioned his name in their house possibly over a dozen times attached to some form of lament or other over the last decade or so.

"Um, no! You absolutely don't know him, Mom. You've never heard his name before. You've definitely never met." Ingrid tugged on her mother's arm to veer her away. "You'd better go help Dad run interference with Aunt Sheila."

Mom nodded. "Oh right." She patted her daughter's shoulder. "Ingrid, the party bags please, A.S.A.P." She turned to leave, but first, leaned toward her daughter with a gesture toward Connell, her voice hushed. "Also don't let him leave without coaxing the recipe for that cheesecake out of him. I don't care if you use any of your illegal psychology tricks. Hypnotize him if you have to. Do you hear me?"

Ingrid laughed. "Yes, Mom."

Once she was gone, Connell gave Ingrid a wary look since he had heard all that. "Illegal what? Should I be scared?"

"Only if you don't give up that recipe." She gave him a mock warning look.

He stifled back a chuckle. "Well then, I'm going to have to disappoint you because the chef is actually my business partner Gail so I don't have access to all these secret recipes."

"Ah, maybe I should go hypnotize her then."

"Unfortunately for you, she's not here right now. She's gone to Philly with our other business partner Nat. They'll be back next week."

"And they left you in charge?" Ingrid clicked her tongue in disapproval. "Possibly not their finest decision."

Still grinning, Connell scratched his head. "Maybe. But what can I do? Those crazy kids are in love." He paused for a moment. "Apparently, it happens when you least expect it."

With the mesmerizing timbre in his voice, Ingrid was the one almost hypnotized. Her gaze was stuck on the vivid blue of his eyes again. It took her a full second to remember the urgent thing she was supposed to be doing right then.

Party bags!

"Oh! I have to go do the thing for my mom." Ingrid pointed toward the entrance as she walked over to where the table of party bags had been laid out.

Connell was right behind her. "What's the deal with these party favors anyway?"

Ingrid groaned. "You don't even want to know. In fact, I wish I didn't know." She was already shaking her head at the mountain of work that lay before her.

He read the distaste on her face correctly. "Well, how about you tell me what I'm supposed to do, and let's each take half and go through them?"

She shot him a questioning look. "Oh, I wouldn't want to bother you. You're probably really busy with work."

He shrugged. "I don't mind. Unless you'd prefer to do it alone?"

Ingrid chewed on her bottom lip. The golden party bags seemed to grow in number right before her eyes as she stared right at them. She already felt exhausted from the work and she hadn't even started yet. "Yeah, okay. You take that side. I'll take this side." She made a face again as she explained what they needed to do.

"I bet you I'll sort my half first before you sort yours," Connell spoke up.

The sudden challenge made Ingrid perk up and she shot him an oh-please look. "Seriously? You feel like losing to me again today? Do I need to do the speech? Sore winner? Obsessive?" She pointed to herself. "You know you can't take me on."

"Oh yeah?" Connell grabbed a few bags at once.

She shook her head in mirth even as she began to systematically go through the bags on her side of the table. She already had the distinct advantage of having packed many of these bags the other day. There was no way Connell was going to win. Although she had to admit, it was entertaining to watch him try.

His forehead was creased in concentration and sort of amusement. "Ohh... I suppose if you're not at all into plants, you could potentially mistake this for a maple leaf," he mused, holding up one of the keychains.

Ingrid just chuckled under her breath.

It occurred to her that the last time they had a contest was when she had ditched him at the bowling alley after making him go through all the trouble of setting an appointment with her.

"Hey, by the way, sorry I hadn't gotten back to you yet about that survey."

Glancing up for a second, Connell's eyes lit up. "Oh, yeah, I did wonder about that. Did you still need me?"

"Well, I wasn't sure if you'd still be interested." Ingrid

grimaced, untying the bows off seven bags one after the other. "The thing is what I need now is a little more involved than just a survey. It's called a case study." Pausing, she put her hands up. "If you're open to it, I'll explain everything as we go through. Rest assured I do replace all the names so whatever information you provide, you won't be identifiable."

Connell's eyebrow quirked up. "Sounds...suspicious."

She chewed on her lip again, hesitating for a second as she remembered what Felicia had said about how flattering it was to be representing this particular stereotype.

But with no Joshua Knowles, Stewart breathing down her neck, and her looming deadline, she had no other choice. She shook off her uncertainty, reminding herself yet again: this was just work.

"It's all very standard," she assured with a nod, giving him her most honest look.

Not seeming to catch on to her consideration, Connell gave her a sideways glance and another smile. "Sure. No problem." He was still preoccupied with the party favor bags, which was probably lucky.

"Great!" A bit relieved, Ingrid turned her attention back to the party bags too.

Either way, Ingrid rationalized, it wasn't like Connell Matthews would be able to make heads or tails of her paper.

Connell tossed one more keychain onto the growing pile of rejected trinkets on the table. "What are you going to do with all these keychains?"

Ingrid bent down to fetch a spare bag from the box of supplies they'd stashed under the table. "I'll drop them off at Grandpa K's. I bet his customers will get a kick out of them."

Connell pursed his lips. "Oh, I haven't been to Grandpa K's since I've been back."

"Oh, I'm there like every other afternoon," she relayed offhandedly. "That's where Felicia and I hang out."

"When I was younger, my absolute favorite dessert was Grandpa K's apple pie. It's such a classic. In fact, we've been trying different variations of apple pie at the restaurant. Some of them are inspired by Grandpa K's pies."

Ingrid beamed. "That sounds amazing!"

Connell's eyes twinkled at her enthusiasm. "They'll be on the menu when we have the launch. You should come to opening night at the restaurant." Blinking as though the thought just struck him, he paused to qualify. "I mean, maybe you and your boyfriend want to come to opening night. I'm sure you two would have a great time."

Just as surprised at the notion, Ingrid's gaze snapped up to meet his and she bit her lip. "Um, yeah, sure."

After a beat, Connell glanced around. "Is he here?"

She shook her head. "No. He's back at school. He's working on our dissertation too. He's busy."

Connell seemed to be thinking the fact over but he didn't say anything.

Maybe he was wondering why her boyfriend wouldn't attend her family's biggest annual Christmas party. But Ingrid hesitated. It didn't matter what Connell thought or whether or not he'd figured out she was lying.

For once, Ingrid was grateful for the distraction of the task at hand. It didn't take much longer for her to finish up her half of the work. "Ahem." Clearing her throat as she finished, she set the last of her party favor bags back down on the table with a ceremonial wave of her hands. "Ta-da!"

He rolled his eyes but it looked like he wanted to laugh again.

She gave him a self-satisfied prompting look. "Do you want me to help you now?"

"Okay, fine. You win again. After this, how about we see how many marshmallows we can get into those cups over there on that table?"

Mirthful, Ingrid shook her finger at him. "You are not going to con me into playing any form of basketball with you."

He blew out a resigned breath. "Ingrid Harmon, you are too smart for me."

"How did you ever doubt that?" she quipped with another chuckle.

The look Connell gave her was so dry that Ingrid had to bite her lip to keep from laughing all over again. But with Ingrid's help, sorting out the rest of the party bags was quick work.

With a final sigh, she set the bag of collected keychains under the table. "What do you think the odds are that this is the last emergency of the night?"

Connell's gaze was already over her shoulder. He pursed his lips. "Um...not good?" His eyebrows rose as he gestured to a breathless Felicia who was charging their way.

Her eyes wide, Felicia grabbed Ingrid's arm. "Okay, I don't want to alarm anybody but I do believe your delinquent little cousins have been switching around the labels on the catering food. I just walked past the roast beef in gravy and it's labeled 'vegan' right now."

That made Connell laugh.

Hanging her head back in annoyance, Ingrid groaned out loud.

"Well, I suppose I'd better go to take care of that then." Connell cleared his throat.

Ingrid gave him an apologetic look. "I am so sorry."

Felicia elbowed her. "Maybe you should go help him out," she suggested out loud. "It *is* your family. You should be uniquely qualified to assist with that, right? Didn't you say the other day that it was your responsibility to rein in the cousins?"

Ingrid shot Felicia a pointed glare but when Connell glanced over, she forced a smile onto her face. "Um."

With Felicia's goading, it was near impossible to say no without looking like a lazy, irresponsible, inconsiderate jerk. "Sure. Thanks for putting it like that, Felicia."

"You are so very welcome." Felicia winked before walking away.

Ingrid met Connell's gaze.

A ghost of a grin was on his face. "You don't have to help."

She waved to dismiss it. "Oh, you better believe those little rascals are going to regret unleashing their cousin Ingrid."

That made Connell laugh again but then he paused, a mysterious glint in his eyes. "I have an idea."

It was easier than Ingrid expected to corral all her wayward cousins, and soon the children were successfully preoccupied with the impromptu Christmas cookie decorating station that Connell decided to set up. Notwithstanding several escape attempts and having to convince at least one responsible parent to keep an eye on them.

Nearly collapsing into a chair near the back of the room, Ingrid shook her head. She could already see the inordinate amount of clean-up required after the party. "They're going to make so much mess," she mused to Connell. "Great idea though. That should keep the little monsters out of trouble for a half hour at least."

Grinning, he sat in the next chair. "Thanks."

Ingrid tapped her chin with a finger. "Now that I think about it, I think we also solved the mystery of the vegetarian truffle mac and cheese from earlier that cousin Monica was whining about." She rolled her eyes. "I have to admit I don't understand why everyone goes crazy over truffle mac and cheese."

Connell made a show of nodding. "Someone once told me it tastes like dirt."

"Fancy dirt."

Laughing, he elbowed her in jest. "Don't tell my chef."

Ingrid burst out laughing too. She gave Connell an apologetic look. "I'm so sorry you had to get caught up in my family's dumb drama."

Connell waved his hand. "Don't even worry about it. It's fine. Your family's...interesting."

Ingrid bit back another laugh. "There's no way that's a compliment. I bet you haven't even met my uncle yet, the loud-mouth know-it-all."

"Oh, is that Uncle Vince? I think I've already had to ask someone to redo his fried egg three times," Connell relayed.

"Oh, just three times? One time, Uncle Vince insisted on going *into* the kitchen to show the chef exactly how he wanted his fried eggs."

"He must have a very delicate palette," Connell mocked in a serious tone.

She couldn't stop laughing.

With a pleased grin, Connell leaned over to prop his elbows on his knees. "Hey, thanks for introducing me to your aunts. You know, word of mouth is still always the best way to get new business."

"*De nada.*" Ingrid smiled.

Connell's blue eyes held hers for a long moment, but before Ingrid's brain could register to be self-conscious, he cleared his throat. "Hey, listen, about that case study." He straightened up in his seat. "With my work at the restaurant and everything, I thought maybe if you had time on Monday, why don't we go through that case study questionnaire you needed? Get it out of the way?"

Ingrid blinked, alerted. "Oh, of course! Sorry. I'm absolutely flexible. We can fit the interview around your schedule, whenever you want. I don't want to take up any more of your time than necessary."

His forehead creased a little. "That's not what I meant. I mean, it just seemed important."

"It is. Um." She glanced around, already wrinkling her nose as she mulled over a few places. "It would be good if we could find somewhere quiet to work." The library was still undergoing construction. Her house—but annoying Sam would be there.

"How about at Grandpa K's?" Connell piped up. "I'd love to see the place again. Don't they have that quiet back area? And since all your work is in the cloud, it shouldn't be a problem to access your files from anywhere, right?"

Ingrid gave him a surprised look. It now sounded like Connell knew what he was talking about. "Have you—did you...google what 'cloud' means?"

A halfway sly grin formed on Connell's face but he started to get up. "I have to get back to work now but I'll see you Monday. Is eleven okay?"

"Um—" But he had walked away before Ingrid could formulate an answer. She sighed again. "Fine. I guess I'll see you Monday."

9

Chapter Nine - Stereotypes

A slow late morning, early in the week at Grandpa K's, meant that Dean's racket from the back of the diner playing co-op first-person shooter videogames welcomed her as soon as Ingrid walked through the door.

Ingrid furrowed her eyebrows. She was sure Felicia shouldn't be here today. She had made sure of it. She knew her excitable friend was just going to get carried away with the whole Connell Matthews thing again...and possibly say things.

But when Ingrid walked toward the back, her jaw almost dropped.

Game controller in hand, Dean was sitting in a bean bag right beside none other than Connell Matthews who was holding his own controller, slumped in his own bean bag.

Connell's forehead was creased in concentration. "On your six!" he yelled out.

Ingrid was unable to stifle her amused chuckle.

Connell's eyes lit up. "Oh, hey, Ingrid!" He jumped up and put down the controller.

There was an explosion in the game.

"I got 'em!" Dean called out. "Eat. My. Lockwood. Boom!" He whooped in triumph as he tossed the controller aside. "Yesss." He looked up to meet Ingrid's gaze. "Hey, Ing."

With a satisfied grin, Connell reached over to shake his hand. "Good game, man."

"Yeah, thanks! You too." Dean ran his hands through his hair.

"So you two have met?" Ingrid gestured to Dean first. "This is my friend, Dean," she said before gesturing to Connell. "Dean, this is Connell Matthews."

Dean's eyes bulged. "*The* Connell Matthews? You mean—"

Ingrid nearly hissed at him to shut him up.

Catching her eye, Dean made a face. "Ahem." Clearing his throat out loud, he leaped from the bean bag to cover. "Um, I mean, hey, Connell. Nice to meet you, man."

Connell glanced between the two of them in curiosity but he didn't say anything.

Speaking to Ingrid, Dean jerked his thumb in Connell's direction. "He's really good at this game."

Connell conceded with a shake of his head. "Not as good as you, man."

Dean gave him a nod. "Hey, we play Halo some nights at the rec center. You should come by and hang out. I've never seen anyone handle himself so well in a melee," he relayed as he went about to put the game area back in order.

Connell looked pleased. "Oh, thanks. I might take you up on that." He shot Ingrid an open-jawed look that was half-surprised and half-self-satisfied with his two thumbs up as though he hadn't expected the compliment or the invitation.

Ingrid could only shake her head in amusement as she set up her tablet on the closest diner table. Leaning over to start up the app, she prompted as Connell walked up beside her, "So, are we ready to get started?"

Coming over to stand between them, Dean slung one arm over Connell's shoulder and the other over Ingrid's. "Cool. What are we working on?"

Ingrid rolled her eyes. "Dean, don't they need you in the kitchen?"

Dean's eyes lit up. Putting his hands up in resignation, he stepped back immediately. "Oh! Of course, you two probably want to be alone."

"What?" Ingrid's face flamed. "That's not what I meant. I just mean we need to do some work. Actual work."

"Sure. If you say so." Dean grinned as he stepped backward to disappear through the back kitchen door but not without wiggling his eyebrows in wicked mischief.

Ingrid could only shake her head in exasperation. She cast Connell a look. "I'm so sorry about that."

Connell waved it away. "Don't worry about it. Your friends are pretty cool. I like Dean. He seems really laid back and chilled out." Glancing to one side, he paused to consider. "Many of my friends are mostly preoccupied with parties, drinking, and one-upmanship."

Her curiosity stirred by the hint of disillusionment on his face, Ingrid tilted her head. She wondered if he was talking about his old high school posse, wondered if he was maybe having some problems with his friends, wondered what she could do to help...

Stop it. This was exactly what made her different from all his other groupies. She'd never purposefully insinuated herself into his life. The things she knew about him were mostly in the public domain, or at the very most, regular school gossip. She'd hardly ever crossed that line to find out certain things about him or nagged his friends with all sorts of questions about him. She'd never put unreasonable effort into discovering all his secrets nor invaded his privacy.

She definitely shouldn't start now.

She needed to keep her eye on the ball.

The faster they started with the case study, the faster they finished.

Without further comment, Ingrid gave him a wan smile. "Let's get started."

Ingrid was fully prepared to deep-dive into terminology, simplify concepts, and answer complex questions about her case study questionnaire. She had cleared her entire afternoon for this important meeting.

But despite his handful of questions right at the beginning, ironically, Connell was surprisingly perceptive about the entire questionnaire and the afternoon had gone a lot smoother than she had thought it would.

Still, she slowly paced the length of the table behind Connell in case she needed to elaborate on any points.

Connell was typing on her tablet while referring to the

paper guide. His forehead was creased in concentration, his wavy hair nearly falling into his eyes.

Ingrid wished someone would just brush it back. Him. Her. Whoever.

Shaking it off, she averted her gaze toward the diner's big picture window to preoccupy herself with something else. School children skipped past the sidewalk, splashing on the slush puddles, little faces turning toward the dinner as the fresh aroma of cinnamon tickled their noses.

It was the first day Grandpa K was serving his special pretzels and the diner had busied up since she had arrived. Dean was back working the long queue at the counter, but not before sneaking Ingrid and Connell a plate with a fresh batch of the deep-fried goodies.

Leaning back to ask, Connell gestured to the screen. "Hey, for this part, what if my answer isn't one of the options?"

Covering her mouth for a sec to finish chewing, she hopped over and peered closer at what Connell was pointing at. "Oh, that could be a scale, so you can just choose the closest answer you think you would give."

"Alright. Cool." Connell gestured to the plate on the table. "Do you want the last pretzel?"

Ingrid glanced over. She'd already had three of them but Grandpa K's pretzels were soft, sweet, and light. It was very likely what pure bliss was made of.

Watching her consideration, Connell's blue eyes twinkled with mischief. "Come on, you know you want it."

Ingrid almost groaned out loud.

Temptation, your name is Connell Matthews.

And pretzels.

He nudged the plate closer to her.

Yep. It was inevitable.

"Mmm," Ingrid murmured as the freaking pretzel all but melted on her tongue. But then she frowned at her sticky hands. The only downside to eating pretzels. "Oh shoot, now how am I supposed to—" She licked the sugar off her fingers.

There was a curious quirk to his smile. "You've got some...on your mouth." He gestured, already reaching for the napkins.

"Sorry." Reaching for a napkin, she licked her lips. "Thanks."

Connell stretched back to give her another intrigued look. "I had no idea stereotypes were so interesting."

At that, Ingrid's eyes lit up in highly elated vindication. "I know, right?" She couldn't help the eagerness in her tone. "This is interesting stuff!"

Leaning against the table, she gave him a wan, self-satisfied look. "You know, not many people would agree with me, but *I* think it's fascinating. All this cult of personalities! And don't even get me started on politicians, scientists—"

Connell reached over to brush something off her cheek with his thumb.

"—um, famous people in movies, pigeonholing their range... It's..." she trailed off.

He nodded in agreement. "Fascinating."

Swallowing her mouthful, Ingrid moved to pull a chair out so she could sink down in it. Her knees were suddenly weak.

Connell had turned back to focus on the questionnaire.

Willing her heartbeat to slow down, Ingrid clenched her fists as she forcibly dismissed the nagging in the back of her mind. This was not the time to get distracted or to regress to flights of fancy.

Either way, once Connell finished answering her questionnaire, her supporting papers would be complete. And all she'd need to do was go through all the responses for analysis and summary, prepare for her advisory presentation and wow Dr. Goya, get a glowing recommendation for Professor Braun's team, and by the New Year be working with the top sociologists in the country.

Job done.

Quickly.

There would be absolutely no reason for her to see Connell anymore and she could go back to pretending none of this ever happened and stop confusing herself.

Connell blew out a breath, sitting back in his seat. "Is that it then?"

Ingrid slid the tablet closer to her and began to scroll through the screen to make sure he hadn't missed filling in any sections. "Yeah. Likely. This is perfect. I shouldn't need to bother you again."

"I told you, it's not a problem."

"Well, anyway. Thank you. For this. It's really a big help."

"You're welcome."

Ingrid was reviewing some notes on the tablet when she swiped one too far that the tablet displayed a screenshot of a Joshua Knowles' magazine cover scan, his name blazoned across the top.

Peering over her shoulder, Connell's eyes widened. "Whoa. Is Joshua Knowles part of your Ph.D. stuff too? He's the youngest ever quarterback to make pro."

"Oh. Yeah. Well, I think it's still a maybe." She shrugged,

swiping the picture away. "He was going to be one of my case studies too."

"Wow. Is that who you've been talking to on the phone?"

She nodded. "His PA—or his agent's PA anyway. He's really hard to access now that he's a big football star. But we went to the same college. So I...sort of know him." She couldn't help the hesitation in her statement.

Recognizing her telltale flush, Connell's eyes lit up and he gave her an expectant bemused look. "Wait a minute. Did you go out with Joshua Knowles in college?" The corner of his mouth was curved up in amazement but also for some reason, a touch of...displeasure.

"What? No! I just..." Ingrid gave him a withering look. She figured there was no point lying to him about it. "Well, I *may* have had a tiny crush on him back then. He was quite the hottie in college."

"Ahhh...is Joshua Knowles your type of guy then?" Connell picked up the tablet and loaded the picture up again as though to inspect it closer. He squinted, pinching the screen to zoom in, and whistled. "This seems a bit intense to compete with. I suppose your boyfriend must have bigger muscles than this."

Ingrid stifled her laughter. "Stewart? Not a chance."

His eyebrows shot up in surprise. "I had assumed your guy must also be some hot blond jock."

Ingrid almost snorted before explaining nonchalantly. "Stewart is a straight-laced social sciences nerd. He's not even blond either."

Connell's eyebrows furrowed in puzzlement. "So that's...different."

Ingrid rolled her eyes. "Come on. Maybe I did like hot blond jocks when I was younger but I don't anymore. I of all people should know better than that."

An odd shadow crossed Connell's expression. "Oh."

"Besides, I knew next to nothing about Joshua Knowles in college. And I now know for a fact that he is a total player and a cheat. He went out with my roommate in college and..." She clicked her tongue in disapproval, unable to keep the venom out of her tone. "Suffice it to say, there is a reason he has a reputation as a legendary playboy. He's a jerk, a bad guy. He steals girls left and right. And he has absolutely no qualms about it. Typical, if you ask me."

"Oh." He cleared his throat, watching her collate the loose pieces of paper back together. "Do you think I'm like that?"

Ingrid froze.

Uh-oh.

Was it possible Connell had figured it all out?

"Umm..." She kept her gaze down. She wasn't sure what to say. Not without lying anyway since the exact reason she was even here was to get his case study for her paper because she definitely knew he was like that.

Or at the very least, she *thought* he was like that before. Ingrid's opinion on the matter had become a bit muddled of late but she couldn't tell him that either.

When her phone rang, Ingrid jumped about a mile high.

So did Connell.

"Oh! Excuse me," She stepped away to take the call—in incredible, absolute relief.

Even if it was just Sam asking to borrow her car because Mom wouldn't let her borrow the sedan despite claiming she would be responsible and careful with it, and wouldn't abuse her learner license this time around, to which the answer was still definitely no.

But even for the two minutes, Ingrid was relieved to be able to duck behind the kitchen wall where she could escape Connell's curious gaze.

When Ingrid returned to the table, Connell was still sitting down. He was browsing through the playlists on the music app on her tablet.

Almost guilty, he blinked up at her when she came back in. "Sorry." He broke a sheepish grin and gestured to a list of songs he was looking at. "I saw the first one on your home screen and couldn't help scrolling through."

Ingrid craned her neck to look. "Are you checking out my Star Wars theme playlists?"

"Yeah." He grinned. "The first track sounded familiar. I'm pretty sure I've heard it in the background for a video clip or maybe a movie or game trailer before. This guy is really good! Although, I still really like the original John Williams score."

Almost bewildered, she shot him a narrow-eyed look. "You're kidding. You...*like* Star Wars?"

"Of course. Why not? The films are pretty epic."

She nodded absently. "Sure, but like you only watch it for the space fighting scenes or something, right? Have you seen the latest trilogy?"

"I've seen Episodes One through Nine. Although strangely, my favorite film is Rogue One. I just can't resist a good heist film." His eyes were wide with enthusiasm. "My college roommate got me into the whole franchise. The shows were always on the TV in the background during finals. Total lifesavers."

Ingrid couldn't quite wrap her head around what he just said. "Right, okay...but you're not like a hardcore fan. If I ask you what race Ahsoka Tano is or what Mandalorians are, you have no idea what I'm talking about, right?"

Connell shot her a plain look. "Let me show you something." He pulled out his phone, swiped it a few times then held the phone out to show her a photo.

The moment Ingrid's eyes fell on the picture, her jaw dropped a little.

It was a photo of someone's room—undoubtedly Connell's since the room had posters of sports teams, basketball trophies, and Lincoln High school memorabilia on the wall.

But across one side of the wall, there was also an entire shelf of sci-fi figurines, collectible items, and bobbleheads—two of Darth Vader. A completely built freaking LEGO N-1 Starfighter was on the top corner shelf.

She blinked twice to make sure she wasn't seeing things. She could barely speak, baffled at the revelation. "Wow..." she breathed.

He smiled, pleased with her reaction. "See? I told you."

Ingrid met his gaze with an amazed smile, but just as instantly, her smile faded into incredulity and disbelief.

It couldn't be. There was definitely something wrong with this picture.

She glanced away to collect her thoughts before looking up at him again in puzzlement.

"It's not much of a collection, I know, but I only started in college."

She shook her head in great disbelief. There was no way. What on earth was going on? Had she been transposed to an alternate dimension somehow? Could that photo have been staged?

Connell's eyebrows had furrowed as he studied the change in her expression somewhat intently.

Entranced for a moment, she swallowed hard. Connell's best feature had always been his eyes but she had also always loved the way his eyebrows arched whenever he was thinking. She had to snap herself out of it again to look away before she kept staring at him like a weirdo.

He tilted his head. "You're looking at me like that again. Have I said something wrong?"

"That's... Are you telling me this is your collection?" She pointed straight at him. "You. Have this stuff. For real. In your room?"

"I swear." His grin widened. "Hey, if you don't believe me, come to my house and I'll show you my room."

Ingrid's flight response was triggered again at the notion of being asked to be shown Connell Matthews's bedroom. It was severely surreal, and despite the years of managing to convince herself to take Connell off that pedestal because he was obviously neither a Hollywood A-lister nor a demi-god in human form, with all the surprising, conflicting information from today, Ingrid couldn't help being flustered.

She pulled her gaze away from his and turning to the big clock on the wall, her eyes widened. "Oh my gosh, is that the time? I think I better go now."

Connell watched her fumble with her stuff. "Sure." He stuffed his hands in his pockets. "Hey, by the way, when are you going to the Winter Fair at the town square this week? Maybe I'll see you there?" Eyebrows raised in a prompt, he shrugged. "Technically, I still owe you for breaking your laptop."

"Oh." Ingrid dismissed it with a wave. "Don't even worry about it. You don't have to do anything."

He shot her a strange look. "I know I don't *have* to. Maybe I want to."

"What?" Ingrid was absolutely puzzled, gobsmacked.

Connell had to chuckle at her bewildered expression. "What is the matter?"

She narrowed her eyes at him again. The logic center in her brain was insisting on trying to make sense of things. For a paranoid moment, Ingrid wondered if Felicia had told him about her juvenile infatuation paper and that this was all some kind of setup. That maybe Felicia had told Connell to pretend to be like this just to mess with her.

"Did Felicia tell you about my paper?"

He blinked in surprise. "Felicia? I haven't spoken to her since the party."

He looked on the level. Also, he was looking at her like she was crazy.

"Never mind. I should really go." Ingrid backed away. She was on edge again. Jittery and self-conscious, as though she was being interrogated.

Connell stood up, his forehead creased in genuine worry. "Are you sure you're okay?"

Ingrid met his gaze, and for a moment, the soft light in his blue eyes sent a wave of calm washing over her.

Taking a breath, she finally managed a smile. "Yes, of course. Thanks again. I really appreciate your help with my paper."

"Hey."

She was almost at the door. "Yeah?"

Connell's expression was a bit uncertain. Probably because she was acting like a lunatic. "I thought maybe...well, I'm playing basketball again at Holly Grove tomorrow. You should drop by."

Ingrid made a face. "Oh, I don't think I want to get hit in the face again."

He grinned with his offer. "I could bring some armor for you."

Her tension dissipated somewhat and she couldn't help a laugh. "No thanks. But good luck on your game." She gave him a short wave.

"Um, okay. Goodbye, Ingrid."

10

Chapter Ten - Winter Fair

"Aren't they going to light the Christmas tree later today?" Felicia asked Ingrid who was rooting into the bag of red vines she was holding out.

Dean craned his neck to read the flyer posted on the street light they'd just walked past. "It says at six tonight."

"I told you it was a good idea to drop off the shopping at home first," Ingrid noted as Felicia pocketed the bag of sweets.

"Well, I still can't believe we'd gotten through all the items on your mom's super pedantic shopping list." Felicia looped her arm around Dean's.

Chewing on a red vine, Ingrid was already giving her a pointed look.

Felicia let out a haggard sigh. "Yes, yes, you are the fastest

Christmas shopper in the world. Oh my god, can you please get over yourself?"

Ingrid chuckled. "Well, it's not like Sam was going to help out. She's already at the Winter Fair for the school fundraiser booth."

"Look." Felicia pointed toward the square as they crossed the street. "I just love these rustic wooden tree decorations. Maybe we can buy some of them to give to your mom. I bet she'd love them too."

Handfuls of stalls turned into neat rows of Christmas popup shops as they neared the town square that had been cheerily decorated with bright pops of red and green everywhere by the vendors selling everything from funnel cake to specialty handmade crafts.

Hale Valley's Winter Fair was an annual event to celebrate the holidays and showcase the local artisan trades.

Felicia shook her head. "I can't believe we still haven't gotten a decent amount of snowfall. All of this would just look so much better covered in tomorrow's shoveling."

"No complaints here." Ingrid shrugged. "I agree it makes a pretty picture but I'm not too good with cold."

"And I can't say I'm fond of all this repetitive Christmas music either," Dean added referring to the tinny music blaring out of the overhead speakers.

"Totally!" Ingrid high-fived him in agreement. "One can only listen to so much Mariah Carey in their lifetime before going crazy."

They both laughed.

Felicia made a face. "You two are worse than the Grinch. Christmas music is so warm and cheery. I love this song! It always lifts my mood this time of year." She put her hand to her chest. "Ooh and I love that roasting chestnuts smell."

"Hey, I know exactly which cart has the best ones. Want me to get us some, babe?" Dean offered.

Felicia beamed at him. "Thanks, Dean." She blew him a kiss as he hurried off.

"You guys are just so adorable," Ingrid exaggerated cooing.

With Dean gone, she linked her arm through Felicia's as they continued to walk past the Christmas stalls to browse and enjoy the ambiance. "I can't wait to finally have a nice long vacation, especially now that my paper is nearly done."

Felicia squeezed her arm. "I still can't believe you had like a study group with Connell Matthews. And I absolutely *cannot* believe he invited you over to see his bedroom." Her tone was stunned and awed and very nearly reverent. "I mean, I feel like we haven't appropriated enough time to let this just sink in. *You* were invited to go to Connell Matthews' house. To see his room. To look at his Star Wars collectibles."

"Ugh. I knew I shouldn't have told you that part." Ingrid smacked her forehead repeatedly. "You know, one of these days, I'm going to have to learn to not tell you everything." She sighed. "You already spent most of yesterday squealing into a pillow about all this. I swear to god if you start squealing all over again, I'm going to find the nearest pillow and smother you with it."

Felicia laughed. "No! I promise. I'm all out of squeals. It's just, seriously, how many times did we ride our bikes past that house in high school?" She threw up one hand in incredulity.

"Too many pathetic times." Ingrid shook her head. "Felicia,

I swear to god, if this is really all some big setup that you've done—"

"I already told you. I would never do such a thing," Felicia vowed. "I may be a bit deceptive at times but that there's a gambit that is way outside of my current capabilities." She pursed her lips. "And I don't even understand what the big problem is anyway. So what if he likes Star Wars?"

"It's not that—well, not just that," Ingrid added. "He's...different."

"Different than what you thought before?"

"Different from what I absolutely knew he was supposed to be!"

Felicia's forehead creased. "Isn't that a good thing?"

Ingrid frowned. "No! That's not good at all. What if I can't use this as a case study? This throws my entire thesis out the window. I might even have to start over with a completely new paper or a brand new angle. I'll never finish in time! He was supposed to confirm my theory, not cause it to completely fall apart."

"Um...I'm sorry?" Her friend smirked, her apology not entirely genuine.

Ingrid threw her arms up again in resignation. "Well, how the hell else do you explain this?"

"People change. People grow up."

"No, they don't," Ingrid argued emphatically. "People don't change. Especially not guys like him."

"Well, there you go with the prejudice again. Maybe that should be your new dissertation," Felicia proposed.

Ingrid groaned out loud. "Whatever. At least it's over now. It hurts my brain just trying to make sense of it all. It's risking my precious mental health. All the more reason to nip all this in the bud."

Ingrid was more than happy to write off the last week as simply a random blip in her life.

She would never have to see Connell Matthews again. And when the holidays were over, she could go back to her normal life and re-train her brain according to the techniques she had formulated from her last paper.

She'd done it before. She most certainly could do it again.

Shaking her anxiety off, she recalled yet another issue. "In other news, I just got a bunch of missed calls from Stewart."

"What did he want?"

"When I finally answered, he just repeated his lecture about me conceding my point all over again." She waved to dismiss. "I told him no. *Again.* I mean, we're both this stubborn. Stewart's not going to give in on this and neither will I."

Venturing farther into the Fair, the throng was beginning to press in on either side of them.

Felicia craned her neck to look around. "Oh, I wonder if Dean can find us in all this," she mused. "Do I need to call him?"

Ingrid whistled. "Wow, this is some crowd."

Felicia jerked to a stop. "Oh my god, is that Connell Matthews?"

Ingrid's gaze snapped over to the distinctively recognizable tall, blond guy on whom Felicia zeroed in, and despite herself, Ingrid had to tamp down the stir in her stomach at the sight of him. She groaned instead. "I am no longer surprised by the crowd. You have got to be kidding me."

Of course, Felicia tugged on Ingrid's arm to walk them over to the booth where Connell was.

Felicia beamed first. "Connell! What are you doing here?"

Connell's eyes lit up upon seeing the two of them. "Oh, hey, guys." He gave out a few more flyers to some passers-by before stepping to one side, out of the mob, so he could talk to them. Raking his hair back with his fingers, he looked at Felicia and Ingrid in turn. "We're trying to get publicity for my restaurant's launch next week. It's a pretty small town so I'd hoped it would be good for exposure." Then his gaze settled on Ingrid. "I told you I would be here, right?"

Ingrid had to nod. "Well, yes, but I didn't realize you would be running a booth."

Felicia had ducked behind Connell and sneaked a piece of sample cheesecake from the tray. "I love these things!" she gushed, putting the entire thing in her mouth.

Connell turned toward the table to shuffle some cards around. "Hey, how about I put you guys down to get invites for the launch?"

Under no illusion that she was going to attend this launch, Ingrid still wanted to be polite and not say no outright, but before she could start, Connell followed up with a question, "Should I put down four? Felicia, Dean, Ingrid, and Stewart?"

"Oh, she's breaking up with Stewart," Felicia put in.

"Felicia!" Ingrid hissed.

Connell's eyebrows merely rose but he didn't comment.

Ingrid shot him a wan smile. "We sort of—we're going through something." She turned back to Felicia with a pointed look, mumbling amidst clenched teeth. "And I don't go spreading it around because it's private." She whacked

Felicia's arm in scolding before meeting Connell's gaze again to add, "Stewart and I are really competitive with each other and so it leads to...fights. They usually blow over."

"He's a big jerk," Felicia couldn't help but add.

Ingrid nearly jumped in alarm. "And Felicia has to go now. Thanks so much for dropping by." She shoved Felicia away despite her protest.

Connell had a smirk on his face.

"Sorry about her. She's never liked Stewart." Ingrid gave him a sheepish look. "It's just like I said. He's also very competitive."

"Like you?" Connell's eyebrows were still raised.

"Worse."

"Oh, dear god." His eyes widened in knowing.

"I know, right?" Ingrid rolled her eyes. "Plus he thinks my dissertation is stupid."

Connell wrinkled his nose. "Whoa. I don't pretend to understand any of this but that's pretty low. Especially for your boyfriend."

"No kidding, yeah, tell him that."

"Is he here?" he asked again.

"No."

Ingrid shifted on her feet at the awkward note. She didn't feel like elaborating on Stewart's current whereabouts or lying about her relationship status again. "Um, I better go." She gestured backward as she moved to leave. "Good luck with your booth."

As Ingrid was about to step away, a tall energetic woman with a short curly bob emerged from the crowd of people in front of their booth and clapped a hand on Connell's shoulder.

"Hey, Connell, did you check with Vinnie about the extra boxes of—" She paused when her gaze fell on Ingrid. "Oh, sorry, you're with a customer. Don't let me interrupt."

Ingrid was already shaking her head when Connell started, "Oh, no, she's not a customer."

He turned to smile at Gail. "Ingrid, this is Gail, my business partner I was telling you about. We met at business school. She's the genius behind the restaurant."

Gail pursed her lips in musing. "Don't believe a word he says. This whole thing was his idea." Giving Ingrid a confident look, she slung an arm around Connell's shoulders. "I've never seen someone so passionate about this work. This guy is definitely a force to be reckoned with."

Connell argued with a grin. "What do you mean? I'm just leeching off of you and Nat's generous spirit and effective teamwork."

"Well then let's just say you have your uses." She winked at him before turning to Ingrid again to remark. "This guy can draw a crowd like no other."

"I noticed." Ingrid nodded.

"Ah." Gail's eyebrows rose in interest at the bemused tone Ingrid hadn't meant to slip into her observation. "Is she the new girlfriend?"

Connell blinked, as though startled, then turned to Ingrid with an expectant half-smirk. "Are you?"

"Don't be ridiculous." Ingrid whacked his arm.

Connell merely chuckled under his breath before explaining, "It was her family's event that we catered at the conservatory last weekend. Her mom would like to request your very special secret recipe for the cheesecake."

"Oh, I see." Gail's eyes lit up in delight.

"And she's prepared to use illegal hypnosis to get your answer," Connell added wryly.

Gail leaned into Ingrid again. "Well, tell your mom, it's just the same recipe as chiffon cake. But the trick is the lining paper needs to be wet. That's what gives it that moist texture." She winked again.

Grateful, Ingrid's eyes widened in satisfaction. "Awesome! Thank you so much! My mom will really appreciate that."

"You're welcome!"

Gail had an approachable, unassuming air about her, but she also seemed sharp-witted. Ingrid could imagine she and Connell would work well together. Ingrid gestured sideways to him. "Connell mentioned you're going on vacation."

Gail grinned and flashed the big rock on her finger. "My partner and I are going on an early honeymoon—because Groupon." She winked. "So I'm leaving everything over to Mr. Matthews over here. We should be back right in time for the restaurant's launch just before New Year's. Let's just hope he doesn't burn down the restaurant before Nat and I return."

"Meanwhile, I have to do all the preparations on the ground all by myself." Connell exaggerated the haggardness in his tone. "Can you say that's fair?"

Ingrid put her hands up in defeat. "Hey, I am always on the side of the person who makes the food." She put her hand near her mouth to whisper to Gail. "Plus, you know, he was totally slacking off at my family's party, by the way."

That made Gail laugh. She thumped on Connell's shoulder again. "I like this one. She calls it like it is."

Ingrid flushed at the compliment.

"Well, I have to get back to work." Gail jerked her thumb back toward the booth. "Rome wasn't built in a day so they say."

"It was great to meet you, Gail." Ingrid gave her a farewell nod, before giving Connell the same smile as she stepped away to leave too. She wasn't a few yards away from the booth when Connell caught up to her.

"Hey."

Turning to see him, Ingrid blinked in surprise. "Hey."

Connell stuck his hands in his pockets as he fell into step beside her. "Would you..." He paused and then sort of shook his head. "I mean, the...restaurant could probably send your mom a box of cheesecake as thanks for using our services. If you like. They say keeping current customers happy is the best way to get new customers."

Ingrid feigned applause. "Wow, you really know this stuff."

"Nah," he dismissed with a small cringe. "Like I said, Gail and Nat are the geniuses behind everything."

Curious, Ingrid tilted her head. "How did you get started with all of it anyway?"

He shrugged. "I guess I've always wanted to start a business of my own and food is always a winner. I met Gail at business school and...the rest is sort of history."

She made a face. "Um, I feel like I should apologize again for not realizing that you *owned* the restaurant at the party last week."

Connell chuckled under his breath. "Well, it was a fair

assumption. And you're not the first person to be surprised. You should hear the shade I get from my own mother. Utter disbelief."

Ingrid laughed. "Oh, I'm sure your parents are very proud of you."

Connell flushed in pleasure. "I hope so."

Ingrid studied the fleeting faraway look on his face. If she didn't know any better, she would have missed it entirely. But of course, she had already known that his parents were divorced.

She tried to phrase her next question without sounding like she was prying. "Do you...have any big family plans for Christmas?"

He caught her glance. "I'm not sure yet."

"Cool." She nodded noncommittally. She wasn't going to press the matter if he didn't want to share.

"My mom wants to go out with her girlfriends and my dad lives in Florida now."

Ingrid simply kept nodding.

It was the first time she had seen that shadowed look on his face.

Despite her knowledge of him in spades, Ingrid didn't know why she had always assumed that he was just one of those typical shiny happy people with no problems whatsoever. Connell just never seemed to show otherwise.

And even as it had been part of her juvenile infatuation paper, Ingrid was still surprised that the fact dug deeper at her, that it was a little overwhelming to be considering there was a real person under his "image."

But Connell went on, unperturbed. "But I'm sort of glad, I

guess. We're really busy with the restaurant and the catering business taking off. It's been a little hectic. Between promotions and coming up with ideas to make our menu stand out from your regular bar and bistro fare."

"But you've got such a unique concept! I remember the party platters—appetizers and desserts. I love that caramel beer idea! It's quite..." Ingrid was honestly so impressed, she couldn't even think of a word. "It's very impressive. You really should be proud."

"Thank you." His smile was so genuinely sincere that Ingrid couldn't look away from it. His smile widened as he held her gaze, and for a moment, his gaze flickered down to her mouth.

Before Ingrid could even attempt to arrest the sudden warmth shooting through her, a high-pitched screech called out her name.

"Ingrid!"

The high-pitched screech could have only come from her sister Sam.

Her gaze snapping to look over, Ingrid found themselves standing in front of the Lincoln High Student Council fundraising booth. "Oh, it's my sister," she told Connell offhandedly.

The charity shop banner hung across the maroon and white striped tent which mirrored the school colors. Several students were milling around asking for donations into their little plastic buckets donning the charity shop logos too.

Sam was standing with a frown, her hands on her hips. "Have you seen Felicia? She said she was going to help me." She made an impatient scan around the crowd.

Ingrid already couldn't help a haggard sigh. "What are you up to now, Sam?"

Sam pointed emphatically across the way. "Would you just look at that? The high school clubs are having a competition for the most funds raised at the Winter Fair and then the cheerleading squad decides to have a 'kissing booth.' Like, can they be any less original?"

"And lame. Let's not forget lame," a boy with a mop of brown hair chimed in from behind Sam.

"Hey, Asher," Ingrid greeted Sam's best friend with a quick nod before glancing over at the 'kissing booth.' She couldn't help a slightly impressed nod. There seemed to be quite a line at one side where a tall, blond guy wearing a football jersey was sitting. "Oh, wait, isn't that the guy you like?"

Sam's eyes widened and she whacked Ingrid on the arm as her eyes darted furtively around the booth. "Shhh! Say it louder, would you? I don't think the entire football team heard. Not to mention the student council."

Ingrid had to laugh.

"Football?" Connell's eyes lit up in amusement from beside her. "I thought I recently heard of someone with a certain crush on the "Youngest Ever Quarterback to Make Pro.' Taking after her elder sister then?"

"I told her it was ridiculous. I definitely don't recommend it," Ingrid told him over her shoulder.

"Felicia was supposed to help me think of a way to beat them," Sam went on.

"Oh!" Ingrid's eyes lit up in recognition. "Sneaky and manipulative Felicia was going to help you beat the cheer-leaders."

"Competitive too," Connell noted in amusement. "Definitely taking after her elder sister."

Sam gaped up at him in suspicion. "Who is this guy?"

"Um, Sam, this is Connell Matthews." Ingrid jerked her thumb back toward him in the least ceremonious manner.

But Sam's eyes bugged out again anyway. "Did you just say 'Connell Matthews'?" she rasped, her statement decreasing in volume and increasing in scandal as she went on. "From Lincoln High of once upon a time in your—"

Oh dear god— Her eyes wide, Ingrid grabbed Sam's arm to cut her off.

"What?" Connell's forehead was creased in question.

Turning back, Ingrid flashed him a big grin. "Nothing." She gave Sam a pointed look to firmly repeat, "Nothing."

Sam merely rolled her eyes.

Ingrid turned back to Sam to talk over the point. "Now Sam, didn't I tell you guys like that fall under a certain textbook stereotype? Their types are blind to their narcissistic tendencies."

Overhearing that, Connell made a face in feigned offense, clutching at his chest. "Ouch?"

"It's true!"

Sam huffed. "Well, those narcissistic tendencies seem to be working in their favor at the moment. Look how many students are in that line."

"Look, I study behavior patterns for a living," Ingrid explained patiently. "The trick is to make it seem like your booth is the bomb."

"Either way, I don't think Asher's grandma's homemade mini cupcakes are doing the trick." Sam gestured toward the table where they were offering chocolate-iced cupcakes on a platter to draw people in.

Connell's mouth was already full of said cupcake. "They're pretty good," he mumbled in praise. "Speaking professionally, I mean."

Ingrid noticed that a couple of pockets of girls had started to huddle around the area and they were all staring up at Connell in some form of awe or reverence or *something* and an idea popped into her head.

Maybe Ingrid was biased, but standing there in his dark blue sweater with the sleeves pulled up his forearms as he licked cupcake icing off his fingers, Connell Matthews was already giving the onlookers a good enough show. She would put so much money on him having no problems whatsoever showing up that little football guy that Sam liked.

Then again Gail did say that he could draw a crowd like no other.

Perhaps they could test her theory?

Connell's forehead creased at the calculating look Ingrid was giving him. "What?"

She quirked a grin. "Feel like doing some charity work?"

Chapter Eleven - To Friends

"There you go."

Ingrid glanced over at Connell's charming smile as he carefully peeled off a sticker from his roll to attach it to the lapel of the generous donor: a giggling teenage girl and her group of friends

It wasn't quite 'kissing booth' material but it seemed dozens of giggling sixteen-year-olds were still more than eager to drop a token donation into Connell's bucket in exchange for a Charity Shop sticker from him, some even asking if he could put it on their collars himself.

Connell straightened up and turned to meet Ingrid's gaze. "I'm running out of stickers."

Ingrid laughed. "Are you keeping count? I think I'm still

ahead of you." She shook the bucket in her hand so the tokens in it rattled. It was also nearly full.

His jaw dropped in indignation. "No way!"

Of course, she was just messing with him. Despite the many donors that she had managed to coax her way, the plethora of awkward teen boys, there was no doubt her theory was a hundred percent confirmed.

After handing in their full buckets of tokens to Asher for the final tally, Connell walked over to Ingrid. Looking triumphant, he twirled the empty roll of stickers around his finger.

She gave him a nod of acknowledgment. "Well done on the tie."

He grinned. "Knowing how competitive you are, I'm counting it as a win. Congrats to me."

"Fine." With a mischievous grin, Ingrid slapped an extra sticker onto his forehead. "Well done to you then."

Not at all hurt, Connell laughed.

Her smile widened as she watched him peel the sticker off and Ingrid couldn't help but feel particularly light.

She couldn't believe she was having fun with Connell.

Again.

Shouldn't it have been harder than this? Shouldn't they have nothing to talk about? Shouldn't he annoy her with his arrogance? Shouldn't she bore him in conversation?

Except she was finding his company unexpectedly settling. It was weird that it felt comfortable. As though she'd known him all her life. Then again, she sort of did.

Sam whooped in celebration as she watched the tokens get counted. "Wow, look at all those tokens! We totally beat those cheerleaders."

Pleased, Ingrid watched the group of students give each other high-fives in celebration.

"I think we even have enough tokens to claim a couple of Christmas trees from the yard," Sam mused. "I'm sure the charity would love to get some. Imagine how happy it would make some of these families to have a nice Christmas tree this year."

Asher wrinkled his nose. "And how would you propose we transport Christmas trees around? We'll barely fit all the foodstuff in the car as it is."

To Ingrid's surprise, Connell put his hand up. "Hey, I know a restaurant that has a pickup you can borrow. If you like, I could help you deliver them tomorrow."

Ingrid blinked and looked over. Wasn't he busy with his restaurant opening? Surely, he had better things to do.

But Connell had begun to discuss tomorrow's arrangements with Asher, a cheerful on his face as though he was more than happy to do it.

Sam beamed in delight. "That's perfect! Thank you so much, Connell."

"Incidentally, it'll also be free advertising for the restaurant as a doer of good deeds this holiday season," Connell added with a smile.

Ingrid's eyes lit up as it finally made sense.

Everyone seemed eager to show their gratitude and it took a few moments for Connell to manage to break away from the crowd of high school girls surrounding him.

The sun was setting by the time they left the student council booth.

Ingrid gave Connell a grateful look as well. "Thanks a lot

for helping my sister out. Sorry, I kind of tricked you into doing it."

"And you claim Felicia is the manipulative one," Connell pointed out, good-naturedly.

"Haha." Ingrid stuck her tongue out at him. "Well then let's just call it payback for breaking my laptop."

His eyebrows furrowed. "Are you sure?"

"Look, you helped out my sister. I'd say we call it even."

"That still doesn't seem fair though." His eyes lit up as they walked past a colorful sign. "Oh, hey, look, one of the 'Hale Valley's Best Hot Cocoa Contest' booths is right there. Have you tried any of them yet?"

Ingrid shook her head.

His eyes gleamed. "Then you should try one today. Look, it's my treat and *then* we can call it even."

She gave him a dubious look. "So you think hot chocolate is a fair payment for a laptop?"

"And marshmallows, don't forget about the marshmallows," Connell added confidently.

Ingrid laughed. "Fine."

Tapping her fingers on the counter, Ingrid waited beside Connell as he ordered the hot drinks.

As usual, Connell was already straining the necks of several passers-by. Ingrid found herself having to field one or two nasty glances from a group of girls who obviously thought they were together and questioning reality as it was.

If only she could stop and tell them the truth.

No, hell had not yet frozen over. The hot guy was absolutely not dating the awkward nerd.

Regardless, she couldn't help but study Connell's profile herself.

The twinkling fairy lights strung above the booth hit Connell in exactly the right places, complementing the angles of his face, and the broad shoulders under that sweater. His eyes were a deep, dark blue in the dimming light of day.

Connell slowly met her gaze at her scrutiny. "What?" he asked, wary suspicion in his tone.

Looking away, Ingrid could only shake her head in incredulity.

After a beat, she decided there was no harm, and she certainly couldn't possibly be the first to ask. "Do you even realize that people are staring at you?" She gestured to the crowd around them. "Like literally every girl walking past us is going to break her neck just to get a look at your face."

Connell's forehead creased and he cleared his throat. "I...don't notice that stuff anymore."

Ingrid scoffed under her breath. Sure, he didn't.

"Besides, they don't really know me."

That addendum drew Ingrid's gaze again. Now she had a whole bunch of other questions.

Connell handed her a steaming cup of chocolatey liquid topped with mini marshmallows. "Here you go."

"Thanks." Ingrid carefully adjusted her hold on the paper cup, and for a moment, she was grateful for the distraction.

"Ingrid!"

And even more distraction.

Felicia was running over to them from across the way and Ingrid's eyes lit up. "Hey, Fi. Where are you rushing off to?"

Breathless, Felicia explained as she fell into stride with

them. "Oh, Mrs. Bradley needs someone to cover the West-field mall booth for a half hour. You guys should drop by. Apparently, we're giving away an outdoor grill for this year's raffle. Check it out!"

Ingrid nodded in approval. "That's better than last year with the air fryer."

"Did you tell Connell you used to work at the mall with me? Christmas time there can be so crazy!" Felicia relayed. "Ingrid and I used to always work the gift-wrapping booth. Ingrid, of course, is the reigning champ for fastest gift wrapping time."

Connell was already chuckling. "But of course she is." He was amused but he also looked mostly impressed. "She has to win at everything, doesn't she?"

Felicia spun to walk backward even as she posed her suggestion. "Maybe the two of you want to drop by the booth. We're right by the Christmas Wishing tree. You might find something of interest there." Her eyebrows wiggled suggestively.

Ingrid gave her a pointed look. She knew exactly what Felicia was up to again. "Get to work, Felicia."

But Felicia just giggled as she whirled around and hurried away.

Connell craned his neck to watch her leave. "And what was that all about?"

"Don't mind her. She's sick in the head."

"What's so interesting about the Westfield mall booth then?"

"Oh. That. The mall supervisor Mrs. Bradley has this thing against mistletoe. So the team would always sort of covertly hide it in certain places and trick people to stand underneath it. I bet you anything it's at the mall booth right now. You know how the tradition goes." She waved her hand in emphasis. "People have to kiss? It's ridiculous, right?" She started to laugh.

"Oh." His gaze dropped to her mouth once more, an odd look crossing his face.

It looked like apprehension. It could have been revulsion.

Ingrid put her hands up emphatically. "Oh, don't worry. We're not going anywhere near the mall booth."

He merely nodded, dipping his head to take a sip of his drink.

A burst of oohs and aahs erupting from across the square grabbed their attention.

The big Christmas tree had just been lit up, lending its sparkle and shine to the rest of the Winter Fair and every bright face surrounding the grounds, and despite the lack of snow, there was no lack of Christmas joy and festivity in the crisp evening air.

Ingrid blew on her hot chocolate as she gazed up the tree in wonder. "I've always loved those lights. Doesn't it look magical in the dark?" She stopped short. "Wait, what time is it?" She checked her watch in aghast. "Oh shoot, I hope Gail didn't miss you at the booth!"

Connell dismissed. "Don't worry about that. She owes me for not working the other party." He added, "Plus I was glad to help out your sister. I gotta say I also remember high school politics all too well."

"Yeah, you remember, right? High school was such a weird place with weird rules. I'm just grateful I didn't get too distracted by so much of that nonsense and I could focus on my studies."

"I sort of understand what you mean. For me, high school was just one massive sensory overload. Everything rushed by so fast. It was hard to find one quiet moment to even stop and look around and...notice things."

Ingrid interjected offhandedly, "And like, for some reason, the most mundane things seemed so important."

Connell took a deep breath. "For sure. Problems are definitely in a different league when you grow up. And I so miss allowance."

Ingrid laughed.

"Especially when you're starting a new business."

Ingrid made a face. "I understand that must be a giant financial undertaking."

"We're fronting up a lot of capital." He shrugged. "We were toying around with the idea of getting some investors involved and growing it more. Gail thinks it's a good move but...I'm not so sure." He ran his hand through his hair. "I wouldn't know how to pitch to investors. I'm pretty sure I'd sound exactly like the dumb moron I am."

"But you're so charming! You would dazzle that panel for sure," she declared before she could stop herself. "I mean—" She cleared her throat, her face flaming yet again. "You already know that."

Connell's cheeks tinged red with pleasure and he dropped his gaze. "Thanks. Again."

Ingrid's arm brushed his while they walked and a shiver ran up her neck right away.

Oh god, get a grip, Ingrid.

She shook her head briskly and made sure to keep enough space between them as they kept walking back to the restaurant's booth.

"Anyway," Connell went on. "We were planning to set up this meeting with a potential VC panel soon but I think I'll just tell Gail we should wait until we get the business up and running to make sure it's worth something before we start getting investors in the picture."

His arm brushed hers again.

Ingrid piped up in alert. "Oh, you know, there are a few tricks to public speaking I can teach you to make it sound like you're not stu—," she stopped short. "I mean, that you're way smarter than you actually are."

Her stumble made him start. "Oh god, you do think I'm stupid, don't you?"

Her jaw dropped in remorse. "Oh, no! Connell, look, intelligence comes in different types," she insisted. "Just because you're not 'book smart' doesn't mean your strengths don't lie with other things. Trust me. I study this for a living—not a great living granted but still..."

He didn't look appeased.

"Ever heard of the fish who failed his flying exam?"

"What?"

Ingrid shrugged. "Well, you know. Fish. They can't fly."

"What?" He wrinkled his nose, even more confused, but he also looked like he wanted to laugh.

"I'm just saying, everyone has different strengths," Ingrid rationalized.

Connell seemed to be mulling it over. He took another

deep breath. "So these public speaking tricks you were talking about. Do they even work?"

"Absolutely!" Ingrid declared. "It was on this video I saw the other day."

"What, like a TED talk?"

"No..." She paused to recall. "I think it was 'College Humor.'"

"College what?" he asked, bemused.

"You know one of those random funny skit videos. It's amazing what you can learn from the internet nowadays," she noted, sipping on her drink.

That made Connell laugh. "I would have thought you exclusively watched documentaries."

"Don't be silly. Even nerds can appreciate a good action film every now and again. There's this one I can watch over and over—Jack Bourne. Do you know it?"

His blue eyes nearly popped out. "You're kidding me."

She shook her head. "No, no, true story. I've always liked the pacing, the storytelling. It's highly underrated."

Connell was still in disbelief. "Jack Bourne is my absolute favorite film ever."

"It is?" Ingrid blinked in surprise.

"This is amazing!" he raved. "Hey, we should see it together. I bet you haven't seen it more times than me."

"More times than I," she corrected before she could stop herself.

That made him laugh again. "Aaand there's Ingrid Harmon from high school."

Ingrid laughed with him.

"So that's a yes?" His eyes were shining.

"Yes...?"

"To seeing the movie," he supplied. "I'm pretty sure it's on streaming right now. How about tonight? We can watch it at my house. We can get popcorn, caramel beer—the works. It'll be great, okay?"

Ingrid frowned instantly.

All kinds of alarm bells were ringing in her head.

Hang out with Connell again? Was he like trying to be friends with her? Impossible. Worst most terrible idea ever.

Ingrid had already started doing it again. Imagining things were there when they weren't. Just like in high school when she believed that Connell had done certain things for her benefit when he so very clearly had not.

She was already at risk of replaying every second of this afternoon in her mind. She was no doubt bound to obsess over and analyze each and every detail of their interaction like a crazed fan. She couldn't afford to add any more kindling to the fire and risk opening herself up to even more delusions, raising pointless hopes.

Already on the edge of a very short tether, it was taking a significant amount of brain power to keep Ingrid's thoughts from jumping to far-off fairy tale conclusions. And the only thing holding her together was the knowledge that this weird blip in her life was all about to be over really soon.

Even if she couldn't account for how nice he was being to her right then. Even if he was looking at her in that genuinely sincere way as though she was the only girl within the five-mile radius.

She bit her lip. "Um, I don't think I can."

Connell nodded right away but he had dropped his gaze again. "Okay. Sure."

Ingrid thought he looked disappointed but that didn't seem at all plausible so she dismissed that thought.

Surely, Connell Matthews had better things to do with his time.

But the seemingly despondent look on his face was irresistible.

Dear god, she had to walk away. NOW.

"I should go." Ingrid cleared her throat and spun to leave. "Maybe I'll see you at the charity thing tomorrow. That is if you think you can still help out?"

Connell gave her a small smile. "Of course. I'll see you tomorrow."

12

Chapter Twelve -
Helping Hands

Sam peered through the misty windshield. "Ingrid, he is just so hot."

Rolling her eyes, Ingrid eased the car to a stop by the curb in front of the charity hall. Right across from Bourbon Streets' pickup loaded with Christmas trees where a certain Connell Matthews was unchaining the back.

With the mid-morning sky overcast, the weather was finally getting much colder despite the absence of snow.

Connell was wearing a hoodie jacket over his sweater and jeans. But even with that simple outfit, he still looked like he'd walked straight off an ad photoshoot. The guy could have been a model for literally anything.

Ingrid shot Sam an amused look. "Hotter than *your* football guy?"

Sam glanced back at her before opening her door. "Don't be silly." She beckoned her friend out. "Come on, Asher."

Asher leaned closer to Ingrid from the backseat. "Not hotter than me, that's for sure," he quipped with a comical wink before hopping out of the car.

Ingrid laughed as she stepped out herself.

A few other cars were parked at the curb. Sam's class adviser was helping her other classmates to drop off their donations to the charity shop and had already formed something like a human chain to pass the boxes and bags along into the shop amidst cheerful giggles and the faint strains of Christmas-y holiday music coming from inside the hall.

Mr. Park from the charity shop was shaking the teacher's hand. "Thank you so much for your help. There's coffee and hot chocolate inside when you are all done, and we'll be serving soup in a few minutes in case your kids would like to volunteer to help out too."

Ingrid stuck her hands in her pockets and walked over to help Sam and her friends. Having gone to the same high school as Sam, Ingrid was also acquainted with the class adviser, Mrs. Hope.

"Good morning, Mrs. Hope," she greeted.

"Ingrid, it's so good to see you again in Hale Valley." Mrs. Hope gave her a kind smile. "What do you think about our new crop of helpers?" She turned to Mr. Park. "Ingrid here used to be one of our most diligent volunteers just a few years ago. I believe she's a Ph.D. now, is that right?"

Ingrid wrinkled her nose. "Oh, I'm still studying, Mrs. Hope."

"Ah, but she is one of my most accomplished former

students." Beaming, Mrs. Hope seemed proud of the fact herself. "What is your Ph.D. for again, dear?"

"Sociology," Ingrid relayed. "Social and market research, communications, public relations, that sort of thing."

"Ah, lovely." Mrs. Hope gave her a nod. "You know, my sister owns this little company. I think she makes quite good money. If you're ever looking for a job, I know she could use someone like you."

Ingrid gave her an appreciative smile. "Thanks for the offer, Mrs. Hope. I'll think about it."

Mr. Park turned to check on the pallets. "I think we are almost done."

Mrs. Hope craned her neck. "It looks like there's one last tree on the pickup."

The lone spruce was sticking out from the pickup's flatbed. Ingrid looked around but Connell was nowhere to be seen. Neither were the charity volunteers who had been lugging the trees into the hall.

From where she was standing, the tree didn't look so big.

"I'll get it." Ingrid walked up to the truck.

She leaned against the flatbed to get a grip on the ropes binding the Christmas tree so she could bring it inside the hall herself.

But the tree was heavier than it looked. There was no angle for her to be able to singlehandedly carry the darn tree off the trailer.

"Need help?" an unmistakeably familiar deep voice called out.

"It's alright, I can do it." Ingrid dismissed.

After yesterday, she didn't really want to have to need to

talk to Connell again. She was perfectly happy to bookend her 'blast from the past' with that awkward exchange at the Winter Fair.

However, the wily spruce had other plans.

Grunting as she tried to dislodge the tree from the flatbed to no avail, Ingrid yelped out when she almost slipped on the icy ground. "Oops, maybe not!"

Connell's chuckle floated toward her as he approached. "Can I help you now? Please?"

With a derisive laugh, Ingrid shook her head. "If you must."

He gave her a meaningful look but there was no condescension in his tone. "I understand you're not a damsel in distress but this looks like a two-person job."

She shrugged in helpless exasperation as Connell established a stable grip on one end of the tree to help her lift it off the pickup and the two of them walked the tree slowly down the sidewalk.

The pine tree branches were blocking her view of him entirely and she was glad for it but she heard his voice clearly enough.

"Hey...did I...?" Connell paused. "Last night, um...I just wanted to check if we're cool."

Ingrid tilted her head. "Cool?"

There was no trace of confidence in his tone. "I hope I hadn't said anything wrong. Maybe I crossed the line somehow if it seemed like I was asking you out, you know when I said we should watch that movie." He spoke a bit louder as though to emphasize his point. "I was just—it was just a casual invite. You understood that, right?" He leaned to one side in an attempt to meet her gaze, his eyebrows furrowed in his prompt.

Ironically, the relief in Ingrid's chest stung, but she forced herself not to look away from his clear blue eyes. "Yes. Of course." It was exactly how she had understood it, which for some reason was what had made his clarification sting more.

"Good." He seemed satisfied with that. "How are things going with...was it Stewart?"

Ingrid nearly froze. "Um...yeah, it's Stewart."

Part of her brain wanted to tell Connell that Stewart was actually out of the picture, but another more dominant part of her brain was going 'why on earth would that even matter to Connell Matthews?'

The truth felt quite a bit complicated to explain right then so Ingrid just gave the easy answer. "Everything's fine."

"Oh, good. Good for you."

Knitting her eyebrows, she second-guessed her half-truth/blatant lie. Ingrid opened her mouth to amend when a bit of cold fluff landed on her nose. Looking up, her jaw dropped. "Oh my gosh, *now* it's snowing?"

Delicate, wispy flakes of ice from the cloudy sky flitted about in the gentle breeze all around them, first a light sprinkling, then heavier.

Connell started, "Oh, we'd better get this tree inside quickly."

Ingrid was getting breathless. "Where did Sam and her friends go?"

"I think they have wisely left the heavy lifting to us."

"Oh jeez."

Fortunately, upon reaching the door into the hall, one of

the charity volunteers arrived and took over to lug the tree the rest of the way to the storage yard in the back.

"Thanks," Ingrid bid him with a grateful smile as she stepped past.

The indoor heating mingled with the chilly air at the doorway threshold. Ingrid must have shivered. Connell glanced over at her. "Are you cold?"

"A little. But I'm fine." She waved to dismiss as she shut the door behind them.

"I'll go get us some coffee." He gestured to the bench seats by the window before moving to step away. "Why don't you grab a seat over there?"

The cheerily-decorated hall was busy with laughing students and volunteers. Cooks sprinted in and out of the kitchen that was steaming with hot food. The charity hall seemed smaller with the tables and benches set out for the lunch service, but it made the average-sized Christmas tree in the corner appear bigger than it was, and the sparse space cozier than it ought to have looked.

Ingrid took a seat by the big round window with a view of the outside garden courtyard. The flurries swirled in the breeze as white flakes settled on the ground and she couldn't help another smile.

When her gaze distracted back to Connell who was walking over to her with two cups of hot coffee in hand, her smile faded a little bit as her pulse began to race. Seven years ago, this situation would have been unimaginable. What was he even doing here with her?

When Connell handed her a cup of coffee, she tried not to notice that his fingers brushed against hers.

He took a seat beside her. "Wow, look at the snow. Everything's going to look so beautiful tomorrow. Finally."

"Yeah."

It was taking a significant mental toll on her to keep her head level. But she assured herself again, that she just had to keep her thoughts in check until the end of the task.

Connell was simply here to volunteer for the charity. His restaurant had a pickup. It was a good deed. Free advertising. For Christmas.

She blew on the coffee in her hand to cool it a little. "Hey. Thank you so much for helping out. I'm so sorry again to be taking up so much of your time."

"Stop saying that." He shook his head. "I told you. I like to help. And I'm having fun."

Ingrid seriously wished he would stop looking at her like that. Connell obviously had no idea the effect he had on women with just that mere look. She clenched her teeth, trying to focus again. There could have been several layers of meaning in his words.

"Um, I hope everything's going well with the restaurant launch," she ventured for a neutral topic.

"Oh." He ran his hand through his hair, and when he answered, he couldn't keep the apprehension out of his tone. "Well, there's so much to do. Some days I do wonder what the heck it is that I've gotten myself into."

He gave her another look. "As you're probably aware, I'm not exactly the hardworking type. One look at me and everyone knows I'm just, you know, somewhat good-looking with no brains."

Understatement. She narrowed her eyes at his jab at himself.

"But didn't you have basketball training nearly every day of the week for at least four years? And then even more those years when you turned captain? I should think that proves your capability for dedication to something."

There was that off-guard look again as though he hadn't realized the fact himself. "Yeah, but that's just basketball."

"That's you," she pointed out, matter-of-factly.

The intensity on his face again made Ingrid drop her gaze to her coffee. "I'm sorry. Felicia did mention that maybe something happened with your scholarship."

A dark shadow crossed Connell's features and Ingrid almost regretted bringing it up but he shook his head before she could apologize again.

"No, she's right. I just...took too many things for granted," he confessed. "In high school, I never had to work for anything and I know teachers took it easy on me because we kept winning basketball tournaments. College was...different."

He took a deep breath. "When I lost that scholarship, I thought it was all over. And Mom, well, she was pretty cool about it. She always just says she wants me to be happy. She's really supportive and I love her to bits but she's...never really pressured me to do anything—more."

The sadness in his voice was overridden by a sort of defensive pride. "But I suppose that gave me an opportunity to try other things, hang out with other kinds of people. And I realized I'd just been...coasting through life. Not really making any decisions or plans. That's what made me go to business school. Apparently, I have a knack for it."

Ingrid wanted to console him. "Well, duh. You're so

socially proficient. You have excellent networking skills and connections. You should lean into those strengths."

"I should, shouldn't I?" The cocky grin was back on his face.

That made Ingrid laugh. She couldn't figure out if he was hiding modesty underneath those layers of arrogance.

He shrugged. "I don't know. I've just always been the dumb jock. Only good at sports. Getting away with murder because of my looks. I guess I just..." he trailed off.

She studied his expression. "You wanted to be taken seriously for the first time in your life."

His eyes lit up, a curious surprise in his ocean-blue eyes at her understanding. "Exactly."

Ingrid held his grateful gaze. The tension in his face had dissipated altogether, his eyes full of wonder, and...somehow relief at finally being able to put into words something he might have been struggling with for some time.

Her heart pounding in her chest, this time it was Ingrid who couldn't help her gaze dropping to his mouth.

Connell's forehead creased slightly as he detected the apparent change in her conviction.

"Hey, guys!" Sam popped up behind them.

Ingrid nearly dropped her coffee. "Sam! What the heck are you doing sneaking up on people like that?" She hadn't even heard her sister approach them.

Connell straightened up in his seat. "Hey, Sam."

Glancing back and forth between Connell and Ingrid, Sam's grin was a Cheshire cat again. The girl had been spending way too much time with Felicia. "Oh, I didn't want to interrupt. I just wanted to tell you that a bunch of us are volunteering for soup duty too so if you want to go first, I can catch a ride back with Lucy."

"Oh, right, of course. Sure." Ingrid nodded, willing her pulse to stop racing from the fright. "No, I can wait. It's not a problem."

"Right! I'm sure you have..." she cleared her throat, "things to keep you occupied. Catching up with old...friends." Her gaze strayed over to Connell for a moment before she began to step backward, waving. "Later."

Ingrid groaned under her breath. There was no way Connell missed that telltale teasing. "Um, maybe I should just finish my coffee and go."

Watching Sam leave, Connell's eyebrows were furrowed. "What was that all about?"

Her eyes widened. "Or, actually, I suppose I don't have to finish my coffee. I'm just gonna go." She jerked her thumb backward and moved to get up.

"Ingrid."

Turning her head away to hide a cringe, she stopped short. "Yes?"

"I've been meaning to ask you about that." Connell shifted in his seat. "At the Christmas party, did your mom say she knows me from somewhere? Your sister also seemed to think so at the Fair yesterday. And I don't know, maybe Dean too? I feel like everyone keeps saying that stuff around me. Do I actually know them? Like have I met them before?"

Giving him a dismissive look, she waved quickly as she sat back down. "Oh, no, no. That was nothing." She hoped her response was casual enough not to arouse any further suspicion.

"Nothing?" Connell peered at her face.

Drat.

She racked her brain for any sort of excuse to explain what her family had said or bring up literally any topic under the sun to change the subject completely, but her circuits were fried, and all her brain wanted to do now was panic. "Nothing!"

Glancing backward, Connell gave her an even look. "Tell you what," he started. "I'll make you a bet and if I win, you tell me."

Ingrid followed his gaze.

A line formed at the kitchen window serving soup was trailing across the hall, out the door, and down the sidewalk. She hadn't even noticed that the hall had already filled with people behind them.

She gave him a wary look. "Alright. What?"

"Alright." He moved to grab one of the flyers from the table and drew a pen out of nowhere. "I bet you I can guess the name of the next person who comes into the hall."

Ingrid blinked. "What?" She wrinkled her nose, looking him up and down. "How could you possibly—" Then stopping short as she worked out the odds, she glimpsed her triumph. She amended to ensure he wasn't hedging on luck or trying to pull one over her head. Maybe he had simply spotted one of his friends outside coming in. "You know what, guess the names of the next *three* people who come into the hall. If you can do that then we'll see."

Connell narrowed his eyes but then to her surprise, he agreed. "Deal." He checked the doorway.

Ingrid watched him, watched the door, watched him again,

her eyebrows furrowing in incredulity as he scribbled down his guesses for the names of the possibly unhoused people walking into the hall for the lunch service.

With a flourish, Connell handed her the flyer. "Done."

Still in disbelief, she looked over the list.

Douglas. Sandrina. Herbert.

Tapping the pen on his pants leg, he tilted his head. "That third guy definitely looks like a Herbert."

Ingrid looked at him strangely. "How do we check if you're right?"

"Like this." Connell raised his hand in greeting. "Hi, Douglas."

"Hey, Connell."

"Hi, Sandrina."

"Oh, hello, Connell."

"Hey, Herb."

"Heyyy."

Ingrid's jaw dropped in indignant protest and serious disbelief as the three people walked past them on their way to the counter. "Wha-what? You already knew—you tricked me!"

"Uh-huh. So I win." Connell's eyes gleamed. "And now you answer my question."

Cold dread filled Ingrid in an instant. Oh, she was sooo busted.

13

Chapter Thirteen - Reveal

"I said it was nothing," Ingrid tried to insist again.

Seeming entertained, Connell stretched back in his seat with a casual smirk on his face. "Hey, I'm not going to stop asking until you tell me, so you'd better just out with it."

Ingrid met his firm, challenging gaze. He looked determined as heck. She considered lying again but she was already hiding quite a few things, she knew it would just bite her in the arse later.

Dear god, she had to tell him the truth. She cast one last desperate glance around. Surely, somebody should be on hand to provide some type of distraction.

Sam and her friends were already bustling back and forth in the kitchen. No one who might be coaxed into saving her was within view.

Steeling herself, Ingrid shook herself out of her cringe and threw up her hands. "Fine! Oh my god, if you won't stop nagging me, I'll tell you."

Why did she seriously never run out of embarrassing incidents around dumb old Connell Matthews? Her mind raced. Her palms were sweating and her heart was pounding in her ears.

His eyebrows rose in expectation.

Ingrid gave him a warning look. "You have to promise not to make fun of me."

"Okay."

"You have to promise!"

Connell's mouth dropped open as if in disbelief that she wouldn't take him at his word. "I promise, Ingrid."

Oh god... Here we go.

"Um, remember how I told you I had a crush on Joshua Knowles in college?"

"Yeah?" His eyebrow quirked.

"Well..." She took a deep breath, making sure her voice was calm and even as she explained as vaguely as possible. "There was also this...guy. In high school. I had a little *teeny* crush on him, that's all. I've probably just mentioned his name one too many times that they can all remember and everyone's just confusing you with *that* guy. His name was also Connell."

Connell scratched his chin in thought. "Hmm... I'm pretty sure I was the only Connell in our high school."

She cringed again. "Um, maybe it was Connor?"

Connell gave her a yeah-right look.

Floored with embarrassment, she glanced away. "Oh my god, look, it's not a big deal, alright?"

"You had a crush on me?" His tone was highly astonished but she couldn't read the expression on his face.

Connell's forehead was creased in puzzlement. Or revulsion. It could always have been revulsion.

"Well...so what? So did every other girl in school, okay?" she pointed out. "It was like a thing everyone did back then. It was nothing special."

The last thing Ingrid wanted to do was freak him out over something that was so much in the past. She was fully expecting to receive an inordinate amount of mocking. How could she have even possibly thought that she was anywhere near even remotely in his league? He probably even thought she was going to jump him just before. She had to qualify ASAP.

"Relax. I'm not going to jump you," she assured, still wide-eyed.

At that, Connell laughed out loud.

Ingrid buried her face in her hands for a moment. "Ohhh...look, just forget I said anything. That was a long, long time ago."

"No, no, I understand." He put his hands up, and after a moment, his grin turned up in amusement. "So you're actually one of my biggest fans."

Ingrid's jaw dropped in stunned annoyance at the nerve of him.

The arrogance and confident condescension.

The absolute gall of him.

Except the easy grin on his entirely cocky, self-assured face —for some strange reason, instead, made her laugh too.

She really should have figured as much. Connell wasn't offended or freaked out at all.

Ingrid let out a loud suffering, aggravated groan. "Oh my god, you are...unbelievable."

"Aww, thanks," he replied, the mischievous glint in his eyes not relenting.

No doubt girls who had crushes on Connell Matthews were a dime a dozen. Just like all those girls at the Winter Fair. He didn't care that she was one of them. He didn't care if an entire horde of his groupies were in the charity hall with them right then and there.

In the grand scheme of things in Connell Matthews's life, it was absolutely not a big deal. To him, it was just another day.

Ingrid had to heave a huge sigh of relief. She had unnecessarily panicked and blown everything way out of proportion.

Lips pursed, Connell's shoulders were still shaking in mirth.

Ingrid gave him a wry, pointed look.

He shook his head, trying to apologize between chuckles. "I'm so—I'm—" He fixed his face to look serious. "I'm sorry. It's not funny. Really." Except he had to bite back another chuckle.

Ingrid moaned in the complaint. "You promised you weren't going to make fun of me!" Rolling her eyes in exasperation, she threw up her hands again. "Besides, it's—it's all in the past now. I...I've—you know..." She shrugged, trailing off. *Moved on*, she was going to say.

"You've...got a boyfriend."

Ingrid's gaze snapped up to meet his. She bit her lip warily. "Um, yeah."

Connell's forehead creased again. "Right."

Awkward silence.

Still a bit on edge about her confession, every nerve in Ingrid's body was frayed. For a delusional moment, she wanted to pretend she hadn't actually told her long-time crush to his face. She wanted to scoot away and hide, but she found she couldn't even move, except to shift uncomfortably in her seat.

Ingrid tried to even the playing field a little bit. "Look, you obviously don't know what it's like to have had a silly crush on someone."

To Ingrid's surprise, Connell's cheeks reddened.

Her jaw dropped with overwhelming curiosity, she couldn't help but ask. "Oh my god, you did! Who was it?"

He looked away. "Nobody."

"Was it Serena?" She narrowed her eyes, trying to guess.

Connell made a horrid face. "God, no."

"So who was it?"

"It was nobody!" he insisted.

Ingrid couldn't help her amused grin. "I cannot believe this. Connell Matthews had a silly little crush in high school too."

He groaned in complaint. "Ingrid."

She shook her head in concession. "Fine, don't tell me. After I've just humiliated myself, this seems totally fair," she quipped.

Connell blew out a breath in resignation. "Look, I can't really tell you because it was such a long time ago. She was just...cute." He waved his hand to point out, "But again, this was like junior high. I really barely remember. I never even got her name. I think she went to a different school."

Her imagination already spinning off on this mystery girl,

Ingrid leaned back in her seat. "Oh, that sounds just absolutely heartbreaking. I wish we could find out more about her."

Connell's cheeks flushed again so adorably that Ingrid had to resist the urge to swoon. How lucky was this random girl?

But Connell's revelation had worked off Ingrid's anxiety. They had never spoken so candidly before. And somehow, now that she had told him the truth and the world had, in fact, not ended, she definitely felt much more relaxed.

It really was a long, long time ago.

His gaze was still on the floor. Ingrid could imagine he'd rarely had to feel this embarrassed in his entire life, whereas she was so used to it by now. Smirking, she elbowed him to divert the subject altogether. "Want to go help with the lunch service? I bet you could do with some good karma right about now."

Connell looked up at her in disbelief. "What is that supposed to mean?"

Standing up, she merely gave him a pointed grin. "Come on," she chided. "A stereotypical narcissist such as yourself will likely benefit from allocating some of your time to helping others for a change."

Ingrid laughed at the hint of indignation on his face but he followed her toward the kitchen without protest.

As they neared the door, Mrs. Hope beamed at them both. "Hey, kids. Go grab some aprons." She gestured toward the far end of the counter. "Tom needs some help plating up over there."

"Great." Ingrid gave her an acknowledging nod.

Mrs. Hope patted Connell's shoulder. "It's good to see you again, Connell. Have you spoken to Mr. Park yet?"

"Not yet, Mrs. Hope."

"I think he said they did end up with extras at the Thanksgiving dinner."

Puzzled by the exchange, Ingrid paused in mid-stride.

Connell shook his head. "Oh, tell him not to worry about it. We were absolutely happy to help out."

"I'm sure he'd love to thank you personally," Mrs. Hope went on with a smile. She cast Ingrid a glance to relay, "Ingrid, did you know Connell's restaurant sponsored last month's charity dinner?"

Ingrid managed to stop her jaw from dropping.

"Make sure Mr. Park catches up with you today, okay?" she bid Connell. "I'm sure he's very grateful for all your contributions for the last couple of years."

Yep, it was inevitable. Ingrid's jaw dropped to the floor.

Mrs. Hope didn't look like she was kidding. Ingrid wanted to smack herself in the face again. Why would she even be kidding around?

But before Ingrid could confirm, Mrs. Hope had already turned her attention back to the kitchen hands doling out the soup.

Connell had a self-satisfied smirk on his face by the time Ingrid met his gaze. To his credit, he didn't rub the fact in her face. He cleared his throat and gestured toward Tom. "Um, I guess we should go help Tom out."

Ingrid had to shake her head in mirth. She simply followed Connell to the end of the counter to help Tom set up the plates and bread rolls for the soup.

Maybe one of these days, she was going to stop underestimating Connell Matthews. Like, *despite* overestimating him.

Behind the service counter, all the volunteers were in good spirits as they washed, mixed, sliced, and served. Mrs. Hope was supervising a few students near the vegetable chopping station. Her sister, Sam was standing by the sandwich assembly area, her hands on hips, as she seemed to be critiquing her classmates' work.

When Sam yelled something about *'skimping on the meat'*, Ingrid rolled her eyes.

Connell had to chuckle. "She really does take after her sister, doesn't she?"

But Ingrid cracked a fond smile. "She's a good kid. And a great deal more socially relevant than I ever was," she added in self-effacement. "I think she makes a pretty good leader, you know, when she's not being such a dumbass."

"I think it's great you're looking out for her," he noted. "I never had that. I'm an—"

"Only child, I know," Ingrid finished.

He looked surprised.

Ingrid gave him a haughty authoritative look. For once, she was happy to be an authority on the subject. "Look, everyone knew everything about you in high school. It wasn't just losers like me." She ticked items on her fingers. "Everyone knew when your birthday was. Everyone knew when you got retainers and when you had them removed. Everyone knew every single detail of your first date with Serena—at the sundae shop," she added, somewhat mischievously. "Seriously, that was top-notch for a first date," she consoled with a cheeky thumbs-up.

Connell gave her a suffering look before his face turned

somber. "I don't know if you've heard but...Serena and I broke up a while ago."

Nodding slowly, she wrinkled her nose. "Yeah...sorry."

"Don't be." He shook his head, concentrating on slicing the bread rolls in half. "I did a lot of growing up since Serena and I—since we..." He trailed off, clearing his throat. "I'd spent so much time trying to make myself good enough for her. But eventually, I realized that I'd changed so much. By then *she* wasn't good enough for *me* anymore." He shook his head again briskly as if to shake off a memory. "She just had different expectations. She wanted to be with the captain of the basketball team with the 87-game win streak."

"85," Ingrid corrected flatly.

In somewhat aghast and great incredulity, Connell burst out laughing again.

"Remember?" Ingrid pointed at herself. "Competitive? You *cannot* beat me at 'Connell Matthews' high school trivia."

"I cannot believe—" He shook his head. "Well, I guess I had *some* idea, but I didn't realize it was like an entire syndicate keeping tabs on me." He gave her a curious look. "*Have* you been keeping tabs on me all this time?"

A little bit guilty, her eyes widened to try to add some perspective. "Oh, gosh, no, look, this was all back in high school, okay? And anyway, it wasn't only all about you. Some of your jock pals also graced the gossip limelight." She paused to recall, waving her hand dismissively. "Hamish. Jenkins... It was just a bunch of silly kids gossiping about other silly kids. Your information was just more diligently collected than others. Seriously, some of the girls kept post-its of your sports stats in their lockers—"

"What?" Connell's jaw dropped.

"Even that controversial incident from your game against Newport when the ref ruled against you but everyone in the stadium saw that foul?"

He looked stunned. "What? Did everyone know about that too?"

"The cheerleaders even kept records of all of your injuries in the girl's bathroom stalls." She chuckled in ridicule as she passed along a plate with a bread roll and a small stick of butter. "I'll tell you, some of these girls seriously had nothing better to do with their time."

Connell still looked stunned. "I don't know if I should feel violated or flattered."

Ingrid laughed. "Go with both."

He snapped his fingers. "Oh, I know an injury nobody would have heard of. What about the game at Fallon Academy during the fourth quarter overtime? I tore a muscle trying to catch an out-of-bounds ball."

She furrowed her eyebrows. "Mm...which one is that?" Peeling off her gloves, she cast a glance around. "I need to get more bread rolls. Tom?" she called out.

Tom's arms were loaded with clean plates from the dishwasher. "It's in the back of the pantry," he hollered over his shoulder.

Wiggling her eyebrows in acknowledgment, Ingrid turned to head for the pantry.

Connell was right behind her. Satisfied with her concession, his grin was wide. "Ah, see? I knew you wouldn't know about that injury."

She shot him an even look. "No. I don't know about it because that probably never happened."

"Nuh-uh," he argued. "Not many people would know about that injury. I didn't even bring it up until lockers."

"Oh, please, I think *I* would—"

"Why? Because you're my biggest fan?" His grin quirked.

Ingrid gave him a suffering look. "Because it hadn't been committed to history onto the locker room walls by your many, many groupies. Plus," she reasoned, "I happen to know that's a pretty serious injury and I still saw you play last week."

Connell threw his hands up. "Why would I make this up?"

She tossed a bag of bread rolls into his open hands before reaching up to grab another. "Put these on the counter."

Turning to plop each bread bag she handed to him onto the kitchen counter beside him, he went on. "It was fourth quarter overtime against Fallon Academy. We were down by three. I wanted to keep the ball in play and try for a three-pointer to at least tie the game. I overstretched and slammed against the wall. Rory Jenkins caught the ball but didn't make the basket."

Ingrid bobbed her head absently. "Sure, I'll pretend you didn't make all that up right now just to try to beat me again."

"Ingrid, I swear to god." He laughed. "You can still feel where the muscle tore. Here." He took the bag of bread rolls she was holding and stepped into her reach. Taking her hand, he pressed it against his side. "See?"

His towering figure suddenly in her space, Ingrid blinked in surprise. Her breath caught in her throat.

With his gentle hand over hers, she had no idea what she was supposed to be finding, except for the firm, toned muscles on his torso beneath his nubby sweater. The heat of him through the fabric caused her face to flush just as hot.

Connell must have belatedly realized how close he had pulled her toward him, his breath hitched as well.

He was standing close enough that if either of them took even a half-step forward, she would be in his arms.

But he didn't move away.

He smelled so good. Like Christmas trees, fresh bread, and spearmint.

Ingrid's mouth immediately turned dry. Tentative, she looked up to meet the intense storm brewing in his blue eyes.

Ingrid was sure he could hear her heart pounding in her chest. His warmth reached out to envelope her and she was severely tempted to come even closer.

And he barely even had to do anything except stand there with that stubborn clench in his jaw, that perfect nose, those sculpted cheekbones, and magnetic boyish charm.

He was just...just so...beautiful.

And she was so gone.

When Connell spoke again, his deep voice was a husky murmur. "Feel that...?"

With the last shred of her sanity slipping away, Ingrid tried to extricate herself from the situation. Except her feeble protest came out a little more breathy than she intended.

"Connell..."

And at the sound of his name soft on her lips, Connell's grip on her hand tightened.

Ingrid didn't pull away. She couldn't move. She wasn't sure she wanted to move.

His eyes hadn't left hers for a second but his forehead

creased ever so slightly. It was as though he wanted to say something, do something...else—something *more*, but he didn't seem to want to move either.

Ingrid wanted to stay suspended in time, at this moment, with him, because right then, it meant nothing, but it also meant everything.

The limbo paradise of not knowing. The "Schrödinger cat" of crushes. The same haze she had been living in for the better part of a decade. Because if it stayed in her head, it could be whatever she imagined it to be, a wonderful permutation of future possibilities of him.

But if she ever took a real step toward it, she knew the dream would no doubt fade away, no doubt lead to disappointment and regret.

She didn't know what her life would be like without that dream. And she didn't want to know.

14

Chapter Fourteen - Relapse

"Good morning!" Sam yelled out.

Nearly falling out of bed, Ingrid startled awake. She raised her hands to block the late morning sun flooding in through the windows in an attempt to glare at her sister. "Cripe, Sam! Do you have to be so loud in the morning?"

"Actually, it's almost lunchtime," Felicia informed her, swiveling around on the vanity chair across the room. "Sam and I had a bet going to see what time your lazy ass would get up."

Still groggy, Ingrid moaned, rolling herself into a blanket burrito. "Felicia! What are you doing here again?"

Felicia waved her away. "Sam and I are plotting New Year's Ball things. What? I can't live vicariously through your sister? You remember how much our prom sucked."

Ingrid laughed as the hazy memories came to mind. Of sitting on the sidelines, drinking too-sweet fruit punch, listening to the worst DJ ever who insisted on playing romantic songs nobody could dance to, and the gym covered in silver foil because of the theme.

"I'm organizing the committees and taking a poll for the theme," Sam relayed.

Felicia's wide eyes were eager. "I have so many fabulous ideas for a theme! I can't believe the geniuses at our prom committee decided on 'Millennium' for ours. That was the most boring ever."

"Then you should have joined the prom committee," Ingrid suggested.

"Hah." Felicia scoffed. "Maybe you don't remember. Back then, you couldn't join the prom committee unless you had the IQ of a celery stick. Sam here is way luckier."

Wading toward the closet past a pile of book boxes on the floor, Sam put her hands on her hips in annoyance at Ingrid. "Are you seriously going to stay in bed? There might be a distinct possibility that at some point during the day, I actually need to use this room, my room?"

Felicia got up from her seat and slumped on the end of Ingrid's bed with an eye roll. "Oh my gosh, were you up all night cleaning after your douchey ex's mess?"

Pausing from tossing several still-in-the-wrapping Christmas presents from the bottom of her closet where she usually hoarded them, Sam cast each of them a scandalous prompting glance. "Stewart did what now?"

Ingrid's frown was already hardened in frustration.

Yesterday, she received a confirmation email from the

university regarding the change in schedule for her dissertation advisory meeting.

For the day after Christmas.

Yesterday.

Or to be more precise, yesterday, two entire hours *after* said dissertation advisory meeting.

Ingrid had missed it.

Apparently, her *incredibly ex*-boyfriend Stewart had taken it upon himself to reschedule the whole thing and had "neglected" to tell her about it.

She'd known it wasn't unusual for her colleagues to take every advantage or go behind each other's backs in an attempt to advance their careers, plagiarizing papers, stealing opportunities, sabotaging grant proposals, but Ingrid had thought that Stewart was above all that.

She had been sorely mistaken.

Stewart had probably wowed their joint advisor with his proposal yesterday morning. And Ingrid not having been there, she had missed out on her opportunity to convince Dr. Goya about the change in direction and the merits thereof.

Ingrid couldn't believe Stewart would resort to this. Then again, maybe she should have already known it too. His competitiveness was one of the things that she'd admired about him. He did anything to get things done. The reality was that, to him, science was a higher calling, his moral cause.

But he was just such a jackass.

So despite her mother's protests about her missing their day-after-Christmas traditions, Ingrid had driven to the university all the way across the state to collate her latest notes into something halfway sensible so she could submit her version to their advisor as soon as humanly possible.

Felicia twirled a lock of her hair around her finger. "You missed our Christmas tradition again too. Don't you remember? Leftover turkey and our movie marathon with the twelve tonnes of popcorn—"

"One for each day of Christmas," Ingrid finished with a sigh. "I know, I know. Of course, I was bummed to miss it! But it's not like I wanted to be stuck at school all day yesterday."

"Is that what you were doing puttering around in here after you came home super late last night?" Sam shook her head. "You should have just stayed at school."

Mom's voice floated up the stairs. "Sam, sweetie, are you up there? Asher's here."

"Yeah, coming!" Sam rolled her eyes. "I told Asher to be here like an hour ago. You would think he has more of a social life than me," she remarked as she made her way to the door.

But Ingrid was glad she didn't have to answer Sam's question.

Ingrid would have wanted to say that she had stayed up late to work on her *very important* thesis presentation. But the truth was that she had stayed up late with anxious pondering about an entirely different, absolutely unimportant, incredibly inconsequential matter.

Ingrid even reread her elective paper twice to determine if she had taken a wrong turn somewhere in her hypothesis or methodology. She hadn't counted on a chance of recurrence for her nonsensical and comprehensively disproven juvenile infatuation at all.

But she had fallen exactly right back to where she hadn't

wanted to be. The deep hole she had already crawled out of. The obsession with a non-existent person.

Felicia bounced on the bed as she sat up. "Have you read any of my messages? I probably called you like a gazillion times and you never picked up. I didn't even get a chance to tell you the latest gossip on Connell Matthews."

At her friend's mention of his name, Ingrid's stomach tightened. She hadn't told Felicia what had happened at the charity hall last week. She knew Felicia's brain would just explode and possibly get too excited about improbable things.

Ingrid pursed her lips again at the entirely too vivid memories that, in retrospect, were wholly ridiculous. No doubt, she'd probably hallucinated the entire thing.

It had been fortunate that Sam, Asher, and Mrs. Hope had also chosen that time to raid the charity hall pantry for cans of peaches, thereby interrupting any stupid daydreaming on Ingrid's part.

Mrs. Hope had asked Connell to help with the peach cobbler service and Ingrid had gone back to help Tom. Once the lunch distribution was done, she had driven Sam and Asher home without any further discussions about sports injuries or hot jock trivia.

In her distracted reverie, Felicia waved in her face. "Hey, hello!" She scrolled down her social feed and held out her phone to show Ingrid. "Yesterday, Connell's check-in said he was in Washington. Do you know what he was doing there?" She gave Ingrid a prompting expectant look. "Have you seen his update yet?"

Ingrid had to grimace when she replied, "Yes." She buried her head in her hands. "I've read all his updates yesterday. I've scrolled through his updates for the last year and a half. I've subscribed to their restaurant's marketing emails."

Felicia burst out laughing. "Oh, Ingrid."

"I know!" Ingrid wailed and buried herself back under the covers.

Despite her valiant efforts for the past few years, Ingrid was now dealing with a total Connell Matthews relapse.

She was back to hopelessly trying to unravel the mysteries of all those little looks, the subtext in his words, or why he did certain things, even when there was no underlying meaning to any of them. Her brain had kept her up all night trying to make sense of a potential mere string of coincidences that by definition were meaningless. She was back to daydreaming about him already. Stalking his social media again.

Yesterday, he had posted a photo of himself with a pretty girl that Ingrid didn't recognize and Ingrid hated that her stomach clenched with jealousy because there was no reason for her to be so.

More to the point, she didn't like him that way anymore. Right?

And it wasn't like he still wasn't way out of her league.

She shook her head to clear it. She had already gotten what she needed for her paper. It was done. The charity event was just another anomaly that would never recur.

She never had to see Connell Matthews again.

Except Ingrid found herself considering stopping by their Winter Fair booth again to do exactly that.

Ingrid's phone beeped and when she glanced over at the nightstand, the preview of a message had appeared on the screen.

A warm rush washed over her upon seeing the name of the sender.

Connell Matthews.

Grabbing her phone, her eyes nearly popped out of her head. "Holy crap. It's a message from Connell."

"WHAT?" Felicia squealed.

Ingrid *almost* squealed.

Jeez! Settle the heck down, Ingrid.

She bit her lip as she swiped to read the message. "He's asking what I'm doing right now," she relayed out loud for Felicia.

"Oh my god, I'm getting shivers. That is so classic text flirting!"

Despite her heart pounding in her chest, Ingrid groaned. "Oh, Felicia, get a grip. He literally just asked the plainest, simplest thing."

"What are you telling him?"

"Nothing. I'm just answering his question."

Felicia was highly elated. "This is so exciting!"

"No, this is impossible!" She pointed her index finger at Felicia's face, unwrapping herself from her blanket burrito. "This is all your fault, by the way."

Felicia flicked her hand away. "Come on, Ing. It's just a bit of harmless fun with your old high school playboy jerky airhead."

"He's changed." Ingrid pursed her lips. "Completely."

"Great."

"It gets worse. I think I like him."

"You liked him before."

"No, no." She shook her head. "I for-reals like him, like him."

Felicia's eyes widened. "Oh, shoot."

"How could I possibly tell him the truth about the dissertation now? He's going to take it completely the wrong way. Not to mention think that I'm absolutely pathetic!" Her stomach was already queasy just thinking about it. "I mean, the subtext of my elective paper was basically about how I'd had a terribly crippling crush on him for years and the onerous undertaking of how I managed to get over it."

Felicia whacked her on the arm. "Who cares about the paper? You should tell him Stewart is out of the picture and ask him out!"

Ingrid's phone beeped again, she almost jumped at the start.

The sender's name was again *Connell Matthews.*

Ingrid made a face as she read Connell's message on her phone. "He's saying he has some sort of news. It sounds important," she relayed aloud for Felicia before shaking her head again. "I don't even understand why he's still talking to me."

Felicia nearly tackled Ingrid on the bed. "Oh my god, Ingrid! For a smart person, how are you so dumb?" she yelled. "Connell likes you!"

"What?" Ingrid twisted away. "No, no, no. It's got to be some kind of dare or a prank something. You know those things they do in movies?"

Or more likely, Connell was probably still laughing at her, thinking he could get away with anything because she'd admitted to having had a crush on him.

Not that she could tell Felicia that part either. She was

busy enough not having to deal with Felicia's no doubt would-be-exaggerated overreaction.

"Oh my goodness, I didn't realize you've reverted into your high school persona with the severe lack of self-esteem," Felicia moaned.

"Hey," Ingrid argued. "This isn't lack of self-esteem. This is just common sense—in that it makes *no* sense."

Felicia put her head in her hands. "Alright then, Miss Everything Needs to Make Sense. Why don't we treat this like it is an experiment too? What does your evidence tell you?"

Ingrid pursed her lips. "I would have to look at the facts objectively. See, I knew this would happen. This is the problem with making a study too personal. My objectivity is totally suspect."

She glanced down at Connell's message again. She tamped down her usual urge to read all sorts of swoony things into it.

For a split second, Ingrid worried that perhaps he had decided to pull his consent on her case study. Or maybe he wanted to tell her that he had finally met someone, that he was dating someone new—maybe that girl in that photo, or maybe even that he had gotten back together with Serena.

Or...maybe Ingrid had finally scared him off and Connell wanted to tell her to stop bothering him.

Either way, whatever his news was, it very likely even had nothing at all whatsoever to do with her. Maybe someone got food poisoning from one of their catering jobs. Who even knew?

Stopping to rephrase her message several times, Ingrid composed her response. She had to reply in an unaffected, neutral way, like any other normal person.

Short. To the point. Casual.

Even if she also wanted to know where he was, what he was doing, if he had managed to come to terms with the pressures of the restaurant launch, what he had for breakfast...

Oh dear god. Help.

Felicia's eyebrows were still raised in expectation. "What is it?"

"It's..." She was feeling weak again from the mere notion of him. It could have been fatigue from lack of sleep. But it was probably more like wearied dread over the puzzle that she just, for the life of her, could not solve. "Connell wants to catch up later today at their Winter Fair booth."

Felicia studied her expression. "Umm...isn't that a good thing? Why do you look like your entire world is crashing down on you?"

"I just...honestly, I'm so exhausted trying to make sense of all this." Ingrid blew out a defeated sigh, tossing her phone away onto the bed. "I'm just going to go, find out what the big news is, and hopefully that'll be the end of it."

"Are you going to tell him the truth about Stewart?"

Ingrid frowned. "Look, I really thought about it—"

"And of that, I have no doubt," Felicia couldn't help interjecting.

Not offended at all, Ingrid nodded. "Uh-huh, exactly! And I definitely think it's a bad idea. In fact, it's the worst idea ever."

Felicia threw her hands up. "Why? Connell should know where you stand."

"For what earthly purpose?" Ingrid tamped down a frustrated groan.

When she was sure she was never going to see Connell again, it hadn't mattered whether Connell did or didn't know about Stewart. But knowing she would keep running into him as long as she was in town, she realized that she had been keeping the truth about Stewart from him as an unconscious layer of protection. Since if she thought Connell 'knew' she wasn't available, her imagination wouldn't have to *go there* with all the possibilities and permutations—yet again.

Felicia elbowed her eagerly. "What if he wants to ask you out? The guy has not left you alone for days."

"Um, coincidence," Ingrid rationalized in a sing-song voice.

"At the very least, he might ask to hook up."

"Whoa, that's—" Ingrid cringed in surprise at Felicia's off-hand suggestion. "Leaps and bounds, Fi."

Felicia made a big show of shrugging. "I mean, from where I'm sitting you and Connell Matthews make a great deal lot better sense than you and your jack-ass ex-boyfriend, the greatest jack-ass who ever lived."

Ingrid's brain was about to implode. Somehow, Felicia's argument was making so much sense. How was that even remotely possible? With a loud exasperated groan, Ingrid slumped facedown on her pillow again.

Felicia patted her back in sympathy. "I know you hate hearing this, but Ing, you need to lighten up," she soothed. "You don't always have to do permutations of each and every outcome of each and every event and decision in your entire life, like they're variables in another one of your experiments. Sometimes you just have to see where things go."

Hunching her shoulders, Ingrid pursed her lips but didn't get up.

Adhering to possibly way too many adages about planning and preparation, spontaneity had never been one of Ingrid's strengths. An ounce of prevention and all that. It was always safer that way.

She'd never known any other way to be.

Felicia let out a loud sigh. It wasn't the first time she had brought the topic up and she was probably certain it wouldn't be the last time.

The door flinging open made Ingrid sit back up in alert.

Sam barged back into the room, declaring, "It's going to work."

"But that's a terrible idea!" Asher argued just as loudly as he followed suit.

Standing in the middle of the room, Sam spun around and put her hands on her hips. "Why?"

Asher's expression was flat as anything. "A Sadie Hawkins Dance? Come on."

"Ooh, that sounds fabulous, Sam!" Felicia gushed, her eyes wide. "I know it's not technically prom but who do you have in mind to 'prompose' to or do I even need to ask?"

Sam's grin was nearly wider than her face but she didn't have to answer out loud.

Asher gave her a mocking look. "Seriously? You would ask that guy?"

"In a bleeding heartbeat."

Ingrid laughed at Sam's enthusiasm. She, too, remembered having a semblance of hope about such things once upon a time.

Asher rolled his eyes. "Did I ever tell you he's a big jerk?"

"No." Sam rushed around the room, putting things in her bag for going out—her phone, a sweater, and some makeup.

"Well, he's a big jerk," Asher relayed.

"Noted, thanks. Has anyone seen my planner?"

Asher threw up his hands. "He's not even really that good at football. He just happens to be this tall, immovable—" He stopped short and shook his head. "Never mind. He's mediocre at best and—and...his grades are terrible."

"Ugh." Sam groaned. "It doesn't matter anyway. Rhys probably wouldn't give me the time of day. If we actually ever do have a Sadie Hawkins dance, can you just imagine how swamped he's going to be with invites? There's no way he's going to notice me amongst his throng of...of..." Palms spread out, Sam seemed at a loss for words.

"Groupies?" Felicia supplied, her eyebrows raised.

"Exactly!"

Ingrid had to snort her laughter and Felicia gave her a pointed look.

Sam blew out a sigh. "Why couldn't I have been a cheerleader?" She clicked her tongue in remorse and stormed out of the room.

Running his fingers haphazardly through his hair, Asher took a deep possibly calming breath then stuck his hands in his pockets.

Ingrid gave him a small, knowing smile. "Hang in there, Ash. She'll come around eventually."

"Hey, for what it's worth, I used to be in the same boat, so—" Felicia fist-bumped his shoulder. "I feel you, dog."

Asher snorted. "Please don't say that to me ever again." He straightened in alert when Sam marched back into the room.

Sam was still going on. "And besides, you know, he'll probably just go to the ball with Tiffany anyway. Popular jock guys always go with the fancy cheerleaders, right? That's just how high school works. It's how the world works. Right? Right?" She cast a glance at each of them in the room for consensus.

Ingrid gave Felicia a meaningful look before giving Sam an emphatic nod. "Yes."

"Hey, but, Sam, what if," Felicia began, glancing over at Ingrid again, "Rhys, for whatever reason, asks you to prom?" She paused for effect. "Would you say yes?"

"In a bleeding heartbeat!" Sam cried out.

Ingrid burst out laughing again.

Asher made a face. "Have you not been listening to a word I've been saying...?"

Their argument faded away as Asher and Sam's ruckus hastened out of the room.

"See?" Felicia gestured to Sam's retreating as soon as the two were gone. "Ingrid, why don't you copy your sister's excellent example?"

Ingrid threw her hands up. "Oh my god, fine! If you want me to embarrass myself even more with Connell Matthews, I'll go step up to the plate, shall I? Never mind that I've probably humiliated myself in front of him about a gazillion times by now."

"Who cares? When are you ever going to have an opportunity like this again? And who knows? It might even turn into something."

Ingrid chewed on her lip. "I'm not banking on Connell. There's another shoe, I just know it. And I really don't want to be around when it drops."

"Then don't." Felicia shrugged. "If you really believe he's like that, then it matters even less, and at least you're going in with eyes wide open. No expectations." She yanked on Ingrid's arm several times. "Ooh, come on, it could be fun! Just take a page off his book! Who says it needs to be serious? He's clearly on a rebound from Serena. Take it. Take the rebound!"

Ingrid considered Felicia's eager appeal. Just casual? Could she really do that where Connell was concerned? Could she ever be just casual with Connell Matthews?

"At the very least, it would satisfy your decades-long curiosity. And it doesn't have to mean anything. Come on," she coaxed. "Your sixteen-year-old self would totally thank you and you know it."

Ingrid bit her lip. Was she actually considering this? What was the harm? Was she going to let Felicia dare her into another embarrassing situation with Connell Matthews?

Her stomach stirred. Oh dear god, she was. She absolutely was.

Felicia nudged her. "Do it. Do it for Sam. Do it for all the nerds everywhere." She gave her a sly grin and a wink. "And may the force be with you."

15

Chapter Fifteen - Not a Date

With the snow falling nonstop for the past few days, Hale Valley had transformed into the perfect winter wonderland. The deciduous trees sparkled with icicles, the snow-covered classic gazebo radiated genuine fairy tale vibes, and the wide grassy expanse was decorated with smatterings of snow sculptures, some carefully built, some haphazardly so.

Although despite the drop in temperature, the Winter Fair still drew an impressive crowd, most notably around Bourbon Streets' booth, which was strange for a late weekday afternoon.

Connell Matthews wasn't hard to spot. Standing near their table, his long fleece overcoat showed off his broad shoulders and tall frame. The cool weather gave his cheeks a ridiculously adorable dusting of color. He seemed to be in a friendly discussion with an elderly customer.

It was truly amazing how people responded to him. Then again, he had such an easy-going, approachable, authoritative attitude with all that charisma. Nobody really stood a chance.

Ingrid had to bite her lip to tamp down the shivers at the sight of him.

Dammit, brain. Get your act together.

She'd somewhat prided herself on being a good judge of character. And being a sociologist, she could usually often see behavior patterns way before anyone else, would know where people were often coming from, and knew exactly what to expect from people.

Could she have gotten this so spectacularly wrong?

Stewart had been an impressive, upstanding, hardworking, caring boyfriend who turned out to be a selfish, condescending jerk who cared less about her than his ambitions.

Then as it turned out Connell 'High School Jerk Jock' Matthews was a surprisingly decent guy.

Then again, maybe people could change.

And that being the case, perhaps Ingrid could change too. Maybe she could even try being a player.

Felicia was probably right. Ingrid should stop torturing herself by thinking about what everything meant. Maybe it really didn't have to mean anything.

Besides, all going well, Ingrid was going to win that TA spot in Professor Braun's lab and be moving away next month. She would never have to see Connell Matthews again.

When the crowd around the booth thinned out for a

moment, Ingrid noticed a striking, pretty woman in a blue designer dress standing next to Connell.

Well, technically, she was standing just to the back of him, phone in her hand taking a photo with a couple of very excited younger girls.

And there seemed to be a small queue of people waiting to take photos with her.

Pausing in mid-stride, Ingrid narrowed her eyes in vague recognition. She could have sworn she had seen her somewhere before.

Her eyes narrowed even further. Though she was not the woman from Connell's social media post the other day.

Then again, no doubt, Connell's days were filled with beautiful women hanging around him, competing for his attention. She really shouldn't be surprised.

As Ingrid neared the booth, the woman was making her leave and waved to the crowd. Turning to Connell, she put her hand on his arm and spoke to him for a moment. Connell gave her a nod in acknowledgment.

As he looked up, Connell spotted Ingrid and his blue eyes lit up. "Ingrid!"

Winding through the crowd, he made his way over to where Ingrid had frozen in awkwardness until he was towering over her again. "Hi."

But the bright smile on his face was irresistible, washing away her every other train of thought.

Ingrid smiled back. "Hi."

Connell grabbed her hand and led her toward the side of the booth.

He was exuding so much excited energy that Ingrid

couldn't help but laugh as she followed in his wake. "What is going on, Connell?"

He gave her a mysterious look. "I have the best news ever."

Ingrid blinked. "Okay."

"Are you ready for this?"

Was she? Not stopping to recount all her worst-case scenario guesses on the matter, she gave him a quiet prompting look.

Beaming, Connell braced his hands on her forearms. "We got the funding approved from the VC panel."

Ingrid's jaw dropped. "What—that's amazing! Congratulations!"

The elated expression on his face was so completely infectious that Ingrid nearly stepped forward for a celebratory hug.

Connell seemed to mirror her movement before he met her self-conscious gaze. His smile faded a bit and he dropped his hands instead. "Um." Glancing away, he rubbed his neck. "Earlier this week, Gail and I caught up with Nat in Washington and met with the panel and it seems they really liked our proposal."

"Oh. Nat," Ingrid echoed as it clicked. "That's your other business partner. The one who wasn't at the Winter Fair." She must have been the pretty girl in Connell's social post the other day.

Irrelevant! She shook her head to focus on what he was saying. "Right. You said Gail wanted to meet with the panel but you weren't sure..."

Connell's smile was lopsided. "I've never considered our little business was good enough to try," he began. "I was so nervous at the meeting but I kept thinking about what you said. When we got the go-ahead, I couldn't wait to tell you. I've never had anyone have this much faith in me before."

Ingrid's chest tightened with a gratifying fullness but she forced herself to stay cool. She cleared her throat. "Well, I am your biggest fan, remember?"

Connell laughed.

She couldn't help laughing with him.

He met her gaze. "Can I... Can I take you out to celebrate? I'd really like to thank you somehow."

Her heart stopped. *What if he wants to ask you out?* Felicia had wildly, randomly suggested. And here it was.

Ingrid must have looked as shocked as she felt.

Connell put his hands up to clarify. "Not a big deal. Nothing fancy." He took a deep breath. "I know...you and your boyfriend are going through something. I'm not asking you out on a date or anything. This is all happening because of you and I just wanted to say thanks."

Ingrid's every nerve was wracked. "Actually...Stewart and I broke up."

His questioning gaze had a hint of wonder in it when it met hers again. "What?"

She swallowed hard, her heart already pounding. "I know, right?" She waved to dismiss it. "Finally. Even Felicia is so relieved. Like why didn't I do it before? I guess he's become more and more of a tool recently."

Connell let out a short chuckle. "Huh." He glanced away. "Well. Good for you."

Furrowing her eyebrows, Ingrid deflated a bit at his down-played response.

It stunk highly and eerily of a certain Joshua Knowles.

Joshua was only ever interested in the chase. He enjoyed the drama. Easy girls didn't interest him. Once a girl was truly free, he dumped her and never looked back.

Joshua had chased after her college roommate Laura for weeks, charming and annoying both her and Laura in the process. He'd been so insistently sweet with all the flowers and gifts. Until Laura finally said yes. But the moment he'd had her, he immediately dropped her and went after the next challenge.

Maybe she had miscalculated Connell once again. Maybe this was a huge mistake after all.

She put her hands up. "Hey, look, you don't have to pay me back for anything. You did all this on your own. You have a really good product. You deserve that funding." She gave him an encouraging nod.

Connell's smile was soft. "Thank you. But I think we should still go out and celebrate."

She tamped down the logic war in her brain. "Don't you want to celebrate with your friends or maybe your family?"

He shook his head. "No."

Ingrid's heart skipped a beat.

Goodness, it seemed it was impossible for her heart to ever be still whenever Connell was around.

*　*　*

It might have been the least fancy dinner Ingrid had ever had but Hale Valley's food truck park had the best takeout she had ever tasted.

Connell said he was doing research for the restaurant too. Showing off his foodie side, they had spent the rest of the afternoon going from one shop to the next trying out both new delicacies and old favorites. According to Connell, there was always some new type of food truck popping up in town and it was good for them to keep an eye on what competition was out there.

Without all the nervous fretting, Ingrid found she was enjoying spending time with him more than she thought she would. It was surprising how easy, how effortless it was to be with Connell when she didn't stop to analyze each and every word he said or second-guess everything he did as suspicious.

Connell had gotten the urgent call just before sunset and since the restaurant was just a few blocks walk away, they had both gone to investigate.

Ingrid was curious to see what Connell's restaurant was like anyway and she was not disappointed.

Bourbon Streets was named for the famous street in New Orleans and the restaurant's theme embodied a very quaint type of décor. Brick archways gave way to a cozy indoor dining space. A great big wooden bar lined the wall, wrought iron balustrades accented the upstairs balcony, and the jazzy frescoes gave the restaurant a classy but homey feel.

Fairy lights strung across the ceiling and the green boughs of red ribbons and little gold toys gave the space a festive seasonal splash. A big box of noisemakers was sitting on the bar, ready to be unpacked for the pre-New Year's launch party.

Ingrid could already tell it was going to be a smashing success. Anything Connell touched was magic.

The neon sign on the wall right above where Connell was

standing gave his form an inviting glow in the darkness as he took another phone call.

Watching him, Ingrid tilted her head. In the past, she would have likely fainted dead away from the view. Connell was still jaw-droppingly attractive as ever, but somehow, it no longer felt as intimidating. Sure, there was this thrilling, electric tension across every inch of her skin, but at least, she could breathe.

Maybe this was how all those popular girls felt around Connell when they weren't daunted by his outright charm and popularity. Maybe this was how Ingrid would have felt if they had been on the same social level back in high school.

Connell's forehead creased as he walked back to where she was sitting at the bar by the entrance.

"I'm so sorry for dragging you all this way. There were a few more gourmet food trucks I wanted to try out but..." He wrinkled his nose in obvious displeasure. "Pete, our foreman says there's some kind of problem with the refits in the back kitchen." He blew out a sigh. "I have to go check it out to see what needs to get fixed before the restaurant launches this weekend or there's going to be trouble."

Ingrid slid off her seat. "Oh, of course, don't worry about it. It's work." Slinging her bag over her shoulder, she gestured to the door. "I should go."

Connell stepped closer. "Wait, I still..."

Turning, Ingrid met his gaze in question.

His eyebrows were furrowed in thought then his eyes lit up. "Oh! I just had the best idea for dessert. Um, if you could hang on for a bit, we can sneak into Gail's special secret stash in the freezer."

Bemused, Ingrid gave him an incredulous look. "What?"

"I mean, it's still early and I've already turned the indoor heating on." Connell stuck his hands in his pockets. "Besides, I'm having a really good time."

Ingrid couldn't help her own puzzled concession. "Yeah..."

He noticed her contemplative expression. "What's wrong?"

"Oh." She blinked. "Nothing." She shook her head, pausing at the odd thought that crossed her mind then said, "Nothing," again.

Curious, Connell tilted his head. "Two nothings. Must be something."

She looked up and met his gaze. She had to neutralize the look of genuine surprise on her face from the realization of what she wanted to say. "I'm having a really good time, too."

He smiled. "Good."

The soft light in his eyes as he gazed down at her was making her stomach flutter. Ingrid had to halt the automatic wheel-spinning in her brain wanting to process what he could have possibly meant by that one word.

Tonight, she wanted to pretend this wasn't simply a surreal, far-fetched illusion that she was misinterpreting.

Just for tonight, Ingrid wanted to pretend that she wasn't just projecting all these noteworthy qualities onto Connell and that all the little meaningless things were actually not.

Just for tonight, Ingrid wanted to live in the ridiculous, incredible dream of 'what if Connell Matthews did like her.'

She followed Connell as he led them past the rest of the dining area. "This place looks so great," she couldn't help her praise. "You guys are going to be the biggest hit in town, I can already tell."

His grin looked pleased. "I know, right? Gail and Nat have done a great job."

Ingrid was almost unable to believe that the words were coming from Connell's mouth. He seriously didn't realize how significant his contributions to the restaurant also were.

"It's going to be amazing." Unrestrained pride in his voice, Connell's gaze was far away. "I feel like I finally know what I want to do with my life. And once we get up and running and the business is stable, I'll move back to town, find an apartment somewhere close by so I'm not cramping my mom's style."

Ingrid blinked. "You want to move back into town?"

"Yeah, why not?" Connell pushed through a door marked 'Staff Only.'

"Oh." She nodded but she didn't say anything else. She, on the other hand, had always set her sights on something...bigger.

Hale Valley was a great place. It was her home. But since grad school, Ingrid had been hoping for a career in a stimulating academic environment that allowed for advancement in her specialty field. It was hardly something a small town such as theirs could provide.

However, Connell's point of view was interesting. And to his credit, she knew it wasn't out of naivety. The two of them had both already ventured out of Hale Valley before and seen what else was out there.

Connell's passions had simply led him back here. Home.

Passing another office, Ingrid stopped short. "Oh gosh, whose office is that?"

The half-open door allowed a peek into the small office

with boxes overflowing on the floor and piles of paper and folders stacked on the table.

Sheepish, Connell bit his lip. "Mine."

Ingrid peered into the door in amusement. "How do you even find anything in here?"

Connell flushed slightly. "Um, that's our paperwork for the whole two years of the business. I just haven't had time to file all the records properly since we moved from our old office." He craned his neck through the door himself. "There's a document management system on the computer. But between the launch and Gail and Nat's upcoming wedding, there's just been not a lot of time. And honestly, not much motivation or technical skill I might add."

Ingrid cast a glance around the stuffy room. He had done so much for her already. She wanted to return the favor. "Did you know I minored in Information Systems?"

Connell's eyes narrowed. "What does that mean?"

"Records management," Ingrid supplied. "If you like, I could take a look at the system and sort out your documents."

He looked surprised. "You'd do that?"

"Sure." She shrugged. "One of my weird hobbies is organizing. And besides, I feel like I've taken up so much of your time."

Grimacing, he shook his head. "Look, stop saying that. I'm the one wasting your time right now, remember?" He beckoned her back down the hall and through another door marked 'Maintenance.'

Trickling water echoed against the section of bare walls and exposed pipes. Ingrid sidestepped the puddle that was trailing across the floor.

"Ah, there's the culprit." Connell approached the wash area.

An open box of tools beside the sink, it seemed some of the restaurant's staff had already tried to fix the leak earlier to no avail.

Connell picked up a wrench and twirled it around as he gave the setup a critical once-over as if forming some plan of attack in his head first. "I'm so sorry about this." He glanced up at her before bending down to check the pipes underneath the sink. "There's like three types of inspectors that aren't going to be happy with us if we open without getting this fixed."

Ingrid waved it away. "Hey, it's not a problem at all."

"Let me just finish and I promise I will make it up to you." His statement was half muffled as he ducked low under the basin.

After a few metallic squeaks, the gurgling of the gushing water died down to trickles and drips.

She tilted her head in marveling. "How do you even know how to do that?"

Connell's head popped up from under the sink for a sec with a sly, pointed grin. "Do you think my mom fixed anything in our house in the last ten years?"

Ingrid's shoulders shook in mirth.

"Almost..." His voice was muffled again.

Ingrid was about to step closer when a small creak gave way to a loud gush. They both yelped out as water sprayed everywhere.

Lucky for Ingrid, she had ducked behind a metal supply closet.

Connell was a lot less lucky.

"Oh, jeez." He straightened up from under the wash basin, wringing his arms out in displeasure.

Connell Matthews was drenched from head to toe, his wet button-down shirt clinging to every tight freaking muscle on his hot freaking body.

Ingrid snapped her jaw back to close. Was this seriously happening to her right now? She looked around. She could just bet that every girl in her high school—nay, *the world*—would love to be sitting where she was.

Connell pushed his blond hair back off his forehead to glance back at her behind the supply closet, his forehead etched with concern. "Are you okay?"

"Uh-huh."

Water was still gushing out from the pipes. With another groan, Connell bent back down to reach under the sink and tighten and seal the leak as much as he could.

Ingrid was still crouched behind the supply closet, watching dumbfounded. It almost physically hurt to watch Connell's muscles play under the wet fabric of his shirt as he worked on—whatever the hell it was he was doing.

Connell stood again, shaking his head. "Well, I guess that's as good as it gets before the plumber gets here." He blew out a breath and met her gaze again. "Ingrid?"

"Yeah." Looking up, she snapped to attention, trying to focus on his face instead of...elsewhere.

Connell frowned as he looked down at himself. "I'm going to go get changed. Would you mind waiting in the hall?"

Oh. Sure. Yeah.

Except Ingrid could see right into his office from the hall

through the sliver of a gap in the door. He was on the phone with someone again. Shirtless.

Dear god, she was in so much trouble.

Connell poked his head out of the office, dismay already written on his face as he met her gaze. "I'm so sorry about this. It looks like the plumber won't make it out tonight. I better go back and check the other fittings to make sure none of them blow out like that one."

"Sure."

He pointed toward the kitchen counter. "Why don't you go browse the dessert menu over there to see what you'd like while I go do this?"

As if Ingrid's attention could be occupied with anything else but she nodded anyway. "I'll be in the kitchen," she replied, relieved she was going to be in a completely different room altogether.

Ingrid picked up the menu and held it up to her face. As if she could read anything on it right then. There was something about cakes, a section on platters... She had to blink several times to focus. It wasn't working.

After a few minutes, Connell came back out, tools still in hand. He had pulled a shirt on over that ridiculously toned and lean figure. "Did you figure out what you wanted?"

The vision of him in the doorway, in dark jeans and that plain white T-shirt, sleeves straining to contain his biceps, his eyebrows still furrowed a bit in frustration, and his jaw set, he looked so hot, Ingrid's face burned already.

She blinked blankly once again.

What she wanted...?

Ingrid bit her lip. "Um..."

Connell noticed her glazed look. "To order?" he prompted. "I know there's always gelato in the freezer. And I think Gail said the watermelons were expensive but nice. Also, persimmons are in season." Coming to stand before her, he peered over at the menu for a moment, deep in thought. "I'm pretty sure she said that was this week. If not, we have some really good cheese platters..."

Ingrid's heart was pounding in her ears and every fiber of her being was humming with pent-up want, possibly a decade long.

For goodness sake. Why did he have to be so beautiful? How unfair was it that he had the longest lashes ever? How was his hair always perfect? Even when it was still all damp and mussed up. She bet it would feel so silky between her fingers.

Ingrid could barely process any other sound except for her own loud breathing.

She swallowed hard, her gaze dropping to his mouth.

No doubt he had kissed dozens of women with those lips by now. What would one more matter? Even if it meant nothing. Even if he flat-out rejected her. She could deal with it. What were the odds that she would be alone with him like this again?

She bit her lip again to check herself. What the hell was she thinking? She absolutely should not be thinking about what she was thinking about.

Connell was still talking about cheese or figs when Ingrid lost the battle with herself.

Screw it.

Reaching up, she grabbed his neck to pull his head down, pressing her lips against his.

It was only for a second but Ingrid's entire body tingled—possibly in triumph, elation, or also perhaps all-consuming nerve-wracking anxiety.

Connell had stilled against her.

When she pulled away to meet his gaze, his blue eyes were wide in surprise—but only for a split second, as in the next moment, his eyes darkened with turbulence and without warning, he dove down to capture her mouth in his once more.

Ingrid gasped, her eyes fluttering closed to the clatter of tools against the wooden floor as Connell's strong fingers plunged into her hair, his other hand cupping her cheek as his eager lips slanted against hers.

Ingrid's mind screamed. Connell Matthews was kissing her!

She should have been cold. His skin was still damp from the plumbing work and he was definitely messing up her hair, but Ingrid didn't care.

She would have melted into a puddle at his feet if he wasn't holding on to her as tight as he was. His one hand was on the nape of her neck, the other slid down to grasp her hip to press her closer against him. She couldn't help but sink into his demanding kiss. He shifted his head to kiss her again, even deeper, even more urgent.

He kissed her like she was oxygen. And he couldn't breathe.

Ingrid shivered in pleasure as he overtook her senses. Connell's insistent lips, his warmth, his cologne, the faint spearmint in his breath, he was absolutely intoxicating.

For some reason, instead of anxiety, there was an

inexplicable feeling of release in her chest. It had been nearly a decade. Had she been waiting for this? All her life? It was like a dream. Maybe she *was* still dreaming. Something in the back of her brain was yelling 'Yes! This!'

Ingrid tilted her face up for more. She couldn't help sliding her hands up his firm chest, his neck, to thread her fingers through his soft hair—even softer than she had imagined.

Connell must have liked that since a low groan escaped his throat and he spun her to one side, pinning her back against the kitchen cabinets, his mouth never leaving hers. It was as if something inside him had been released as well. He kissed her fervently, and hard, that surely her lips would be swollen if he pulled away.

Ingrid lost all track of time. Was it still Christmas? What year was it?

Connell's next groan hinted at displeasure as he broke off. Breathless, his eyes were still closed, his forehead pressed against hers.

Ingrid was breathing just as hard. She was sure her face was flushed scarlet. She had no idea how she was standing upright. She was pretty sure her bones had all liquefied.

Connell rumbled out his tortured question. "Why did you do that?"

The blood drained from her face and Ingrid's throat constricted. Why on earth *did* she do that? He didn't sound too happy with what had happened. She wasn't sure what to do now. Floored with embarrassment yet again, she pushed away. "I'm so sorry—"

But he held her fast. "Don't." He let out a half-sigh, half-groan. "I was telling myself off."

"Oh."

"Ingrid..." Connell pulled away just enough to look into her face. "Look, I know...you're probably just upset about your break-up and I'm—I'm sorry, I was taking advantage." His gaze was imploring, stricken. "That thing you said about Knowles keeps haunting me. I don't want you to think I'm that kind of guy."

"But I just..." Connell's gaze was pinned to her mouth. He stroked her bottom lip with his thumb, his voice husky as hell. "God, that felt so good..."

Ingrid's entire being turned into jello.

"Was that okay?" He met her gaze, his forehead creased in worry.

She couldn't speak. She could only nod.

"I don't want this to be just some kind of rebound." His fingers brushed her cheek so gently it almost made her heart ache. "And I know you said you didn't like jocks anymore but...do you think you could give me a chance?"

16

Chapter Sixteen - State of Bliss

Ingrid needed to write a whole new paper.

'How Not to Float on Cloud 9 After the Best Kiss Ever.'

Tugging her coat closed over her neck, Ingrid brisk-walked down Main Street on her way to the bake sale fundraiser at Grandpa K's, taking care not to slip on the snowy sidewalk.

Her chest tightening again, she tried to shake off the overwhelming sensations. She needed to think. She needed to make sense of things.

Do you think you could give me a chance?

There had been no teasing in Connell's eyes and the sincerity in his voice made her chest ache.

Was this really happening? And even if it was, *why* was it happening?

But she couldn't muster two seconds of clear-headed

thinking to sort it out before floating off into dreamy, dreamy fantasy land again.

Oh god. She buried her head in her hands as she walked.

Rebound.

The word, ironically enough, bounced around in her head.

Connell was on the rebound from Serena.

But was he right? *Was* she on the rebound from Stewart too? Oh jeez.

She touched her mouth. Stewart had never kissed her like that before. Connell was obviously, and of course, he was, really good at that. It was everything she could have dreamed of and more.

Ingrid seriously needed to explode at someone about this. She needed a major reality check.

The throng of people at Grandpa K's helped a little. Such noise and ruckus would never exist in dreamy, dreamy fantasy land.

The dining area had been rearranged to fit tables of candy, frosted cookies, fudge, and delicious baked goods on sale for a good cause. Even Dean was struggling to tend to one of the booths with the longest lines, serving Grandpa K's delicious pretzels.

Ingrid craned her neck to spot her friend. She could almost already see Felicia's possibly wily Cheshire cat grin again.

Except Felicia wasn't in the building.

Seriously? Every other day in her life but today?

Frowning, Ingrid parked herself at the last empty booth table near the back, right by the unusually tidy gaming beanbags.

When the bell above the door jangled again, a swirl of

snow accompanied Felicia into the diner as she came in. Her forehead was creased, dimming her usual positive glow.

"Hey, Felicia!" Ingrid jumped up from her seat to wave.

Felicia approached her with narrowed eyes. "You...look happy."

Her cheeks reddening, Ingrid bit her lip. Was it that obvious?

Felicia slumped in the booth across from her with a huge sigh. "I'm guessing you haven't perused social media today yet."

Ingrid froze in dread. "No. Why?"

"Do you remember Verona Muller? From high school?"

Her name clicked in Ingrid's head with a flash of her pretty face, that blue dress, and those long legs. "Oh my gosh, that's who that was. Verona Muller from high school." She nodded. "She was at Connell's Winter Fair booth yesterday, taking selfies with people."

Felicia gave her a look. "You saw her there?" Pursing her lips, she drew out her phone. "She's a famous influencer now or something. She's been posting all about Connell's restaurant and the launch." She held out a photo of Connell and Verona together except it wasn't from the booth yesterday.

The two of them were sitting at some fancy café, large steaming cups in each hand, big smiles on their faces, the gorgeous snow falling outside the framing window right behind them. The photo looked like a bunch of professionally-shot models advertising coffee.

"Oh...she's probably helping out with the publicity for the restaurant," Ingrid rationalized, despite the sinking feeling in her stomach. "That's nice."

Studying her reaction, Felicia's eyes narrowed again. "It's probably nothing." She put her phone away. "I thought you might have seen it already. Maybe I shouldn't have shown it to you."

Ingrid dismissed with a grimace. "Well then, I feel like that sort of colors my news a little bit."

Felicia's eyes lit up. "What? What news?"

She cocked her head. "Last night, with Connell... It...went well."

"What?" Felicia's jaw dropped.

"We went out last night. I mean it wasn't like a date or anything but...um, it was good."

"WHAT?"

Ingrid laughed. "Stop saying 'what'!" Her cheeks flushed again, her heart beating faster with the visceral memories from the night before. "Let's just say Connell had some *really* good news yesterday."

Blinking for a moment, Felicia needed a moment to absorb the news. She leaned forward, her elbows on the table. "So you told him Stewart is officially out of the picture?"

"I told him Stewart and I broke up. He said he didn't want to be just some rebound and then he asked me out again." Tentative, Ingrid studied Felicia's face. There was a lack of squealing given what she had just shared.

"Wha-what—" Felicia couldn't seem to wrap her mind around her revelation. She blinked a few more times. "Wait, lemme just make sure—you said yes, right?"

Ingrid paused. "Yeah. Of course, I said yes. Look, I followed your advice, okay? I'm just seeing where things go. I'm trying not to overanalyze it." She picked at the table's surface. "I...like him. Last night was fun."

Felicia's eyes widened at her vagueness. "You kissed."

The bright red on Ingrid's cheeks probably said enough.

And then Felicia squealed. "Oh my gosh, I'm so glad! I'm so happy for you!"

Ingrid chuckled in great relief, especially given Felicia's earlier demeanor.

But now that she had told Felicia, everything seemed all too surreal all over again. Ingrid furrowed her eyebrows. "Is this really happening? I'm not hallucinating, am I?"

Felicia raised her hand. "Quick, how many fingers am I holding up?"

Ingrid laughed again. "That's not the right test."

"Then look at your phone right now." Felicia waved her instruction as she jumped up to sit beside her on the other side of the booth.

Ingrid shot her a look as she reached for her phone. "Why?"

Felicia nodded down at it. "Is your last message from Connell?"

Ingrid swiped to check. "Yes."

Connell had been her last text last night and first text this morning. His last message was about how he was looking forward to seeing her again tomorrow.

"Was it from the last half hour and does it have *any* kind of smiley emoji on it?"

She gave Felicia a quizzical prompt. "Yes. So?"

"Dude." Felicia gave her a flat, no-nonsense look that said everything.

Ingrid colored again. "Alright, fine. I'm not hallucinating."

She put her phone away. "But do you think...?" she hesitated. "What do you think he and Verona—Should I—maybe I should just..."

Felicia braced her hands on Ingrid's shoulders. "Look, if he asked you out then it means he likes you. You're probably right. Verona is just helping out with the publicity for the restaurant. You know how social media is nowadays. Nothing's real."

But something was still nagging at the back of Ingrid's mind. "So you're saying I should give Connell Matthews 'The Biggest Jerk in High School' the benefit of the doubt?"

Felicia chuckled. "I think we shouldn't discount him quite yet."

Ingrid shifted in her seat. "Maybe I'm not emotionally stable enough to do this. I'm not thinking clearly enough."

"Well, welcome to being every other girl in the world." Felicia clapped her hand on Ingrid's shoulder. "None of us can think clearly with regards to the tricky opposite sex, as you well know, with being a mediator to my own relationship."

Ingrid shook her head in mirth.

"Now we need to buy you a new dress for that party."

"I have dresses," Ingrid reminded her.

Felicia disagreed. "You have work interview outfits and pantsuits. In which case, we'd better do that shopping right after this." She rubbed her hands together. "Ooh, this is going to be my new mission."

"Hey, Sam is the one going to a New Year's Ball. Why does it feel like I'm the one who's going to do a dressing room montage?"

"You never know, we might need *two* dressing room

montages," Felicia mused. "We'll devise the perfect ensemble for you, all day tomorrow if we have to."

Ingrid laughed. "As much as I would love not to miss out on that sort of torture, I still have to pop around the restaurant in the morning to organize some files first. So we'd have to defer all the 'devising' until the afternoon."

Felicia's jaw dropped. "Organizing files? Wow, you are one full-service nerd."

"Shut up." Ingrid rolled her eyes.

"This launch is probably going to be the biggest thing Hale Valley is going to have all year. It's so exciting!" Felicia gushed.

"Connell says the whole town is invited and then some."

"Then how could we possibly miss such a prestigious affair? I should buy a new dress too." Felicia's eyes lit up at more scheming.

"You mean, any excuse to buy a new dress?" Ingrid prompted.

Felicia corrected, "Any excuse for three dressing room montages?"

They laughed.

***

Full-service nerd.

Ingrid had laughed at the notion but she had indeed spent all morning organizing the files she had hauled from Connell's to Gail's office.

Gail and Nat were expected to arrive back from their

vacation this morning as well but Ingrid hadn't seen them yet so Connell had said she could use Gail's office in the meantime.

The desk was piled high with folders and files, Ingrid could barely see over them as she sat behind the laptop.

With the restaurant's launch being that evening, the whole place was bustling with activity. Serving staff and delivery people had walked up and down the hallway outside the office Ingrid had been working, rattling carts of fresh fruit, meat, bottles of wine, and other supplies.

Being swamped with work, even Connell only had time to say hello when Ingrid arrived in the morning and she hadn't spoken to him since.

He'd brisk-walked past the office door multiple times, his forehead creased in preoccupation.

Ingrid was grateful for the pile of files blocking her view, since every time Connell passed by, she couldn't help but glance up. The crisp button-down shirt he was wearing looked too similar to the shirt he had worn the night of the burst pipe and the sight of it sent butterflies to her stomach all over again.

Plus Connell was pretty inspiring to watch. He moved with confidence and authority, coordinating everyone pretty well, like the captain of a team.

Ingrid could imagine he was probably busier than ever. This was the biggest night of their business endeavor.

Standing up, Ingrid stretched out her arms. Filing the records wasn't particularly difficult but it was meticulous work. Work she had underestimated. She had to let Connell know that she was going to need more time, possibly come back again another day to finish.

She thought he might be out in the restaurant's dining area, but passing by his office, Ingrid couldn't help herself stopping at the door at the view.

Connell was leaned back in his chair, resting with his eyes closed, broad shoulders slack, head tipped back, displaying that gorgeous throat. He was just so beautiful. He almost glowed in that tiny office with the rare winter sunshine from the skylight washing over him.

She must have made a sound. Connell opened his eyes, tilting his head ever so slightly to look over, and when his gaze met hers, the most dazzling smile formed on his face that Ingrid's heart skipped a beat.

And then, not moving an inch otherwise, he held his hand out. "Come here."

Warmth flushing right through her, she tried to get a hold of herself, shaking her head in feigned disapproval even as she approached him. "This is just sick. Nobody should be this attractive."

Connell swiveled in his seat to get up when she took his hand. His smile widened, his blue eyes studying her face as he tugged her close. "You're absolutely right."

Ingrid was so lost in his eyes. It was hopeless.

It was crazy how simply being near him mesmerized her and all she wanted to do was to be even closer.

She couldn't help reaching up to brush his hair back off his forehead, her fingertips playing at the incredibly soft hair near the nape of his neck. When her fingers grazed his ear, Connell's breath caught in his throat.

Ingrid's stomach stirred in the encouraging thrill that not only was she allowed to touch him, to be this close, but he maybe actually even liked it.

With every bit of extra daring she could muster, Ingrid stood on tiptoes to pull his head down toward her.

His mouth already curving into another smile, Connell obliged, leaning in to meet her lips with his in a sweet, slow kiss.

Ingrid's eyes fluttered closed, shivers running up and down her spine as she breathed him in.

This time, Connell let her lead, let her set the pace, let her lips part across his, let her discover how achingly perfect their lips fit together. He merely kissed her back, brushing his mouth softly against hers over and over in response.

Pressed against him, Ingrid could feel his heart pounding through his shirt. Connell's unhurried, leisurely kisses made her almost dizzy, heady. She was surely floating, except his arm was curved around her waist to hold her tight, keeping her grounded.

He felt so good against her. She could just keep kissing him all day.

After a long moment, a low groan rumbled out of him. He tilted his head to nuzzle her nose with his, his voice husky. "You should probably stop or I'm going to end up just kissing you all day." He met her gaze with his smoldering, heavy-lidded one, a smile reappearing on his lips. "And I won't even regret it."

Flushing slightly at their shared sentiment, Ingrid straightened back up. They must both be crazy.

Connell wrinkled his nose. "Sorry, I thought we could

spend more time together this morning." He reached over to tuck her hair behind her ear. "Thanks for checking in on me."

"Well, I just came in here to tell you I need to do more work with the records, but..." She cracked a small smile. "This is good too."

His phone beeped with a couple of messages but he ignored them.

Ingrid glanced over at his phone, sitting on the desk. "Shouldn't you get that?"

Connell was still studying her face like he couldn't get enough of how she looked. "You wouldn't believe how many times I wanted to call you the other day. Just so I could hear your voice. Gail's basically had enough of my being so restless because, for the last few days, all I've been able to think about is you."

A pleasurable tingling shot up Ingrid's spine, she could barely breathe.

For a moment, Ingrid wondered what her life would be like if she didn't always have this reaction to Connell Matthews. Just the sheer amount of time she would have gotten back from her childhood would be phenomenal. She would probably have been more productive. She would have been more logical and never been stunned into silence whenever he smiled or said things like—

"It means so much to me that you're here." He cradled her cheek in his hand. "And I don't want to have to make any more excuses just to see you.

Ingrid shot him an incredulous look. "You haven't been doing that."

"Oh, you don't even know."

She gave him an incredulous prompting look. "When did you make excuses to see me?"

Connell couldn't quite meet her gaze. "You know, I finished that case study questionnaire in like fifteen minutes."

Her jaw dropped. They had been at Grandpa K's for over an hour. "You did not!"

"And I obviously had no friends to meet at the bowling alley. I just...wanted to hang out with you." Visibly coloring, he hung his head. "I can't believe I just told you that."

Ingrid bit her lip in empathy. Taking a deep breath, she peered into his face. "Back in high school, do you remember your sophomore terrarium project? You were supposed to demonstrate a type of rainforest process all week?"

Connell's eyes widened. No doubt he was recalling the enormity of the task. "Yeah, it almost died. But somehow I managed to keep it barely alive that week and I passed." He whistled. "That was a close one. I really thought it wouldn't last past the first day." He tapped his chin. "But actually, I figured out a week later that I should have been making sure the water somehow filtered all the way down to the ground, like a real rainforest."

"That is correct," Ingrid confirmed. "It definitely *wouldn't* have died if you had watered it correctly."

His eyebrows furrowed. "But...it *didn't* die. How did it stay alive?" It struck him after two seconds and he gave her a gobsmacked stare. "Did...did *you* do that?"

Ingrid tilted her head. "The science club has access to the labs after school. I didn't want you to fail science." She shrugged. "You were so close! You just...needed a little help."

Connell's blue eyes were filled with wonder as he studied her face. "You...did that for me?"

She flushed in embarrassment. "I'm sorry. I feel like such a stalker. But I didn't want Mr. Jacoby to discount you as just that dumb jock. You've always been more than that."

With her pressed against his chest, his heart thundered harder against hers. Connell visibly swallowed. He wanted to say something. "Ingrid, I..."

The sweet, sincere look in his eyes...Ingrid wanted to drown in it.

His forehead creasing, his face pulled into determination, as though something shifted within him. An inkling. A realization. A finality.

Holding Ingrid's solemn gaze, Connell opened his mouth. "I..."

His phone beeped again.

Ingrid jumped in the startle. "Holy—!"

Dropping his head, Connell chuckled. "Worst timing ever." He heaved a resigned sigh and then met her gaze again. "I guess I...better get back to work."

She opened her mouth to say something but he interrupted, "Please don't say you're sorry for taking up so much of my time again." He gave her a look. "If it was up to me, I know exactly who I want to spend all my time with."

She bit her lip in wry mischief. "Gail?"

Connell had to stifle his sudden laughter. Shaking his head, he stroked her cheek with his fingers as he gazed down at her. "Later, Ingrid Harmon." His focus dropped to her mouth again with a promise. "I'm going to want to kiss you again later."

Ingrid shivered again as his thumb brushed her bottom lip.

"So hard you're going to forget your own name," he spoke barely above the groan in his throat.

She swallowed hard, her gaze pinned on his mouth. "Will I remember you?"

A grin formed on his lips. "Like no one else exists."

Several more beeps.

Connell groaned out loud.

Ingrid laughed and pulled away. "Holy cow! Seriously, what is going on over there?"

When Connell picked up the phone, his forehead creased instantly like a shadow fell over him.

She frowned too. "What is it?"

"It's all from Gail," he relayed as he scrolled. "She says her phone must have been stuck at a dead spot. No wonder all of these messages just came through." His eyebrows furrowed even deeper as he read on. "Oh, shoot. Gail and Nat are snowed in at Bermont. They won't make it to the launch opening of the restaurant."

Stepping back, Connell rubbed his face with his hand. "Well, this is going to be interesting." His expression didn't betray any panic but his anxiety was clear.

Ingrid clasped her hands together. "Do you need help? Is there anything I can do?"

He shook his head at once. "No, no. I'm sure I can do it."

"Hey." She elbowed him to reassure him. "I'm sure you'll be fine. You did great all by yourself at my family's party, remember?"

He broke a smile at that. "Thanks, Ingrid." His smile faded a little. "Listen, about tonight, I was planning to pick you up at your house, but it's looking like I won't be able to get away. Do you mind just coming to the restaurant?"

"Of course!" Ingrid assured with a nod. "I understand. You're busy. Don't worry about me. I can come over with Felicia so we'll just see you later."

17

⤫

Chapter Seventeen - Roaring Party

Pushing through Bourbon Streets' double swinging doors was like entering another world.

Strains of soft jazz music, the clinking of expensive glass, and the scent of vanilla, mint, and party poppers wafted past Ingrid as she came inside.

The upstairs balcony trellis had been adorned with fake ivy and fairy lights. The long wooden bar shone under the neon and chandelier lights, accented by the multi-colored liquor bottles decorating the shelf behind the bar. A tower of champagne glasses was stacked like a pyramid at a round table near the back. Silver and gold balloons with curly trailing ribbons lined the ceiling.

Several of the glittering guests holding sparkling, long-stemmed wine glasses had even come dressed in theme.

Felicia cast her eyes down at Ingrid's feet. "I still can't believe you wore your goth combat boots to a Gatsby New Year's party."

"What?" Ingrid argued. "It's black so it matches my dress. And if you all want to walk around in that six-inch snow in your four-inch heels, that's your problem."

Surveying their surroundings, Felicia's eyes widened in awe. "Wow, look at this place."

Electric excitement ran up Ingrid's spine. She nodded in agreement. Despite the last-minute issues and incidents, everything looked absolutely magical. She couldn't wait to congratulate Connell. He must be so stoked.

Venturing farther into the party, Felicia whistled, but she kept her voice to a low hush as she remarked, "It looks like all of Connell's fans turned up, including every town debutante and cougar."

Ingrid had to stifle her chuckle. "I can't believe you just said cougar."

"Ooh." Felicia's eyes followed one of the servers in shiny black tuxedos swerving around the room with their platters of sampler delicacies. "There's the reason I came with you tonight."

"I thought you came with me for moral support?"

Felicia didn't even wince. "What the heck made you think that? You don't need moral supp—ohh..." she trailed off, her attention captured by something across the room.

Ingrid glanced over. "What?"

"There's Connell." Felicia gestured with her chin. "And yup, he's surrounded by women."

Ingrid craned her neck and easily spotted his tall figure

and blond hair. Connell's back was turned but he was indeed amidst a glittery group of people. "Men *and* women," she corrected. "It's a party. Look, everyone's just having fun."

"There's a bunch of girls from our high school here! It's like a freaking reunion." Felicia made a face of distaste as she tugged them both in the other direction. "Ugh. I didn't miss our high school reunion on purpose to end up at another. If you ask me," she began, her tone authoritative, "high school reunions are for those people who were actually there." She let out a wry laugh. "I'm sorry. I was too busy earning my honors diploma."

"That's funny," Ingrid mused. "One of the first things Connell said he remembered about me was that I'd won many awards in high school."

"That *is* funny." Felicia nodded. "Being that he's not going out with Angela Moskowitz, our class valedictorian, the actual one with the most awards. So at least you can be sure, he wasn't just looking for the biggest nerd in the—"

"Nice," Ingrid interrupted, putting a hand up to Felicia's face. "That's great, thanks, my best friend."

Felicia chuckled.

Still shaking her head, Ingrid glanced back toward the offices. "Let me just pop in the back for a sec. I need to double-check that I didn't leave some records open in the system when I was organizing this morning."

"Sure, knock yourself out." Felicia's gaze was already turned toward the finger food buffet by the wooden bar.

Before Felicia could whirl away, Ingrid grabbed her arm. "Behave, please?"

Cheshire cat grin was back on Felicia's face. "No promises," she quipped as Ingrid let her go.

Blowing out a breath, Ingrid headed into the darkened hallway. Not wanting to call attention to herself, she didn't turn the lights on in the office.

Ingrid was pretty confident in the quality of her work but being that it was really important to Connell, she wanted to make sure again. She leaned over the computer to do a quick scan.

Connell's office was adjacent to the dining area, and with the bright lights filtering in through the drawn blinds, she happened to see him walk past the office.

Another thrill shot through her again. Connell was wearing black on black once again, a suit jacket and tie, the overhead lights glimmering in his hair. Respectable and formal, he wasn't dressed in theme, but he still looked super hot.

A few other guys came up to greet him with handshakes and fist bumps.

Ingrid narrowed her eyes as she recognized two of Connell's best friends from high school in the group, Hamish and Trevor.

Strange. From what she could overhear of the conversation, Connell hadn't caught up with them in a while.

Ingrid was preoccupied with work so she wasn't intending to listen to them but the word 'scholarship' slipped through to her awareness.

Hamish was saying it to Connell. "I only just heard about your basketball scholarship. That sucks, man."

A shadow crossed Connell's face but he smiled after a

moment. "I'm not going to say it didn't suck, but I...think I'm fine with how everything's turned out."

Trevor slung his arm around Connell's shoulder. "This guy —this guy used to bring the best stories at Friday drinks. The sheer amount of women he picks up every night is legendary. And yes, that can be plural some nights." He regarded the others with a grin.

"No kidding! Though I don't think we've even seen you at drinks since before Thanksgiving," another guy noted.

Connell shrugged. "Sorry, man. I've been busy with the restaurant and...other stuff." There was a slight hesitation in his voice as he finished his sentence.

Hamish clapped his hand on Connell's shoulder. "So you *are* dating somebody again? After Serena? Finally!"

Connell nodded. "Yeah, she's really great." A curiously odd look flitted past his face for a split second. "I think she really likes me."

Hamish cheered. "Hey, who doesn't?"

"That's what you call a sure thing. Pow!" Trevor quipped, shaking his shoulder.

"You guys are still idiots." Connell twisted away, shaking his head in amusement.

"Word is you stole her from her boyfriend. Is that true?"

Connell seemed to think this over. "Hey, look, I'm not going to brag about that. But I think technically...yes."

Hamish whooped. "My man!"

A nerve in Ingrid's neck ticked. She supposed the conversation should have been flattering for her but when heard within that context, the statement struck her as a bit devious, bordering on sleazy.

She shook her head briskly to clear it. *That's what you get for eavesdropping on people.* She wasn't surprised at all that Hamish and Trevor were still the wildly immature jerks they were back in high school.

Focus! She smacked her hand on her forehead. She still needed to close out the system.

By the time Ingrid stepped back into the dining area, Connell was by the bar, engaged with a different group of well-dressed people she didn't recognize.

She wasn't going to interrupt them but Connell's eyes lit up when he spotted her walking across the room. "Ingrid!" He gestured around. His smile couldn't be any bigger. "What do you think?"

Truly happy for him, Ingrid beamed as she arrived at his side. "This is seriously so amazing, Connell."

Sliding his arm around her waist to tug her closer, Connell turned to introduce her to someone. "Mom, this is my girl-friend, Ingrid."

Ingrid nearly had a heart attack.

"H-hi..." She could barely form a stammer. Shoot, maybe she *was* having a heart attack.

The confidence with which Connell just so casually threw the 'G' word out there, no hesitation, no mocking, absolutely caught her off guard.

Not surprisingly after such an introduction, everyone in the group peered at Ingrid in great curiosity as well.

And his mother... Tall, blonde...

Ingrid snapped to attention enough to manage a polite smile. "It's very nice to meet you, Mrs. Matthews."

"Lovely to meet you, dear," she replied.

Ingrid couldn't help but notice the striking resemblance between them. Connell's mom was incredibly beautiful, same cheekbones, same dimples.

"Ingrid's a Ph.D. candidate at Hartford." Connell cleared his throat in jest. "I even helped her with her doctoral dissertation."

His mom's eyes narrowed. "Sure, you did."

Ingrid couldn't stifle her laughter fast enough.

Connell rolled his eyes. "My mother, ladies and gentlemen."

The rest of the group laughed.

Mrs. Matthews shook her head in mirth but her eyes were twinkling with pride. She leaned up to kiss her son on the cheek. "Now, sweetie, I have to go meet Dana. I just dropped by to congratulate you on your special launch. Enjoy your night." She gave Ingrid another cheery smile. "It was very nice to finally meet you, Ingrid."

"Thank you. You have a good evening," Ingrid bid as the whirlwind of his mother exited the scene.

Ingrid almost wanted to shrink and disappear. The whole encounter had only taken about a minute but she already felt shell-shocked.

And it wasn't over yet. Connell walked them around and introduced his girlfriend to a few more groups of people. Ingrid almost wished she had not worn her goth combat boots tonight.

Coming around the next corner of the wooden bar, two servers came up to Connell at the same time.

"Excuse me, Mr. Matthews, some of the VC panel have just arrived."

"Mr. Matthews, Louis needs you in the kitchen. It's an emergency."

With a slightly overwhelmed groan, Connell met her gaze. "Sorry, I have to go deal with this."

Sympathizing completely, Ingrid gave him a light push. "Of course. I understand. Go."

Connell gave her a helpless look. He didn't want to leave. He leaned closer, his face nearly brushing her cheek, close enough just to whisper, "You look beautiful tonight, by the way."

Tingling all over, Ingrid watched Connell turn and walk away. She had to shake her entire body briskly to snap back to the present.

That guy. Smooth, as always.

Ingrid blew out a breath, casting a glance around the room. Felicia was by the dessert tables.

Ingrid had to shake her head in ridicule as she caught up to her. "Felicia," she hissed. "You are not supposed to doggy-bag those."

Turning around, Felicia's question was muffled by the cake in her mouth. "What?"

Ingrid stifled her laughter with a heavy sigh. "Connell's super busy tonight. I feel bad for him. He's got his hands full with Gail and Nat not here."

"He's doing great though. This party is just fabulous." Felicia gestured to the lush ambiance surrounding them until her gaze caught on something across the way. "Oh, there's Verona. She's talking to some people near the foyer."

Ingrid turned to look. "Oh, those must be the people from the company that's offered to invest in the restaurant."

Felicia curled her lips. "They look uber fancy."

Connell must have finished dealing with the kitchen business. He strode over to Verona's side and the two of them engaged the distinguished group in conversation.

Verona gestured toward several interesting or noteworthy features of the restaurant while Connell explained...something. Then he must have made a joke and the group laughed.

Verona's giggle was lighter than air.

Verona also looked very beautiful that night. With her gold feather fascinator and gold lace and sequin dress, her classy outfit was a perfect contrast to match Connell's all-black look.

"Connell and Verona have them all eating right out of their hands," Ingrid couldn't help but note.

Peering over her shoulder, Felicia feigned a retch, her mouth full of cake once again. "Charming."

Ingrid's lips pursed in consideration.

Stewart most definitely did not draw crowds of beautiful women around him. There was never any time in their relationship when Ingrid had to consider what to feel whenever he spoke to another girl, laughed with another girl, or stood beside another girl.

Her stomach sank at the nagging realization.

Connell had called her his girlfriend.

She had never dared to contemplate it before.

Felicia had told her to stop trying to project outcomes, permutations of possibilities, implications, consequences...

But this was how it would always feel like to be Connell Matthews's girlfriend.

The logical part of her brain she had put to sleep for the last few days was stirring awake.

****

"Oh my gosh, I ate too much cake." Felicia hung over the metal rail of the much quieter upstairs loft of the restaurant where they had gone to escape the crowd.

Laughing, Ingrid gave her a wry, pointed look. "No, you think so?"

Her face in agony, Felicia tugged on Ingrid's arm. "I have to hit the ladies' room."

An inkling of impending doom at the notion nagged Ingrid's mind. "Oh, no, I'm not going to the bathroom with you here. I don't want to run into any of those preppy girls. That's for sure where they're all hanging out and I loath to think what they're gossiping about in there right now."

"Your brain is so weird sometimes." Felicia rolled her eyes. "Fine, I'll be right back then," she bid, turning to descend the wrought iron staircase.

Leaning against the balustrade, Ingrid couldn't help a smile. Everyone looked like they were having so much fun. She almost couldn't believe what a smashing success Connell's restaurant launch was. Giddy with exhilaration, she was already replaying the events of the evening in her mind. Everything was so perfect.

"Yeah, Connell was parading her around before. Poor guy. It was like he wanted to hold up a sign 'No longer pining over Serena. I can score a nerd too.'"

What the—?

Glancing down, she furrowed her eyebrows in aghast.

Thanks, or maybe no thanks, to the fantastic acoustics in the architecture of the restaurant, the dripping judgment in the person's statement had sailed clear up the supporting wall right next to Ingrid.

She could only see the tops of their heads but she could tell they were those preppy girls from her high school. It seemed they were, in fact not congregated in the bathroom, but sitting in the booth directly beneath her.

She almost moaned in disbelief.

Just her freaking rotten luck.

"Oh, you mean the rebound from Serena?"

"What kind of nerd is she?"

"Some kind of Ph.D. or something."

Ingrid couldn't help an eye roll. To these girls, those were just letters. They didn't have the tiniest idea what sort of ambition, drive, and hard work was required in its pursuit.

She already knew the sensible thing to do was to stop listening. This conversation was not going to end in her favor. She should go and find Felicia and maybe eat some more cake. But Ingrid couldn't quite drag herself away from the wall.

"Well, if Serena dumped my ass for a doctor, I'd probably be looking for some kind of geek to go out with too just to prove I could."

"Come on. The odds of a dolt like Serena landing that doctor was like a million to one. And now Connell's found himself some kind of smarty doctor too. That scans for me."

"Oh my god, wait, I think I remember now. That girl, she went to school with us! She was that computer nerd that got all those awards or something."

"Oh, hey, wasn't she one of those girls obsessed with Connell? Remember the bus incident on that one school trip? I saw her staring at him."

Ingrid's face burned. She supposed that while it may have been possible she had flown completely under Connell's radar in high school, she may not have escaped the radar of these nosier girls.

"Did she get a makeover or something? Did you those hideous shoes?"

"I think she works here. I saw her in the back before."

"Oh wow, is Connell still getting the nerds to do his homework?" One of them laughed.

Full-service nerd.

All the blood drained from Ingrid's face at the metaphorical punch in the gut.

Oh, dear god. Had the unspeakable finally happened? Had she finally turned into one of Connell's 'groupies'?

Thinking back to the last couple of weeks, Ingrid's realization sank like an onion in a martini. There was no denying the facts. She was always more than happy to do anything for Connell.

One of the girls' next statements made Ingrid's stomach turn right over.

"I wonder if she gets any additional perks with this job."

They giggled hysterically at the notion.

"Verona said she was planning to ask him out. Maybe he'll be so grateful for all her help with the publicity for the restaurant."

"Maybe I'll ask him out too. Verona doesn't have dibs on him, you know. Just because she's a famous influencer now."

"You're a tramp. Maybe I'll ask him out. He's always liked me better, that's for sure."

Her heart pounding in her chest, Ingrid pushed away from the balustrade.

Was this seriously happening right now?

Prickling ran up her spine and Ingrid hurried down the stairs. She almost bumped into Felicia coming back up.

"Whoa." Noticing her distress, Felicia caught her arm. "What's up with you?"

Shrugging her off, Ingrid wrung out her hands. "Nothing, it's fine. Those girls from high school are down there," she relayed, offhand. "And I just heard some...stuff."

Felicia's face crumpled. "What, are they talking smack right now? Should we go throw champagne in their faces or something? You know, I'd totally be up for that."

The indignant tone in Felicia's voice, the aggressive look on her face, somehow, at that moment, struck Ingrid as absolutely comical, and she nearly burst out laughing.

Tension instantly dissipated from her shoulders, and the fog in her mind cleared away, making room for some rational perspective. Ingrid shook her head at how ridiculous this all was.

These preppy girls lived in their little echo chambers where they were the stars of the show. They'd led sheltered lives, oblivious to the workings of the real world. They'd never been exposed to things that challenged their views, their opinions. These were the sorts of people who would never change.

More to the point, Ingrid had now grown a backbone— sure, not a formidable one, but a backbone nonetheless. She had enough sense of self-worth. She didn't need the approval of these people, nor should she put any stock in their cage-rattling opinions.

Ingrid blinked as another thought occurred to her.

Surprised, Felicia craned her neck as Ingrid kept going downstairs. "Where are you going?"

Ingrid waved her away as she purposefully strode toward the group of girls who were already giving her wide-eyed, scandalous looks as she came closer.

"Hi." Ingrid gave them a perfunctory smile.

Reaching into her shoulder bag, she began to distribute several calling cards. "My name is Ingrid. I'm conducting a survey for my dissertation and I think you guys would be perfect candidates for this study."

She gestured to the cards in their hands. "The QR code on the card will take you directly to the survey. It shouldn't take you more than five minutes to answer." Her smile widened. "I would really appreciate your time."

The girls could only stare at Ingrid as she walked back to meet Felicia who was waiting by the bottom of the staircase.

Her friend was giving her an incredulous expectant prompting look.

Ingrid threw her hands up. "What? They were the ideal sample population for my stereotypes study. I could always use more respondents. I'm just glad I have those calling cards with me all the time."

Felicia burst out laughing. "You are crazy and a half."

"Look, they were either going to offend me or be of use," she reasoned with a shrug. "I just prefer to choose the latter."

"Ah, the high road." Felicia stuck her nose up. "Nice."

That made Ingrid laugh.

Gaze past Ingrid's shoulder, Felicia tugged on her arm. "Oh hey, Connell's talking to Verona again. Do we need to do something?"

With no enthusiasm whatsoever, Ingrid turned to look.

Every high school party memory flashed back in her mind of a shiny Connell Matthews surrounded by his shiny posse, all the pretty girls hanging all over him while his drunk friends roughhoused all over the place.

She always wondered what it would have been like in high school if she'd managed to enter his social circle.

Was this the world she would now be a part of? With all the backstabbing, the shallowness, the hypocrisy? She would never last any measure of time with these people. Surely, this should have already been glaringly obvious to Connell.

Then it dawned on her.

Of course, he knew that already.

But he also knew she'd do anything for him.

This morning, it was to organize records. Tonight, it was to help him save face from having been dumped by Serena for that doctor. Tomorrow, maybe he would find something else to brag about to his friends or boost his reputation at her expense.

Connell wasn't looking for a real girlfriend. He needed a crutch. Someone to lean on until he recovered from his rebound.

Meanwhile, all the smarmy other women would be slinking around him and bad-mouthing her, it would only be a matter of time until—

Stopping that thought, Ingrid sucked in a breath as a fresh wave of realization washed over her.

This was the other shoe.

The buzzing in her purse jerked her back to the present. She frowned upon reading the message. "Oh, it's Mom. The condenser flooded the laundry again and Dad and Sam have gone to the movies."

Slinging her bag of purloined cheesecake over her shoulder, Felicia exaggerated her moan of dismay. "Oh nooo, we have to leave? That's too bad. I really wanted to sta—race you to the door!"

With a laugh, Ingrid watched her friend scoot away.

Ingrid was certain Connell wouldn't have missed her at all tonight if she left right then but she still wanted to do the polite thing and say thanks anyway. He was the host of the party after all. And despite everything, she sincerely wanted to congratulate him again on the fantastic launch.

When Ingrid spotted him near the table in the back, Connell's eyes were darting furtively around as though still checking to make sure everything was going well.

He seemed a bit haggard, worse for wear, his hair a tad bit mussed up, but not any less hot that all the girls around him had stopped staring.

Ingrid tilted her head in mocking incredulity. With her conclusion settled in her brain, strangely, she was calm and relieved.

Just because she somehow could date Connell Matthews now didn't mean she *should*.

The relief in Connell's eyes was visible when he spotted her crossing the floor toward him again. "Ingrid." His smile was sincere but tired.

Ingrid returned his smile, graciously. "Congratulations, Connell. You've done so well. This was a great party."

Connell noticed her glance at the door. "Are you leaving?" Before she could respond, his eyes lit up. "Hey, how are you going with those records?"

Ingrid blinked, almost surprised at his query. "Um, fine, I think. But listen, Fi and I have to leave now. My mom needs me."

He nodded, even though his gaze was elsewhere. "Oh, alright. Make sure you finish sorting out those files. I told Gail everything would be peachy by the time she and Nat come back. Everything needs to be cool."

A bit jarred by the directive in his tone, as though she was his employee or one of his grunt nerds doing his homework for him, Ingrid stifled her scoff under her breath. "Um, okay, sure, you got it." She patted his arm casually before turning to hurry past the crowd toward the exit. His change in demeanor didn't even faze her as much as she thought it would. It was all water off a duck's back.

"Ingrid, wait," Connell called across the room.

Ingrid almost winced as nearly everyone else in the restaurant had also turned to look.

But Connell strode toward her with a mysterious smile on that ridiculously handsome face, his gaze pinned only on her.

"What is it?" Her eyes were wide in expectation.

A corner of his mouth turned up and he leaned closer. "I almost forgot." He tipped her chin up and gestured to the door frame above them.

Ingrid looked up but barely had time to register what the

object hanging above their heads was before Connell covered her lips with his.

Mistletoe.

His arm slid around her waist to pull her closer, and despite her convictions, Ingrid still shivered against him. He really was still so very good at that.

It wasn't slow like this morning but it wasn't urgent like the other night. It was firm, chaste, definitely showy.

When Connell finally broke off, Ingrid was sure her face was flushed. She ignored the deadly stares from that same group of preppy girls from the dimmed booth across the dining area.

With that heavy weight back on her shoulders, Ingrid stiffened. "I should go."

Connell reached up to pluck the mistletoe down from the door frame, and then taking her hand, he closed her fingers around it. "Well, then I don't need this anymore."

Ingrid couldn't bring herself to say anything more. She merely gave Connell a slight wave and turned on her heel to join Felicia who had been waiting in the foyer the whole time.

"Well, that was horrible and a half," Felicia noted as she buttoned up an extra one before they ventured out into the cold night.

Ingrid shook her head. "I thought it was quite a successful event."

The evening definitely helped Ingrid accomplish one important thing.

Finally, everything made sense.

18

Chapter Eighteen -
Follow-up

Bourbon Streets was the word in everyone's mouth the next day.

Or at least, everyone who had come into Grandpa K's that chilly morning since Ingrid had sat down at one of the diner tables.

Such high praises for the food, the ambiance, the cake.

Likely all of Connell's dreams come true.

Speaking of dreams, Ingrid was staring at the email on her laptop again. The one she had received early this morning.

Subject line: Congratulations on making the shortlist for Professor Braun's team!

Even Felicia who had dropped by her house before leaving for work had whooped in celebration. Ingrid could hardly believe it herself. She supposed that the selection panel must have liked both her and Stewart's versions of their paper.

Although, what was even more interesting news was that the shortlist had not included a certain Stewart Talbot's name.

Meaning that if Ingrid was selected for one of the highly coveted two positions, she would get to work her dream job starting right after New Year's and there was no risk that she would be stuck working with the biggest jerk ever for the whole year.

A vague disquiet nagged in the back of her mind, but it was overwhelmed by a sort of vindicated relief.

Dismissing its indeterminate nature with a sigh, she switched screen tabs from her email back to her dissertation again to do some more work since she couldn't afford *not* to impress Professor Braun's team.

Or at least, Ingrid had planned to do work this morning.

She had started on a completely different, absolutely un-important, possibly ludicrous questionnaire.

On tenterhooks about the *other* thing she had planned to do today, Ingrid focused to drown out the ambient noise in the diner, of the jarring bell above the door from the multiple eager customers coming in and out for the last time this year, since Grandpa K's would be shut for two weeks from tomorrow for the New Year's break.

She gasped as arms wrapped around her from behind, a husky voice in her ear.

"How's my biggest fan this morning?"

Turning slightly, she glimpsed the dazzling smile on Connell's face. She hadn't heard from him at all since the party last night. Understandable, since he must have been exhausted.

Ingrid couldn't help closing her eyes to savor the moment

—his warmth on her back, his jaw pressed against her cheek, that stupid cologne of his getting more and more familiar to her by the day, the tingling she got everywhere, every second he was anywhere near her.

And that was enough.

Pulling herself back down to earth, Ingrid mused wryly, "Am I going to keep running into you like this?"

Connell shrugged. "Maybe you're just lucky."

Her chest constricted at the potential accuracy of his statement. "Is that right?"

He chuckled low, withdrawing his arms. "No, I'm actually here for Dean. We're supposed to go meet up with the others again for Halo."

The others? *Again?* "Oh. Really?" Ingrid's eyebrows furrowed in genuine surprise.

"Yeah, they're pretty cool. They're letting me hang out. Dean and I are supposed to leave from here this morning." Connell moved to sit beside her. "But honestly, I was also hoping I'd run into you."

He reached for her hand, his smile softening. "Listen, I..." He stroked her palm, his fingers playing with hers. "Was thinking last night didn't really count as our first official date since I know it didn't turn out as well as it could have." That disarming, imploring gaze met hers. "Could we try again? Please?"

Willing her pulse to stop racing, Ingrid sat back in her chair. "Um, Connell, I think...we need to talk."

"Pardon?"

Connell's face was bright, at ease, so relaxed, Ingrid almost changed her mind. But despite the urge to spontaneously catch on fire so she could somehow avoid doing this, she knew the honorable thing to do was to tell him to his face.

Expediently. She clenched her jaw in resolution. There was no point dragging it out.

Ingrid was more than perfectly happy to bookend her 'blast from the past' with that amazing mistletoe kiss at the restaurant launch party.

Turning to her laptop screen, Ingrid steadied her chin. "I...needed to ask you some follow-up questions for my study."

Connell only looked puzzled for a split second. "Oh. Okay, shoot."

She spun the laptop around so he could read them off the screen.

"Okay, number one," he started, his tone casual. "Last night, did you introduce me as your girlfriend to make it clear to everyone that you were over..." he flinched but he finished, "Serena...?"

Connell's eyebrows furrowed as he kept reading. "Number two, did you think dating a Ph.D. candidate would one-up Serena getting engaged to that doctor?" His voice hushed as he went on, "Number three, was being able to say that you stole me from my boyfriend a nice little bonus?"

Sucking in a breath, he dropped his gaze as he recited the last question. "Number four, is that why you kissed me in front of everyone?"

An already suspiciously guilt-ridden look on his pale face, Connell met her prompting gaze. "Ingrid, I can explain."

Ingrid tamped down the squirming in her stomach, the constriction in her chest, that strong urge to yield to that pleading look, those gorgeous eyes. She had resolved to see this through and by glory, she was going to.

She put her hands up in resignation. "Look, you don't have to go through any trouble for me." Closing the lid on her laptop, she nodded. "I understand. I get it. You must have been hurt when Serena left you for a doctor and now you're just trying to get even, trying to win at relationships."

Connell's forehead was still creased. "Okay," he began. "I admit that did occur to me in the beginning. And for the record, we would totally beat them at which of us makes the best couple." He gave her an emphatic nod. "We *would* win. Please don't be mad."

"I'm not mad," Ingrid reassured him, determined to keep her head clear. She dropped her gaze. "But I think this is probably a good point for us to—"

A burst of raucous laughter from the door interrupted Ingrid.

Still laughing, Dean was charging through the door, his head turned to one side as he spoke to the person behind him.

Ingrid had started to wave at him when her eyes met the distinctly familiar brown eyes of the lanky brown-haired guy with the ascot and she froze.

Oh, holy crap—

"Hey, Ingrid!" Dean gave her a cheery wave. His eyes popped wide upon seeing Connell standing by Ingrid. "Oh, holy crap."

Stewart's visit was probably instigated by that surprising 'short list' email from this morning. But despite his name somehow missing from the list, Stewart's smug, sardonic air still clouded his form as he approached.

Ingrid gave him a dull look. "What are *you* doing here?"

Easily sensing her tension, Connell took a half-step forward as though to keep Ingrid partway behind him. "Who is this guy?"

Ingrid put a hand on Connell's arm to dilute his intimidating presence in case Stewart was also in a mood. The last thing she wanted today was to instigate some sort of fight. Gesturing to Stewart, she pursed her lips together. "This is my friend—"

Connell's forehead creased. "Your friend—"

"Her boyfriend," Stewart supplied.

"*Ex*-boyfriend," Ingrid corrected loudly.

Connell blinked as he connected the dots. "*Ex*-boyfriend? Stewart?"

Not pleased at all, Stewart's lips were a thin line. "Via memo as it were. You should have seen it. And here I thought Ingrid couldn't have any less class."

"I think you take the cake for that award, Stewart." Ingrid rolled her eyes. "Now if that's all, would you quit bothering me? I have too much work to do."

Stewart tossed a glance at Connell before glaring at her. "Oh and he doesn't bother you?"

She shooed Stewart away. "He's part of it, now would you please?"

He glanced up at Connell again and Stewart's face lit up in recognition. When he grabbed Ingrid's arm to pull her aside, Dean had to hold Connell back, the displeasure clear on his face.

But Stewart's incredulous question was as urgent as it was

hoarse. He was reluctant to make a big, loud scene. "Is this the jerk from high school that you wrote your last paper about?"

Ingrid crossed her arms across her chest but she didn't say anything.

Stewart threw up his hands. "Oh my god, are you still on that stereotypes thing? There's nothing more to find there, Ing!" he argued under his breath. "You already know what your study is going to turn up so why even bother? Guys like him and Joshua Knowles are a dime a dozen. Playboys and liars and cheats."

He leaned closer in mocking disbelief. "Or have you actually fallen for his tricks? Let him wow you with that shiny hair and shiny words? You already know how this is going to end. You wrote an entire *thesis* on how this is all going to end."

Indignation rose in her chest. She couldn't let Stewart talk about Connell that way. "That's just one interpretation."

Stewart put a hand to his forehead. "Good grief. *Now* she's doubting herself." He shook her head. "Look, I'm trying to save your career here. I'm trying to help you. My version of the paper is the only acceptable one. And nobody will ever take you seriously if you keep going off on these tangents of contemporary sociology."

He rubbed his face with his hand. "Do you think the esteemed academics on Professor Braun's team all just play around? That is serious scientific research, Ing. You need to play the classics like everyone else."

She rolled her eyes. "That's exactly why I don't want to do that. Everyone else has already done it. And it seems the selection panel agrees with me."

Stewart grimaced. "You know I'm going to file an appeal

to the panel. For sure, this is just some minor oversight. I just wanted to give you a heads-up before you embarrass yourself."

"Do what you want." Starting to get irritable, Ingrid made a face. "Look, is that all you're here for? If it is, then I think there's nothing else we need to talk about. I'll talk to our adviser about splitting up our study."

"So instead of working together, now you want to compete with me for the TA slot?"

Stubbornly, she tilted her head to meet his even gaze. "I guess that's what we have to do."

Stewart glanced from Ingrid to Connell to Dean then back to Ingrid again. With a helpless shrug, he adjusted his fancy ascot. "Fine then. As much as I would love to stick around and watch you destroy your career, I have better things to do."

"Shut the door on your way out. It's cold today," Ingrid called to his back as he exited.

Stewart slammed the door shut but didn't bother looking back.

A handful of Grandpa K's patrons nearby craned curious necks to watch the angry person who had stormed out, darting discreet looks at Ingrid, but fortunately, their attentions were fleeting.

Dean blew out a breath before he patted Connell's shoulder. "Well, I'm sure Felicia would be gutted to have missed all that." He met Ingrid's sullen gaze. Grimacing as he read the room, he piped up, "Or maybe I should go away and transcribe these events for Felicia," before whirling around to retreat into the kitchen.

Connell's forehead was already etched in concern as he strode right up to her.

Still on edge, Ingrid put her hand up before he could ask. "Yes, I'm fine."

He shook his head in resignation. "Obviously. That was a little impressive to watch."

"Thanks."

"So that was Stewart."

Pursing her lips, Ingrid nodded.

"He's...kind of—" Connell wrinkled his nose as though to think of the right words.

"A jerk?" Ingrid supplied.

"A jerk! Yes," Connell finished resolutely. "Thanks for clearing that up." His forehead was still creased but he grinned to ask, "So...what was his problem?"

Ingrid blew out an exasperated breath. "He's just sore because I'm in the running for a spot in this prestigious research team in Berkeley in January and he's not. This could be a really big stepping stone in our careers."

"I see."

"You know," she went on, a sour taste still in her mouth from the encounter, "he could have just humored me and been willing to work together. Then maybe we would both be on the shortlist. And all this controlling, pig-headed behavior was exactly why I broke up with him last semester."

Connell looked stunned. "What?"

Ingrid blinked. "What?"

He stared at her. "You broke up when?"

Uh-oh.

Her eyes widened in dread. "Oh, I mean—"

Confused, Connell dropped his gaze. "If you've been broken up since last semester, then that means..."

Ingrid tamped down the urge to cringe. "Well, we were sort of on a break but we both knew it was over. It's—it's complicated." She waved to dismiss it.

When he looked up again, his blue eyes bore into her. "So technically, I *didn't* steal you from your boyfriend." His forehead creased deeper. "But...you wanted to make me think that I did?"

"No, no!" She shook her head in protest. "I just—I didn't want to... I didn't want to leave that chance open for..." Groaning, she buried her head in her hands. "It's hard to explain."

Connell's face was flushed. "I wanted to steal you from your boyfriend. It did cross my mind." He shook his head briskly. "I'll admit it. I'm not a nice guy. But only because I could tell he didn't deserve you, Ingrid. You deserve so much more than him." His face was stricken. "But you—you set me up! You were purposefully trying to make me like Joshua Knowles so you could use it against me."

Ingrid's heart pounded in her chest, her mouth dry. She couldn't argue with any of it. "I know. You're right!"

Connell's gaze had daggers in it. "And what was that paper he was talking about?"

Ingrid stilled. He had heard that too?

Fidgeting in her stance, she chewed on her bottom lip. "The paper I wrote last year. It was...about proving that—well—" She blew out another breath. "It was about me realizing the truth about this guy that I liked, that you weren't perhaps as noble as my biased, rose-tinted glasses made you out to be." Guilt-ridden, she bit her lip again. "The stereotypes case study is sort of similar in that I was looking for people with...certain qualities. Popular, self-absorbed, arrogant, disingenuous..."

He took a few seconds to process her words, what they actually meant, as though realizing why she had been spending all this time with him, to begin with.

She watched his face. She knew it sounded bad, and while it was all legitimately academic, and mostly theoretical, sweeping generalizations, her conclusions didn't portray him in a favorable light at all.

Connell's eyebrows furrowed. "Let me get this straight. You...*did* like me in high school when you thought I was an immature jerk. And now you've come back to make sure I was still an immature jerk? And you've been going out with me so you could have a chance to dump me?"

Her eyes widened. "Oh. No. That's not—" She wrinkled her nose. "I mean, I never said we were dating. You assumed we were. I just needed to interview you for my dissertation."

He scoffed as if he'd been punched in the gut. "And now that you've got what you need, what, you're just going to leave? You said you're moving to Berkeley next week? Possibly even to work with your jerk ex-boyfriend?" He shook his head as if to clear it. "You're still messing with my head, aren't you? Is this still part of your experiment? Are you still testing me?"

Ingrid swallowed hard. "No!"

His face was ashen, desolate, his voice hushed. "You said you had a crush on me. I thought..." His forehead was still creased in deep thought. "I thought you liked me."

She averted her gaze. "Look, the truth was in high school, I had a crush on who I thought you were. It wasn't really you. It was just the 'you' I imagined in my head! It wasn't real."

Connell shook his head. He wouldn't meet her gaze. "All this time I thought you saw me." He was still shaking his head to himself in disbelief. "God, I really am stupid."

Ingrid's chest constricted tight. She tried to find the right words to say.

Connell may have used her for his own ends but to some degree, she supposed she had used him too. He was well within his rights to be angry.

Then again maybe it *was* better if he was angry with her. The whole point of this conversation was to give Connell an out after all.

She kept her chin up. "Then you agree? We've both accomplished what we need. We don't have to keep doing this," she rationalized. "Last night was proof enough that you live in an entirely different world from mine, and I honestly can't see myself being any kind of part of it."

Studying her blank expression, Connell shook his head. "You don't even seem upset about all this."

She pursed her lips. Upset? No. More like numb. Cold. She had to be. And surely, he also understood why this would never work out anyway. She steeled herself, gathering up the courage to finish what she'd started.

"We're going to be fine," she assured, hoping her voice was even despite the constriction in her chest. "We were never friends. You didn't even remember I existed until a few weeks ago."

Almost wavering at the stark truth in her point, Ingrid clenched her fists at her sides to stay focused. "Let's just say I was the first girl you saw after you broke up with Serena.

Let's call this what it is. A rebound. And now I'm letting you move on."

She gave a dismissive shrug. "This was great and I really appreciate the opportunity. But I can't be what you need right now. I know you'll find another girl who would do anything for you—way better than me."

Connell's glassy blue eyes met hers. He was studying her face intently, as though trying to uncover her real meaning. "Ingrid, is this really what you want?"

Ingrid tilted her head. He seemed concerned that she would take the loss hard. "Me? I'll be okay," she assured with a nod. At this point, she was so used to disappointment, it was no longer a big deal.

Her eyes lit up as it struck her what he still could have been worried about. Something else he needed from her. "Oh, and don't worry about those records. I'll still drop by to finish filing them this week. You don't even have to meet me there. I'll do what I said. I promised you I would do it so I will."

Connell's glare turned to disbelief.

Pursing her lips, she broke a casual, sympathetic smile. "You've done such a great job with the restaurant, Connell. I'm really happy for you. I hope everything stays on track with the investors. I know you can do it."

That statement struck a different chord with Connell, as though he found her words patronizing. He shot her a dark look, spun on his heel, and then he was gone.

The jangling of the bell above the door faded into the overhead din in the diner as the world resumed its normal speed.

With the biggest sigh ever, Ingrid sank back into her chair.

Shaking off the prickling running all over her skin, she wanted to curl into a ball in the corner booth. Though, the painful stabbing in her chest had subsided somewhat.

She had to let him go. It was the right thing to do.

She was sure she would get over it, given enough time and distance—which she would definitely get.

Turning her laptop back toward her, she flipped the lid open once again, and with loud, repeated clacking, she deleted the new questionnaire before switching over to her proper dissertation notes.

It was finally over.

Taking a deep, calming breath, she took careful stock of the situation.

She was on the shortlist for the TA position, and against all odds, her paper was complete—thanks, in part, to Connell. She almost couldn't believe she had even accomplished all that.

While the time she'd spent with him was a nice little walk down memory lane, it was time to focus on the future.

She needed to walk away.

To put the genie back in the bottle.

Put Connell back in the past.

19

Chapter Nineteen - Empty

Bourbon Streets' mid-afternoon scene had an opposite vibe from the launch party.

Since the restaurant didn't officially open for another few weeks, chairs were neatly stacked above the tables in the dining area. With the main ceiling lights on, the huge space was stark and sterile, the long wooden bar plain. Nothing shone nor glittered. Only a couple of cleaning staff were meandering through the front of the restaurant.

Ingrid's shoes clacked on the floor almost in time to the decorative brass clock ticking above her head as she walked to the back offices.

Her eyes darted around furtively in case Connell was in the building, even though since he knew she would be dropping by, he'd probably made himself scarce to avoid her like yesterday's bad oysters.

Peeking into Connell's office, she sighed in relief to find it empty. But her eyebrows furrowed when checking next door, Gail's office was empty too.

Ingrid had wanted to make sure Gail was aware she was here tinkering in her office again to finish organizing those records.

Heading back down the hall, Ingrid called out. "Gail?"

"In the kitchen," the disembodied voice yelled out.

Gail met her gaze with a smile as Ingrid walked into the kitchen. She put down the menu clipboard she was holding. "Ingrid! I'm so glad to see you again."

"Hi, Gail."

Before Ingrid could confirm her permission to access her office, Gail spoke up first. "You know, I'm not sure where Connell is. He hasn't been answering any of my messages since yesterday."

Holding back her flinch, Ingrid waved it away. "Oh, don't worry about that. I'm just here to finish sorting out those records. Is it okay if I used your office again?"

"Absolutely!" Gail said with an enthusiastic nod and a wink. "Hey, if you ever need a job, we would love to get you on the team with a contract to manage them. You just let me know."

Ingrid chuckled. She couldn't tell if Gail was serious but it was sweet of her to say. "I'm really glad you guys got out of that freak snowstorm. I hope it wasn't too bad."

Gail huffed to dismiss it. "Oh, yeah. Nothing Nat and I couldn't handle. We even got a complimentary night's stay at that gorgeous B&B because we basically couldn't leave. It was fantastic." Her tone turned wry as she considered, "Never mind that our little Mini was buried in snow, froze overnight, and nearly fell off a cliff. These are stories you tell your grandchildren."

That made Ingrid laugh.

"It was just a bummer that we missed the launch party," Gail went on. "But I hear everything went off without a hitch?"

"Yes! It was amazing." Ingrid agreed with a nod. "But of course, it was. You said it yourself. Connell's a force to be reckoned with."

Gail's face warmed and she put her hand on Ingrid's shoulder. "I'm so glad at least you were there to support him the other night. I'm sure he needed that."

"Of course." Ingrid's nod was sincere. "I'm always happy to help out. But I'm sure Connell would have been fine by himself. He is really good at this," she pointed out.

Gail clicked her tongue. "I tell Connell all the time how good he is but he never believes me. Good thing he has someone like you to tell him the same thing who he'll actually believe." She gave Ingrid another pleased smile. "You guys are so great together."

Ingrid blinked. "Oh... I think you misunderstood." She shook her head. "We're not together. We're just friends."

Her forehead creasing, Gail blinked. "But I thought... Connell said he asked you out." She broke a quirky, mischievous grin at the recollection. "I distinctly remember because he wouldn't shut up about it."

"Oh." Ingrid almost chuckled. "Um... It...didn't work out?" She shrugged with a sheepish smile.

"Oh." Gail made a face. "That's a shame."

Ingrid couldn't understand the disappointment in Gail's expression. "Why?"

Gail straightened up. "Well, I know I've only known Connell for a few years, but I'd never seen him as happy as he's been these last few weeks." She gave her a pointed look. "And I know you're the reason why."

Ingrid almost soared at the notion, but checking herself, she dismissed it with a wave. "Oh. Well, I'm sure he'll be fine. He's...you know, Connell Matthews. Surely, he would have no trouble finding someone else."

Gail tilted her head. "But I thought you liked him?"

"Not really," Ingrid tried to clarify. "I did explain that to him. It was just a silly little crush. The guy that I liked in high school, I had imagined all sorts of nice, noble qualities—you know, the most thoughtful guy ever, having the best sense of humor, confident without being arrogant..." She rolled her eyes in mocking.

Gail narrowed her eyes in thought. "But...Connell is all those things."

A bit taken aback, Ingrid's eyebrows furrowed.

"I know people think Connell had the best time of his life in high school," Gail began. "But from what he's told me, he seemed lost those days." She hopped up to sit on a bar stool by the kitchen bench. "Coming to business school, he already had a bit of a rough start. His self-confidence was shot by losing that sports scholarship. But he worked his ass off. Harder than anyone else I knew." She lifted her shoulders.

"But I could see it in him, that drive, that passion, like he finally found a sense of direction."

Ingrid's conviction faltered as she recalled the way Connell would get that shadowed look on his face sometimes, how he would often joke about how he had no idea what he was doing, his apprehensions about people thinking he was simply a talentless, pretty face.

Gail was studying Ingrid's expression as though she had figured out some things on her own. "I'm guessing Connell must be in worse shape than I thought."

Ingrid couldn't help a derisive scoff. "Why? I was just the dumb girl with the stupid crush on him all those years ago."

"I know." Gail nodded. "I bet this hurts him more because it *is* you."

Ingrid dropped her gaze. Remorse stabbed at her chest. She wasn't sure what to say.

"Are you sure there's no chance?" Gail prompted.

Uneasy with Gail's whole line of questioning, Ingrid edged back against the table. "Well, it just didn't make any sense..."

Sensing her retreat, Gail took a deep breath, not wanting to intervene any further. "Sure, I suppose it's not my place to say. I hope you had let him down easy." She picked up her clipboard again. "Feel free to use the office however long you need," she instructed, patting her shoulder again. "And thanks for the great work, Ingrid."

Ingrid could only nod.

"Oh, hey, by the way." Gail hopped off the stool and walked across the kitchen. "Can you tell me..."

Her eyebrows up in expectation, Ingrid met Gail's questioning gaze.

Gail pointed the toe of her shoe to a small spot on the hardwood floor by the cabinets. "Why is there a dent on this floor? It's like someone dropped a big wrench or something. Did something happen in here?"

***

Felicia's eyebrows rose as she found Ingrid in the kitchen. She put her hands on her hips in disbelief. "Are you eating ice cream on a plate right now?"

Glancing up, Ingrid mumbled through her mouthful of Ben & Jerry's. "We're out of bowls but the dishwasher's still running. I didn't want to wait."

Felicia clicked her tongue as she came up to lean against the kitchen counter beside her. "Dare I ask?"

Ingrid took a deep breath. "Gail said Connell really liked me."

Felicia's eyes widened.

"She said Connell really liked me and I didn't believe him." She threw up her hands. "Why wouldn't I believe him? Why, Felicia? Why?"

"Because you overthink things." Felicia ticked off her fingers. "Because you're Type A, because you're still insecure, because—"

"Ahh!" Ingrid cut her off, even though she knew Felicia was right.

Putting away her empty ice cream plate, she sighed yet again. "I feel like such a jerk. I assured him *I* would be fine. It didn't even occur to me that maybe he was struggling too. Gail said she hoped I had let him down easy. I'd basically told him 'thanks but I politely decline' like it was a job offer." Burying her face in her hands, she groaned out loud. "I am a jerk."

"Are you going to do something about it?" Felicia's eyebrows rose.

Ingrid made a face. "I mean, it's Connell Matthews!" she declared. "Everyone knows who that's supposed to be. But sometimes when I'm with him, it's like...I can't even believe it's the same person." Subdued, she went on. "He's...clever, thoughtful, dedicated..." She shook her head. "I have got to be simply projecting these qualities onto him, right? Is it possible I'm not just seeing what I want to see again, just like in high school?"

Felicia seemed less sympathetic. "Ohhh...I'm so sorry the guy of your dreams turned out to be a real guy."

Ingrid glared at her. "It's not funny."

"I think it's hilarious," Felicia drawled. "Your entire life has been focused on getting over Connell. And now that you can finally have him, you want to let him go?"

Fidgeting in her stance, Ingrid frowned. "Yes! Don't you understand? I have been trying to get over the guy for seven years and I'd barely even known him! My entire theory was based on the proposition that the only way to get over a juvenile crush is to realize that you never really knew the person to begin with. I don't have a working theory of how to get over someone you've gotten to know. Someone you've realized who for real is incredible, and generous, and kind, and sweet. How would I ever get over him then?"

Felicia whacked her arm. "Duh. The same way everyone else does. This is real life, Ing. This is how real relationships work. It's unpredictable. It's messy. It's unexpected. You take your chances and you deal with the consequences. You don't preempt a thing because you've foreseen every single bad thing that could happen along the way. That's how you miss out on the wonderful parts."

"Why did I never have this problem with Stewart?" Ingrid mused in puzzlement.

Felicia scoffed. "You want me to say it? Fine, I'll say it." She smacked her fist on the kitchen counter. "Because you never really liked Stewart. He's impressive, no doubt about that, and you wanted to be around that. But there were no feelings involved there. Just brains. Just thinky logic nonsense."

"Huh. No feelings?" Ingrid echoed in consideration.

"Well, except maybe loathing," Felicia added, offhand. "Look, forget Stewart." She slammed her palm on the counter again. "Honestly, Ingrid. When you barged into Grandpa K's that day after the basketball game, I saw you were a little upset. But you know what? I also saw you were happy. Every single time you talk about Connell—and you talk about him *a lot*, you really should see the look on your face. You..." she paused, her eyes glazing over, "come alive."

Ingrid met Felicia's gaze. It was weird but throughout the years, even the mere thought of Connell, all those lame, tiny nuggets of memories from high school that she held on to, had always brought her comfort. She wouldn't know where he was or what he was doing, but it never mattered.

Pursing her lips, she pulled out her phone. She considered sending Connell a message but the truth was she wanted to see him.

Felicia craned her neck to look. "Are you checking Connell's check-ins right now?"

"He's at some place called 'Nice Stems'," Ingrid mumbled, frowning over the screen.

Felicia rubbed her chin. "Oh, I think that's the flower shop at the end of Main Street, near the school."

Ingrid grabbed her bag. "I have to go talk to him."

"Really?" Felicia jumped in excitement.

Ingrid gave her an oh-calm-down look. "I'm not saying I want to be with him. The odds are he already has a new girlfriend by now. I'm just saying maybe I could have been more...understanding when we spoke last. And I probably should apologize."

Felicia's excitement dampened and she faked a cheer. "Oh, yay."

Not giving Felicia a chance to protest, Ingrid grabbed her arm. "Come on."

'Nice Stems' was at almost the opposite end of town from Ingrid's house. Across the street from the school, it was far enough that in those days, Ingrid would sometimes take the bus to get home.

But despite Felicia complaining about the long trek through the town and last night's fresh dump of snow, Ingrid forged on until they reached the end of Main Street.

The boutique flower shop was among a row of low, color-ful buildings. Crates of flowers and plants covered the front-age underneath a retractable canopy awning.

With the big picture window overlooking the street made of glass, from across the street, Ingrid had no trouble spotting Connell inside the shop even with his back turned.

Ingrid's heart pounded in her chest in anticipation. She had to forcibly tamp down the smile breaking on her face, her thoughts pre-emptively spinning into dreamy, dreamy fantasy land again. That maybe she could still have a happily ever after.

Then a familiar face stepped out of the arched doorway behind the counter inside the shop and Ingrid stopped short as though the wind got knocked out of her for a moment.

With a charming smile on her face, Verona's arms were already outstretched as Connell handed her a giant bouquet of pink and red roses.

Turning around, he gave her a smile just as charming, then he probably said something funny, making Verona giggle.

Ingrid's stomach churned hollow.

She supposed she should get used to it by now but she still really hated when her theories were proven correct—especially in this case.

It had taken Connell no more than twenty-four hours to find someone new.

Then again, given who he was, Ingrid supposed she should have expected less.

Despite her convictions, the mere sight of that perfect smile even from afar sent a warm rush straight through her from the flood of memories.

You should have my number. Do you think you could give me a chance...? Stop saying that. If it was up to me, I know exactly who I want to spend all my time with...

Ingrid's heart dropped to her toes. Her loud breathing in her ears fogged out the rest of the world.

I'd never seen him as happy as he's been these last few weeks. And I know you're the reason why... For a smart person, how are you so dumb...?

Her chest ached with bitter disappointment. Both she and Connell had come so far since high school. Was this really the end of the road?

Then again, the two of them might have had a moment, a window, to step out of her imagination and into the real world. If Ingrid had just had a little more faith in him, in the both of them, maybe they could have been together.

Except her stubborn brain had let the moment pass her by.

Felicia peered at her face but didn't say anything. She put her hand on Ingrid's shoulder.

Ingrid kicked at the snow on the sidewalk with her toe as she spun on her heel. "Let's just go home. The dishwasher ought to be done by now."

Shaking her head, Felicia stroked her back in consolation. "This is all my fault. When I asked you to hunt Connell down for that survey, I was just thinking it would be something fun to do. Something we could laugh about for a day or so." She shrugged. "I had no idea it would evolve into this huge drama where my friend gets hurt. I'm so sorry."

Ingrid gave her an understanding smile. "I know you meant well, and honestly, it was fun. Neither of us could have predicted this outcome. This is totally unprecedented." She jerked her thumb backward. "Hence, more ice cream therapy."

"So you *are* giving up?" Felicia prompted, her eyes lighting up as she hazarded a challenge. "And here I thought you were the most competitive person I'd ever met."

Ingrid knew exactly what Felicia was trying to do. "The thing about that, Fi, is I don't usually enter something I know I can't win."

Felicia elbowed her. "Want to go through your elective

paper again? That always cheers you up," she joked. "Maybe we can formulate some kind of corollary to your theory and see where it might have gone wrong."

Ingrid shook her head. "No. I think the truth is I did get over him—the imaginary version of him back in high school, the one I concocted in my head. So there was nothing wrong with my theory. The only problem is I think I really like the real him. The real him right now." She blew out a breath. "And unfortunately, I blew it."

***

Chapter Twenty - A New Year

"Happy New Year!"

With a slight frown, Ingrid tilted her head at the little potted plant in Felicia's hand as she stood in the doorway. "Is that...basil?"

"Uh-huh." Felicia stepped past Ingrid closing the door and poked her head into the living room. "Happy New Year, Mr. and Mrs. H," she greeted with a big smile.

Sitting at the coffee table, Ingrid's parents were surrounded by several boxes of board games and puzzles. Seeming to be concentrated on a type of Rubix cube game, Mom only glanced up for the briefest moments. "Oh, hi Felicia."

Dad didn't look up at all. His eyes darting to the sand timer instead, he went on to rearrange the cubes on his game to fit the pattern.

"My mom had an extra plant so she thought you might like it," Felicia went on, gesturing to the basil in her hand. "Also she says you guys shouldn't buy kale for a while. Our home garden is exploding with kale right now."

Forehead creased in concentration, Dad waved his hand as he shushed the room.

Blinking in surprise, Felicia pursed her lips in amusement as she met Ingrid's smirk. "I see we are starting our day with a fresh batch of crazy," she mumbled under her breath.

Ingrid rolled her eyes and beckoned her into the kitchen. "My mom wants to start this tradition of post-New Year game night for our family. Mom and Dad were going through to pick which board games to play but I guess they got distracted." She shot her friend a pointed look. "Can you believe it? My family? Competitive games? I feel like we're wanting to shoot ourselves in the foot."

Felicia's eyebrow rose. "You mean, your whole entire family? Are they all coming today?" Dread was clear on her face as she deliberated the arrival of the rest of Ingrid's highly judgmental family.

With a snort, Ingrid shook her head as she poured two glasses of sparkling cider. "Fortunately, no. Just us." Glancing over her shoulder, she asked, "How was the weekend in the mountains? You guys missed the blizzard. The New Year's Eve fireworks got snowed out so they had to postpone the event."

Felicia's eyes lit up. "Yeah, I heard, but three days in the mountains with my family? It was all Scrabble and diet Coke. Not very festive. I'm glad we got back in time for the fireworks tonight." Her eyes caught the decorative cheese platter on the kitchen bench. "Hey...cashews."

Ingrid took a sip of her drink. "I can't even believe the sun is out. After that freak blizzard, I thought this week would be just as dreary."

"Ah, a sign of better things to come," Felicia noted, raising her glass to clink with Ingrid's.

Ingrid raised an eyebrow instead. "You're in a good mood today."

Felicia gave her a suspicious look right back. "And I see you're definitely not."

At Ingrid's glare, Felicia put her hands up in defeat. "Okay, pivoting right now." She looked around. "Is Sam here? I told her I'd bring her back a souvenir from Bermont—oh, there she is." Craning her neck, she peered down the hall leading to the sheltered deck behind the house. "Huh. What do you suppose is going on over there?"

Ingrid was busy rearranging the cheese platter to disguise Felicia's thievery. "I don't know. Asher dropped by earlier to hang out or something."

Popping some cranberries into her mouth, Felicia hummed in intrigue. "Mmm...a sign of better things to come indeed."

Ingrid glanced over toward the back porch. "What are you talking about—oh!"

Sam and Asher were sitting on the porch swing in intense conversation.

They were also holding hands.

Ingrid swatted Felicia's arm. "Oh my goodness, Fi. Don't watch them."

Felicia shoveled more food into her mouth, her gaze still pinned on the two. "Sorry, I can't help it. You know I live for this stuff."

When Asher stood up to turn to leave, Felicia and Ingrid scrambled around in the kitchen in an attempt to look inconspicuous.

Leaning against the oven, Ingrid gave him an innocent wave as he shuffled past them. "Hey, Asher. What's up?"

Asher's head was ducked down, his bashful face beet red, but his grin was almost wider than his face. Not stopping as he walked through, he simply waved back. "Hey."

Felicia rushed over to Ingrid and grabbed her arm in excitement. "Oh my gosh! Do you think what just happened is what we think just happened?"

By the time Sam strolled past the kitchen, Ingrid and Felicia were almost already in squeals.

Ingrid cleared her throat all casual. "Hey, uh, how's it going?"

Felicia couldn't help herself. "And why was Asher's face all red before?"

Sam's cheeks were flushed as well, but like Asher, she couldn't bite back the big smile on her face. "Sssooo...yeah."

Felicia moved to eagerly grab Sam's arm in turn, peering at her face. "Oh my god, tell us already!"

Sam couldn't help a euphoric laugh, but before she could tell her story, Asher swung back in through the kitchen door, a bit breathless.

Sam's eyes lit up. "Asher!"

Running his fingers through his disheveled hair, he bit back another nervously fervent smirk as he approached Sam again. "Hey, I forgot to ask if you wanted to go into town to watch the fireworks with me later tonight."

Ingrid's heart squeezed at the way Asher and Sam were

looking at each other. It was like they were seeing each other for the first time, even though they had known each other for years.

Sam's happiness had been right under her nose this whole time.

"I'll walk you out," Sam offered, a shy tinge in her voice. But Asher couldn't look any more pleased as the two of them exited the kitchen.

Leaning back against the kitchen counter, Felicia met Ingrid's gaze as soon as the two were gone. "So that was interesting."

Ingrid signaled two thumbs up in derisive mirth. "I see someone has some sense in her head picking *not* the stereotypical hot high school jock."

Felicia gave her a pointed look. "That's what you got from that?"

"Why? Did you see something else happen there?" Ingrid prompted as she went to refill the cheese platter. "Sam just forwent the hottest jock in school in favor of her nerdy best friend. We both did call it. It was just a matter of time." Shutting the pantry door, she sighed out loud. "I should go find myself a different nerd."

"Yeah, 'cause the last one went so well," Felicia murmured into her drink.

Ingrid whacked Felicia's hand away from the cheese board. "I think we should go upstairs before you eat all the food for dinner."

They ran into Sam coming up the stairs. Her eyes were glazed, still all dreamy. "Hello, friends. How are you all today?"

"Well, we're back down here on earth in case you'd like to join us," Ingrid joked.

With a knowing scoff at Ingrid's tone, Felicia shook her head but then she stopped short at the doorway. "Whoa." She held up her hands. "Is it my imagination or did your room just grow even more boxes?"

The entirety of the bedroom was now piled high with even more boxes. Even the vanity chair was stacked with old, ratty cardboard containers. There was barely anywhere to sit.

Sam's glazed look morphed into dismay and she put her hands on her hips. "Ingrid, you are aware this is a bedroom and not a storage unit, right?"

"I swear I had nothing to do with it," Ingrid promised. "It seems Mom is starting spring cleaning way early. She unleashed a whole bunch of stuff from the garage this morning to see what we want to throw out. I guess she wanted to do that while I was still here too."

Sam's eyes widened. "Oh my gosh, I think I know why. I saw her watching some Marie Kondo videos on YouTube the other day. I bet you anything we're about to be bombarded with questions of whether or not all of this stuff sparks joy."

"Oh boy." Ingrid waded past a pile of boxes to squeeze over to the bed.

Sam rolled her eyes. "I'm telling you, Mom's going on some sort of OCDC kick for New Year's."

Sam's error combining a behavioral disorder with a band's name made Ingrid snicker. "Sure, the heavy metal band has perfectionist syndrome."

"Whatever." Sam made her way past the mess to the closet.

"I need to find something to wear for my date tonight." She tossed several outfits onto a pile already on the bed.

"Hey, you'd better not be expecting me to fix all this by myself," Ingrid called out, unable to help the resentment creeping into her tone. "I have enough of my own mess to deal with."

"Whoa, okay." Sensing her tone, Sam turned to Felicia, jerking her thumb in Ingrid's direction. "And what's wrong with Little Miss Cranky Pants?"

Slumping into bed beside Ingrid, Felicia grinned. "Ingrid's still being a sore loser about that jock from school she has a crush on."

"I am not," Ingrid insisted then pausing, she chewed on her bottom lip in consideration. She supposed there was no use denying it now. "And even if I was, there's nothing I can do about it now. That ship has sailed. The horse has bolted. Insert lame metaphor here," she declared with a wry wave of her hand. "So just please drop it, okay?"

Felicia moaned as she all but collapsed onto Ingrid's bed, her wailing all muffled. "Oh my god, Ingrid. The truth, it's staring you right in the face." She gave her a no-nonsense look. "Look, the fact of the matter is, you've gone out with nerds too and that didn't work out either. Why don't you do yourself a favor, stop moping, and go fight for this guy? You know you want to."

Arresting the tightness in her chest before it could take hold, Ingrid tapped her chin. "Well, how do I put this plainly—because I already screwed that up, remember?" she declared. The mere memory of every stupid, condescending thing she had said to him at Grandpa K's last time almost made her nauseous.

Since the flower shop encounter last week, she had actively tried to busy herself to stop thinking about that certain jock from high school. She was waiting for the day when she would stop getting the urge to check his social feed.

It wasn't today.

Ingrid's stomach churned. "What you're proposing makes absolutely no sense."

"That's exactly my point." Felicia tapped her chest. "Heart things, they're not *supposed* to make sense. These things just happen. And sometimes it *does* happen with the person you least expect. With Sam, it was her best friend. But for you, why can't the person you least expect be Connell Matthews?"

At the mention of his name, Ingrid's heart thumped harder.

Apparently, it happens when you least expect it...

Even Connell had been perceptive enough to acknowledge it before.

Ingrid pursed her lips in annoyed but resigned amusement. "You mean, why can't I just admit I'm falling in love with the person I've been obsessed with for nearly a decade?"

Felicia started laughing. "What do you think?"

"Yeah, jeez," Sam interjected, unable to help rolling her eyes. "You've been mooning over Connell Matthews forever. Seriously, you should get a prize for longevity or dedication or patience or something."

Ingrid rubbed her forehead. "You should have seen how hurt he looked when I..." She swallowed past the lump in her throat. "He's not going to want to see me. Let alone want to date me again."

"How do you know for sure if you don't ask? Maybe you can still change his mind." Felicia was already scrolling on her phone. "Okay, he's checked in at 'Nice Stems' again."

Ingrid pointed at her. "See? He and Verona make much better sense together anyway," she claimed despite her stomach rolling right over at the mere notion.

Then Felicia's eyes popped wide and she shot up in her seat. "Oh shoot, Verona just posted about an announcement there on her live video in five minutes. She's hinting at something big." She looked up to meet Ingrid's gaze. "Do you think she's going to announce they're a couple on a live social stream?"

Sam cringed. "Ooh, that's so tacky. I would barge in there for no other reason but to stop that."

"I'm not going to barge in there!" Ingrid waved her hands despite the wheels in her head already spinning up in contemplation. "And, okay, let's say I really wanted to talk to him—not saying I do, but just for instance if I did, honestly, the sensible thing to do is to call him later."

"But what if by then it's too late?" Felicia propped her chin on her hands.

"Yeah, what if?" Sam chimed in.

Ingrid looked from her sister to her friend in absolute incredulity. "You are both crazy. Besides!" She threw her hands up. "I could be moving to Berkeley next week. Does this even matter? This is a chance of a lifetime!"

"Oh, which one?" Felicia couldn't help but prompt. "The TA slot or Connell Matthews?"

Ingrid made a face. "Oh, haha."

"That has got to be the weirdest toss-up I've ever heard."

Sam shook her head as she stepped out of the room. "Good luck with that."

Tapping her fingers on a cardboard box, Felicia's tone resolved. "Well then, how about we take our girl Marie Kondo's approach?" She paused for dramatic effect before leaning over to ask, "Ingrid, which one of the two sparks joy for you?"

Ingrid furrowed her eyebrows.

Joy...?

She cast a glance over to the corkboard wall where she had pinned the sprig of mistletoe from the restaurant launch party.

This is my girlfriend, Ingrid...

The mere memory sent a pleasurable shiver up her spine.

Connell had said it with such confidence, such unfaltering conviction. He was braver than her that was for sure. And thoughtful, and funny, and passionate...

Ingrid picked at the bedcovers. She had already resolved to let Connell go. But was she doing it for the right reasons or was she just afraid again?

She'd said she never usually entered competitions she knew she couldn't win. But she also knew in her heart that Connell was well worth this risk. Aside from her career, she had never wanted something for so long in her life.

Besides, how pissed off would she be with her sore loser self if she didn't give this one last shot?

She didn't want to find out.

Did you figure out what you wanted...?

Clenching her teeth, Ingrid groaned in annoyed resignation. "Screw this." She jumped out of bed and grabbed her jacket and phone. "I'm getting my prize."

"YES!" Felicia pumped her fist in the air. "Oh, I am just so happy for you, Ing. You're going to get your dream guy. And you totally have me to thank."

"Are you coming?" Already a bit breathless, Ingrid gave her an expectant prompt as she headed for the door.

Felicia made a show of slumping back deeper in the bed to get comfortable, her phone propped in front of her. "What, and miss the live stream? No way!" She gave her a mischievous look. "You better hurry."

Ingrid rolled her eyes in mirth and hurried out the door.

21

Chapter Twenty-One - Sparking Joy

Ingrid tore off her Bluetooth earphones with an annoyed groan. Sam must have borrowed it and forgotten to charge it last night so Ingrid couldn't keep listening to Verona's live feed while she ran. She just hoped that she made it to 'Nice Stems' before she missed anything good—or bad.

Winter had definitely arrived. Ingrid rushed past the snowy landscape, past the handful of people tightly bundled up in thick coats headed to the square for the evening's fireworks display.

Her heart pounded in her chest. She was sure her face was red, her frizzy hair all sticking out. Her anxiety grew as she neared the end of Main Street.

With every step forward, she almost wished she was stepping back. She didn't have a plan. She hadn't run through any potential scenarios or thought of any contingencies, and given the stakes, it seemed highly counterintuitive and ill-advised.

She shook it off and kept moving.

Sometimes you just have to see where things go.

When Ingrid burst through the door like the ghost of Christmas future, not only did she startle Verona enough to stop her talking, but everyone else inside the little boutique flower shop turned to gawk at her.

Including Connell who was standing by the counter, a fresh giant bouquet in his hands, his eyes popped wide in surprise.

The two guys holding light domes had inadvertently turned their focus toward the door.

Ingrid's face flamed. Oh, hell. Here she was again. In another absolutely embarrassing situation in front of Connell Matthews.

Ingrid clenched her teeth.

There was no turning back. She was doing this.

Verona's quizzical face with those big eyes made her look like a sleep-deprived owl. "Oh, goodness." She put her hand to her chest. "It seems we already have one very eager customer. Are you in the market for some lovely flower arrangements today, Miss?"

Breathless, Ingrid couldn't seem to form words just yet.

After an expectant prompting second, Verona pursed her lips. "Um, perhaps, we'll let her get warmed up first." Then turning back to face the camera, she donned a bright smile. "The weather outside is positively chilly today, my lovelies!"

She waved to her crew again to reposition the lights. "Now, maybe it's time to do our big announcement."

Verona waved her hand in a beckoning gesture toward Connell and Ingrid jumped to a start.

Except Connell's gaze had not left Ingrid since she'd burst in.

Ingrid met those gorgeous blue eyes in determination as she marched straight toward him. With an authoritative nod, she tugged on his sleeve. "I need you."

Connell's eyebrows rose but he didn't resist. He tossed the bouquet onto the shop counter while Ingrid dragged him off toward the exit.

"Um, hey, wait a minute. Where are you going?" Verona called out in protest. She turned to the camera again with a sheepish look. "I'm so sorry, my lovelies, but this girl seems to be stealing my model." She hastened across the shop to chase after them, and hiding her annoyance with clenched teeth and a fake smile, Verona hissed under her breath, "Don't you have anyone else to stalk today? He's supposed to be my model."

Ingrid whipped around. "Yeah? Well, he's supposed to be my boyfriend so back the hell off."

One of the catty girls from high school standing near the door couldn't help her quip of bemused disbelief. "Oh, no, she didn't."

Her stomach churning, Ingrid forged on as the door swung shut behind them. She didn't even want to consider what those preppy girls were all saying behind her back.

All going well, she would never have to see them again for the rest of her life. Or if this all blew up in her face, Ingrid could always live in her lab for the rest of her life too.

Coming up to the next block, Connell finally cleared his throat even as she dragged him along. "Um, where are we going?"

Ingrid made a face. She had no idea.

He chuckled low under his breath. Moving to take her hand that was grasped on his sleeve, Connell took the lead and began to pull her in another direction. "It's freezing out. Let's go this way."

Having already used up most of her conviction with that publicly humiliating chaotic entrance at the shop, Ingrid didn't have enough left to protest.

Walking them past a snowy courtyard, Connell pushed open a door to a big building. The unmistakable odor of old plastic seats and rubber hit Ingrid with an instant flood of memories.

The big banner across the wall read 'Go, Lincoln High Ravens!' An open crate of basketballs sat haphazardly on one side of the bleachers, neglected while the school was out for the Christmas break.

It was the gym of Lincoln High, their old high school.

Connell stopped walking in the center circle of the basketball court. He faced her, his eyebrows raised in a prompt.

"What are you doing, Ingrid?" He stuck his hands in the pockets of his long fleece overcoat.

Those bright blue eyes, that hint of a smirk on his mouth, that shiny hair under the court's glaring floodlights amidst the backdrop of the high school gym, Ingrid's heart nearly stopped.

But there was also that telltale apprehension in his eyes

as he chewed on his inner cheek. Hesitation. Uncertainty. Diffidence.

They don't really know me, Connell had said at the Winter Fair once about all the random girls.

Ingrid's spirits lifted in reassurance.

She wasn't just one of his groupies. She wanted to know him. The real him.

But her thoughtful silence might have been too much for Connell.

Scoffing, he rolled his eyes. "You don't even know what you want," he mumbled as he turned to walk away.

An orange ball zipped past his nose, so close the air stirred the wavy hair nearly hanging over his eyes.

"Hey—!" Connell whirled around in indignation.

The bouncing of the ball echoed hollowly before it rolled to the foot of the bleachers.

Ingrid's frown deepened when he met her gaze despite the next words she yelled out. "I want you!"

He blinked, stunned. "What?"

Clasping her hands, she took one step closer. "Look, I know I screwed this all up." She dropped her gaze. "I wanted to apologize. I understand I could have handled the last conversation we'd had a little more sensitively than I did. I...I told you there were different kinds of smarts—"

"Your apology has an I-told-you-so?" Connell couldn't help but interject in amusement.

Ingrid gave him a pointed what-else-did-you-expect look. "What I'm saying is I wanted you to know...I do see you. Not the fake you I'd made up in my head. But you." She took another step closer to him. "The guy so passionate about his work, he single-handedly launched his dream restaurant. The guy who was happy to help out someone's kid sister for charity. The guy who wasn't intimidated by my dumb theories and called me out when I was clearly wrong."

Connell's forehead creased at her words. He didn't say anything but at least he hadn't stormed off.

She pursed her lips. "Ironically, you've been the one constant thing in my life," she began with a shrug. "You've always been the dream. But I've also always made sure I kept you at arm's length. And...I realized I didn't want to stand too close because I thought I would be disappointed with what I found."

She wrung her hands out to shoo away the nerves. "But the truth was...I was afraid I would still like you anyway, regardless of what I found." She swallowed hard. "I had a crush on the guy I knew you were deep down. The guy I knew you were meant to be. The guy you were *going* to be." She gestured toward him. "This guy."

The awkward silence in the empty gym that followed tormented her already weakened, frayed nerves. Her feet were heavy with remorse and refused to move any farther.

Connell's gaze on her was wary when he finally spoke, "I read your paper."

Ingrid blinked in full incredulity and couldn't help her remark, "No, you didn't."

Conceding, he rolled his eyes again. "Well, I read the start of it. And I also spoke to Gail."

She bit her lip. "And? What were your conclusions?"

"Well." He waved his hand. "We think you completed a week's worth of records management in two days. But besides that…" He took one step forward. "I think…you do belong with Stewart."

The statement stabbed at Ingrid's chest.

But Connell wasn't done. "On paper, Stewart is safe, convenient. And you didn't want to take a chance with me because you were scared." He gave her a meaningful look. "Well, you know what? I'm a little scared too. I know you're absolutely out of my league. I already knew I wasn't good enough for you. I'm just a stupid jock, right?"

Ingrid grimaced at his glaring error. "Are you crazy? I think you've got that backward. You're the one who's out of *my* league. And it's you who thinks I'm the safe, easy option. For god's sake, I already told you I've liked you for years."

Connell's eyes popped wide again in incredulity. "Oh my god, you think you're easy? Have you *met* you?" His voice rose as he took another step forward. "You are—infuriating, exasperating, confusing, fascinating…and I can't get enough of you." He threw up his hands. "So maybe yeah, I am crazy."

Ingrid's mouth went dry but a tiny bit of hope stirred inside her.

He said what?

Connell's chest began to heave. "I'd been…kicking myself all this time, racked with guilt for having kissed you right after you just broke up with your boyfriend. Because I didn't want to be that guy—that guy *you* thought I was, the one who steals other girls."

He ran his fingers through his hair in frustration. "I'd been feeling so guilty about it because kissing you was the best thing that's happened to me in so long. But it turned out I didn't even need to feel guilty about it in the first place."

"I'm sorry," Ingrid implored. "I didn't mean to set you up like that. I should have told you the truth." Shifting in her stance, she bit her lip. "I don't want to give up on you. After nearly a decade of trying, I think it's pretty clear I can't." Almost already resigned, she shook her head. "But if you like Verona...if you're with her now... I think that's great. You guys really looked good together at the party the other night."

The glare he gave her was one of slight distaste. "I'm not with Verona."

Ingrid furrowed her eyebrows. "But you'd been spending so much time with her, I thought..."

"Verona owns the flower shop. I owed her a favor for the launch marketing." Connell's tone was calm as he explained. "Did you think I was going to give up on *you*? I haven't called because I needed time to think about what you said."

He peered at her face. "The restaurant launch, that was one night, one party." He averted his gaze for a moment. "You said my world is so different and you couldn't see yourself being in it." He shrugged. "Well, that's great because I don't want you to be a part of my world. I want to be a part of yours. I know I'm not perfect but this is who I am. And I don't want to miss out on us again."

Ingrid could hardly believe what he was saying. But the funny thing was, in his own way, Connell had already been telling her these things for the last few weeks. She just wasn't hearing him.

"Plus I had this grand plan to wear you down with flower deliveries every day for the next three months. You would have been so impressed," he assured with a playful tone. "Or...would have gotten sick of it."

Ingrid's jaw dropped in bemused disbelief.

With the next step closer he took, he was within arm's reach. He gazed down at her. "You think you're competitive and obsessive? Try me."

Ingrid's chest bloomed with a bittersweet ache as she drowned in those earnest, blue eyes.

Connell touched her cheek. "I've already won. My prize is you. You are what I've never realized I've been working so hard for. I know I don't deserve you yet. But I will." He tucked her hair behind her ear with a diffident smile. "I want you to challenge me, encourage me, be proud of me. I want to be the guy you've always wanted because whether you intended to or not, you've made me into him. And I don't want to be anyone else except him."

With his comforting touch, his perfect smile, and that familiar intoxicating scent that flooded her senses while his precious words washed over her, Ingrid's heart soared.

His blue eyes flickered as he dropped his agonized gaze. "And I know you're leaving next week but I still wanted you to know."

Chance of a lifetime...

And in that moment, Ingrid's true answer to Marie Kondo's question struck her. The heavy weight on her chest instantly bubbled away. She felt so light, she almost felt like laughing.

Ingrid peered into his face with a new resolve. "I'm staying."

"What?" Connell's eyes narrowed. "For real? Why?"

She bit her lip, rolling one shoulder. "Because."

His mouth formed another slow smile, of relief, of elation. Because.

That was enough.

Beaming, Connell pulled her close and Ingrid reveled in the strength of him wrapped around her.

His gaze dropped to the smile on her lips as he bent his head.

Tilting her chin up in thrilled anticipation, she watched his mouth as he closed the gap between them. She was ready for him to obliterate her every thought, ready for her world to consist entirely of him.

His phone beeped in his pocket.

Ingrid jumped in the startle but Connell held her steady against him. "Goodness, you need to change your message tone to something less jarring."

He gave her a look. "Oh, are you going to start ordering me around now?"

That just made her laugh.

With an equally mirthful shake of his head, Connell glanced down at his phone. His eyebrows furrowed as he read the message. "Um, my mom wants you to come over for dinner. I think she saw Verona's Live feed."

Ingrid's eyes widened. As if on cue, her phone buzzed in her pocket and she checked. "Oh shoot, looks like my mom watched that video too." Groaning, she covered her face. "Oh gosh, I'll never live this down."

Connell grinned. "Then I guess it's official." He put his arms back around her and tugged her even closer. "I'm supposed to be your boyfriend so everyone needs to back the hell off."

Ingrid narrowed her eyes at him but spoke fully in jest, "Yeah, speaking of orders, I forbid you to work with that Verona, by the way."

He leaned down to kiss her but she twisted away. Chuckling, he called after her. "What, were you jealous?"

Ingrid went to pick up the ball that had rolled to the foot of the bleachers. Not quite wanting to give in completely just yet, she paused to consider his question. "Possibly."

But Connell was pleased enough with her response. He watched her dribble the ball out to just inside the curved painted line. "What are you doing now?"

"Want to play basketball?" Ingrid prompted, offhand.

He gave an incredulous look. "Do you even know how?"

She pursed her lips and dribbled twice more before she set up to launch the ball into the air.

Swish.

Beaming in triumph, she cleared her throat as she met him as he walked up to the halfway line again. She gestured to herself. "Competitive, remember?"

Connell's jaw had dropped in wonder and disbelief. "Wha—that was amazing!" Stepping back up to her, he cupped her face in his hands, a soft smile on his lips. "I'm learning so many new things about you."

One corner of Ingrid's mouth curved up, much like a Cheshire cat's. "We're just getting started, Connell."

22

Epilogue

"I still definitely need a jacket." Ingrid was digging inside a drawer for something to wear over her cocktail dress. "You know, they've already been on an early honeymoon. You think Nat and Gail could wait a few more months to get married."

Connell seemed entertained by her flurry. In his tailored black three-piece suit, arms crossed over his chest, his broad shoulders nearly filled the doorway to Ingrid's room as he leaned against the frame. "Fine," he declared. "Next time, you tell Nat and Gail they should be married in summer."

Ingrid's eyes lit up. "Or! They could have planned for a location wedding," she piped up, crossing the room toward him. "New Zealand is gorgeous this time of year. You know because it's in the southern hemisphere? The seasons are reversed. Did that not occur to you?"

He couldn't help a shake of his head. "You really are way too smart for me, Ingrid Harmon."

Leaning up to give him a quick peck on the cheek, she patted his chest as if in consolation. "Of course, why do you think I picked you to be my boyfriend?"

"Because you think I'm hot," Connell declared, matter-of-factly. "Duh."

Laughing, Ingrid stood in front of the mirror to put on her earrings. "I guess to some degree, I'm glad the wedding is today. That new job starts next week and I wouldn't want to disappoint everyone in my first month."

His gaze on her was steady, unflinching, and full of pride. "I cannot imagine a scenario when you are going to be anything less than perfect."

Basking in his praise, Ingrid couldn't help a smile. She could hardly describe the relief, the elation, the confidence she felt in knowing that Connell would always support her, always be on her side.

It had been three weeks since Ingrid had conceded the coveted TA spot in Professor Braun's team to Stewart who was more than happy to take it.

But after successfully gaining her Ph.D. from her contemporary sociology paper, Ingrid was surprised and certainly grateful to have had her pick of job offers.

"Who would have thought Mrs. Hope's sister runs a Fortune 500 company, eh?" she mused aloud.

Slipping his arms around her from behind, Connell met her gaze in the mirror, his eyes solemn. "I'm just glad it's across the state, not across the country."

In full agreement, she signaled an emphatic nod at their reflection. "I'm glad too."

A shadow of guilt crossed Connell's handsome face. "Aren't

you disappointed about Berkeley? What about, you know, working with the leaders in your field of specialty?"

Turning around, Ingrid clasped his cheek so he would meet her gaze. "Did you not hear what I just said? Fortune 500. That's five-oh-oh. And they have some rather interesting compensation numbers as well from what I've been told."

Stepping away to rifle through the pile of clean laundry on the bed, Ingrid mulled something over. "Besides, with the restaurant officially opening next week too, I bet we are both going to be so busy." She sighed. "Then I have to find an apartment so I can finally get out of Sam's hair. It's just lucky my whole family's gone looking at colleges for Sam all weekend so good luck to them—" She spun to go look in the closet again.

Connell caught her hand and tugged on her arm until she was flushed against him. "Hey, I know of an apartment you might be interested in."

Her shoulders shaking in mirth, she gave him an amused look. "Oh, really?"

"Really."

Ingrid blinked, stunned. "Really?"

His mysterious smile stood in for his words. Playing with the tendrils of her soft hair, he cradled her face in his hands. "You are so beautiful. I love your hair like this."

Shivers ran up and down her spine from his compliment. *This guy. Smooth, as always.*

Ingrid tugged lightly on his lapels. "I love this suit on you."

"I love your eyes."

"I love this tie."

"I love your mouth."

There was that knowing quirk to his smile again.

Meeting his challenging gaze, Ingrid bit back a smirk.

She wanted to say it. Her entire being was already filled with it.

Connell would have to be a genuine dumbass if he couldn't already tell how much she overflowed with what she was feeling for him.

But they were playing the chicken game of who would say it first. And Ingrid was determined to win. Of course.

Instead, she pulled his head down to catch his lips with hers. That same delicious warmth shot up and down her from the sweetness of his kiss. He was her world.

It was all she needed to know.

For now.

When she tried to pull away, Connell murmured in protest, leaning back in to keep kissing her, his hold around her waist tightening.

Ingrid pushed harder with another chuckle but he wouldn't let her go. "You're going to make us late. And I definitely have no qualms telling Nat and Gail that it's your fault if we are."

That annoyingly charming smile was still on his face. "Sure, as long as you also tell them why."

"You're the best man!" she cried out. "We can't be late."

"Alright, fine," Connell conceded with a sigh, straightening up. "Just for the record, I'm not the one still not ready."

Ingrid waved him away. "Then stop distracting me with your hotness."

Chuckling to himself, Connell glanced around the room. His gaze fell on one of the last few half-open boxes beside the bed. "What's with all these boxes anyway?"

"Oh. Yeah, Mom was wanting us to sort through all our old stuff for spring cleaning. You should have seen how many there were, to begin with." Ingrid dismissed with an eye roll.

"Is this yours?" Connell had picked up pair of glasses from inside the box, the pale pink frames dangling from his fingers. "I didn't know you wore glasses."

"Used to," she relayed as she finally picked out a sweater. "That's an old pair. I had to wear them for like six whole months back in junior high when I first got them. I only have to wear them every once in a while now."

"Oh." Connell nodded as he set the glasses back down. He was walking to the door when he paused in mid-stride as though something struck him and he turned back to her. "Did you say junior high?"

"Yeah." Ingrid's eyes narrowed at the look on his face. "Why?"

His forehead creasing in thought, he put his hand up for her to wait as he strode purposefully across the room toward the bookshelf.

Tilting her head, she watched him in bemusement. "What are you doing?" She put her sweater down and walked over to see.

Connell was running one finger across several rows of book spines on her shelf, from left to right, top to bottom. He visibly jerked to a stop at one particular book.

Ingrid peered up at him. "Connell? Are you looking for something to read? Right now is not the time."

But he seemed frozen in his stance, except for the smile that was slowly spreading on his face, his voice tinged with reverence when he finally spoke, "It was you."

Ingrid looked around, at a loss. "I was...what?"

Straightening up, Connell beamed at her, and before Ingrid knew it, she was once again in his embrace, her face in his strong chest.

"I should have known." He shook his head almost in disbelief, incredulity. "That cute girl I once told you about. The one I kept seeing at the bus stop who I thought went to a different school in junior high. It was you, Ingrid."

Ingrid pulled away a bit to look up at his face, her jaw had dropped. "What? No way! I can't believe this! I must have waited for you at that bus stop dozens of times all through high school."

And the one time she hadn't been looking, he had seen her instead.

The light in his eyes was soft, brilliant. "It was you. The only girl I'd ever had a crush on. It's always been you, Ingrid."

Ingrid's chest was so full of love and contentment, she was unable to tamp down her elated smile as she gazed right back up at him—naturally, not to be outdone. "It's always been *you*, Connell."

The End

Don't miss a happy ending!

SARA BREAKER lives in New Zealand with her husband and two kids. She writes offbeat young adult/contemporary sweet romance.

Suburban mum by day and author by night, she loves to live vicariously through her characters. They don't have to vacuum all day long and are always guaranteed happy endings no matter how melodramatic she writes them. Easy to read, feel-good love stories that break your heart, puts it back together, bam! happy ending— but then still have enough time to wash the dishes after.

Subscribe to her mailing list and get a FREE e-book!

https://subscribe.breakerworlds.com/romance

Read on for a sneak peek. . .

Sneak Peek: Holiday Blues

Snowed in at school over Christmas. What else is there to do? Maybe fall in love with the guy you least expected? Too bad he's dating your roommate...

***

I just wanted to walk on by, pretend he wasn't there, and deal with it another day.

But Lachlan had a different notion. "I think maybe we should put your stalker guy in his place."

"How?" I made a face, already uncomfortable about the idea. "I have no idea what to do."

"Maybe I do." Lachlan reached over to take my hand.

I bit my lip to laugh but didn't pull away. "What are you doing?" I hissed.

He grinned, not wanting to look right at Gilbert. "Is it working?"

I pretended to stretch my neck and spotted Gilbert again, shocked, dazed, and shaking his head.

The guy stood stock still, still puffing slightly in disbelief for a few moments before he finally turned and walked away.

I blew out a breath in relief. "He's leaving."

Lachlan let out a deep, throaty laugh. "I do admire his perseverance."

"Man, that is one tough customer." I shook my head again. "He's actually a nice guy. He's just...a little too intense."

Lachlan blew out a breath. "Wow, you're defending him. Alright."

I cringed again. Jeez. Was I?

My hand felt cold when he pulled his away, and when we crossed the next street, Lachlan put his hand on the small of my back to lead.

I figured he must have done it before. Except for this time, I was acutely aware of his touch.

I walked faster but he matched my pace and when a breeze blew past, I caught his scent—freshly-showered and all minty from that Christmas drink—and I couldn't help an involuntary shiver.

Uh-oh.

Then a heavy warm coat settled on my shoulders. "Hey—"

"You looked cold."

I blinked at him, surprised. "Oh. Thanks."

Goodness. This guy was chivalrous too?

I sneaked a sideways glance at him but he met my gaze and smiled.

Another shiver ran up my spine and I looked away.

Uh-oh.

We arrived at the front steps of our dorm building and I paused to shrug off his coat to give it back.

"Well, um, that was fun." Lachlan slid his coat back on,

shoving his hands in the pockets again. "Thanks uh...for keeping me company."

"And thanks for helping me out with...you know." I curled my lips in distaste.

His smile widened in mirth. "My pleasure," he said again, his voice lowered.

My pulse was racing again. I couldn't help it. The combination of those puppy dog eyes and that deep, rich voice was a killer.

Uh-oh.

***

Enjoyed the preview? **Holiday Blues** is available to purchase at your favorite bookstore.

Sneak Peek: When They Do

Can you handle a bit more steam? Try this quirky, offbeat romantic comedy **When They Do** by Sara Bellcamp.

Alex Keaton is the hottest playboy on the West Coast, living the carefree single life. That is until his best friend decides to get married. And he finds himself chasing after the absolute last girl he would have ever imagined.

***

I was getting some drink refills for me and my date (which was code for flirting with the hot female bartender) when Janice found me at the bar.

"Hey," I greeted over the noise of the party. "Tyler here yet?"

Janice yelled in my ear. "He's on his way," she said. "He's picking up Claire from some law school alumni event. Where's Candace?"

"Charmaine," I corrected.

"Oh, so you do bother to know their names?" Janice mused.

I had to laugh. "Why do you always underestimate me?" I asked her. "I can be a perfectly decent gentleman when I want to be."

She wiggled her eyebrows in agreement. "Yeah," she said wryly. "I can see that from your unnecessary tipping at an open bar—oh, finally!" she exclaimed, starting to wave both hands as if to get someone's attention from across the way. "Ty!" she called out.

And when I glanced over, I had to blink myself out of a startle. Tyler was making his way up to the pool area where we were. But my eyes had snapped straight to Claire who was right behind him.

She looked jaw-dropping hot!

She was wearing a low-cut snug little white number and her light brown hair was down her shoulders, wavy and tousled.

"Damn girl, you lookin' fine tonight," Janice commented, giving Claire an appraising look as she and Tyler approached us.

Claire gave her a deadpan look before stealing her drink. "Is that alcohol? Great." And she chugged it down quickly.

Janice's forehead creased. "Something wrong, sweetie?"

"No, no, just busy," Claire dismissed quickly. "Some of the senior partners just decided to throw this case referral down the ranks, and between that and dealing with the interns—"

I wasn't listening to the conversation but I was still staring at Claire. I would never have imagined that that body had been hiding under her usual three-piece business casual attire. Tyler had to elbow me to snap out of it.

He shot me a strange look. "Bro, you checkin' out Claire?"

"What? No," I replied quickly, instinctively, before I stopped short. "I mean, yes. Hell yes," I amended, figuring there was no shame in admitting it.

"She does look different tonight, doesn't she?" Tyler commented.

"Different," I echoed. That was an understatement.

"Have you seen Marco yet?" he asked me.

"Oh, uh." I blinked a few times to clear my head. "Not yet actually." I panned my gaze around the crowd and spotted Nina quickly. She was wearing a shiny silver dress so it was easy to spot her. "There's Nina though. I bet if you stand close to her long enough, Marco will turn up," I remarked with a bit of sarcasm.

"Come on, Jan." Tyler took Janice's hand to pull her along in pursuit of Marco and/or Nina, leaving Claire standing beside me.

She didn't say anything. She wasn't even looking at me. But she took one of the glasses I was holding and drained it quickly. I had to grin. "I see time away from Marco is agreeing with you," I commented, giving her look another once-over.

"Oh my god." Claire shot me an annoyed look. "Would you just shut up? I don't want to talk about it."

"Jeez, someone's having a really bad day," I noted passively, then offered the other glass of wine I had to her. "My offer still stands, you know," I said with another grin. "Whenever you want to get that palette cleansed."

Naturally, I had seen Claire's look of scorn before but it was particularly prickly tonight. "It's that fast, is it?" she cut in, before declaring. "Just because Marco's got a new girlfriend doesn't mean you're suddenly allowed to hit on me."

Just then, I noticed Claire's gaze distract somewhere and I looked up to see what it was.

Tyler and Janice had found Marco and Nina. Marco,

inexplicably, was also wearing a shiny silver shirt for tonight's party.

I was about to snicker and remark something insulting about matching couple outfits to Claire, but before I could say anything, Claire grabbed my second glass of wine, chugged it down quickly, then whirled around to walk away.

I tried to see where she went but she was quickly swallowed up by the party crowd.

***

Enjoyed the preview? **When They Do** is available to purchase at your favorite bookstore.